The Time Mistress

Book Five in the Time Mistress Series

Georgina Young-Ellis

LTB Publishing

Copyright © 2020 Georgina Young-Ellis

All rights reserved

The characters and events portrayed in this book are fictitious. Any similarity to real persons, living or dead, is coincidental and not intended by the author.

No part of this book may be reproduced, or stored in a retrieval system, or transmitted in any form or by any means, electronic, mechanical, photocopying, recording, or otherwise, without express written permission of the publisher.

*This book is dedicated to Jonathan Ellis
– my all and my everything.*

Acknowledgements

I would like to thank, first and foremost, my husband, Jonathan Ellis, who not only designed the cover of this book, but is my overall tech guy, and just simply the best in every way. I'd also like to thank my mother, Patricia A. Young, for being a dedicated early reader and for her input on WWII. I'd like to particularly thank my editor, Rich Mattiello, technical writer and editor in Silicon Valley, for his keen insights, constructive criticism, and all his help in making this book the best it could be. I'd like to thank my dear friend Eric Johnsen, historian and musician, for sharing his expertise on jazz and musicianship for this book; Regina McCaughey-Silvia for her careful line-editing; and, finally, author/designer Candace Bowser for her original design concept.

In spite of the notice stating, "no accreditation required" - the Corner Ornament 4 By Rebecca Read is from Pixabay. Thank you.

The Time Mistress

by

Georgina Young-Ellis

Chapter One

From the memoir of Akito Wakai - undated

I met my wife on what was a terrible day for my country. I was working on the Empress of Australia, which sailed between Yokohama and Vancouver, B.C. It would have been my second passage to Vancouver. We had spent a week in Yokohama, replenishing our supplies. The passengers, Americans and Canadian, had been boarding all morning. They had remained in Japan for military, business, and other reasons after 1918, the end of the Great War. Many of our countrymen were also heading east to start a new life. They'd heard much about that strange land since our country had been an ally in the war, and had come to know many of those easterners.

I was twenty-six. I had served in the Imperial Navy in the last year of the war, where my job then, as now, was nothing more than assistant to the cook, chopping vegetables all day long. After the war, I worked on my family's farm. The rural life was boring to me. I wanted to travel again. When I heard the Empress was hiring Japanese for menial tasks, I seized the opportunity, and was hired because of my experience in the Navy.

The ship was to leave port at twelve-thirty in the afternoon. I had been visiting my family, and it had taken hours to get from their farm back to the harbor. I was late and running to be there well before the ship launched. I remember seeing, out of the corner of my eye, a dog that had been sleeping suddenly leap to his feet and run off as though devils were chasing him. People all around me started to laugh. Their laughter died only a minute later when the ground began to move. In front of me the street cracked and the two edges ripped apart in opposite directions. If I had been standing a finger's length to my left, I would have been swallowed by the earth. That very thing happened to many of the people who had been on the street only seconds before. Now, only screaming and crying remained. Everyone ran in confusion. No one knew what to do or where to go, or even in which direction to run. Buildings were crumbling all round us. Dust was so thick in the air we couldn't see anything, but we ran anyway.

My only chance was to make it back to the ship. Somehow, I knew my way to the harbor, maybe because it was all I knew in the city. I ran toward it with thousands of others running in the same direction. I fell down and many people stepped on me, but a man helped me to my feet. I turned to thank him, but he had disappeared. Everything was burning. Fires were everywhere. We believed the safest place was near the water but we were wrong. Everyone was trying to get to the Sumida River, where it opened to the ocean. Many pushed others out of the way to be first over the bridge, but even as they hurried to cross, it fell from underneath them. Hundreds were in the water. Their screams were terrible as the river churned violently, pulling everything into its depths.

Those of us left behind gathered in an open place nearby. Flames had sprung up all around. I had never seen this before: a wall of fire, hundreds of feet high, began to twist like a dragon. It devoured everything and everyone in that space. There may have been many thousands of us trapped there, yet in minutes only a couple hundred still remained alive. I cannot know why I was one of those spared. All I wanted was to get away. I began to run again. I found my way to a raft filled with people heading across the river. I held onto a rope someone tossed out to me and I was hauled behind them, gripping with all my might. I fought to keep my head above water until we came near to the other side. I stumbled onto the river bank. I saw the harbor through the smoke, and there was my ship. I was heading for it when a sound penetrated beyond all others in that terrible chaos and fear. It was the sound of a woman crying. She was covered in thick white dust and mud, partially buried beneath the remains of a building. I knelt to help. She looked up at me with eyes so wide and fearful I had no choice but to do what I could to get her free. Her right leg was trapped beneath a heavy beam. I could not move it myself so I screamed for someone to help. No one even looked in our direction. She clutched at my arm, afraid I would leave. I told her to be strong, that I would find a way though I had no idea how. She pulled at my arm again and pointed to a pile of poles that had once been the roof of a vegetable stall. I realized what she had in mind and I ran to get one. It was very hard wood—it would work—but I needed something more. Again, she pointed to a large wheel of a cart that had fallen nearby. Holding up my hands to let her know I understood and that she should lie still, I rushed to it. I will never know where I found the strength to lift it but I did, and rolled it close to her leg. Jamming the pole beneath the beam and the rim of the cart, I pushed down hard with all my weight, and it rose a bit. It was enough for her to pull herself free. She had a terrible bloody gash on her leg. Blood was pooling around her. I pulled off my tunic and bound the wound as best I could. With an effort, she was able to put a bit of weight on it. I put my shoulder beneath her arm and we ran together until she cried out from the pain and very nearly pulled us both down. I balanced myself and pulled her over my shoulder. I knew it could not be comfortable, but I had no choice. Strangely, I will always remember, even as I tried to be careful not hurt her further, the smell of fresh flowers filling my nostrils.

Nick Stockard limped around his Boston apartment in a frenzy of thought. Only a few weeks before, he'd recovered from a life-threatening stab wound to his chest, and it still bothered him when he exerted himself. He didn't have time to pamper himself any further though. If he was going to kill Akito Wakai, he needed to get to it. The two men he humorlessly thought of as his henchmen, the two who were in charge of his time portal, were ready to send him on the next trip where he planned to accomplish just that. He had decided the only way to have Cassandra Reilly to himself once and for all was to get rid of the person who had been the cause of their break-up: Evie Johnston. To get rid of Evie, he had to make sure she never existed in the first place. That meant killing one of her ancestors—someone history wouldn't miss—not that he cared. He had no desire to go to another uncivilized period in time though, having just returned from 16th century England, one of the filthiest times and places to ever exist—and one of the most dangerous. He wouldn't have to though. Evie's many-times-over-great-grandfather, Akito Wakai, was a young man in the 1920s, living in the U.S. Nick considered the 1920s the era when civilization basically began, in that there were cars, telephones, clean food, washing machines…the things you needed to exist comfortably. It would be a quick trip. He'd easily found out about Wakai by tracing Evie's ancestry. He'd kill him before his son was born, thus wiping out the lineage. He had already found out Wakai's address. It was an obscure piece of information, but somehow the lease with Wakai's name on it was part of the scant evidence about the man's life that was searchable. He'd go there, gun him down, and Evie Johnston would cease to exist. Then, he and Cassandra would still be together as if nothing had ever happened to come between them.

Chapter Two

From the memoir of Akito Wakai

They were pulling up the gangplank when we got to the ship. Two of the crew were fending people off, telling them there was no more room. Many crowded forward anyway and several fell into the water. Some were crushed between the ship and the pilings. We couldn't move on our own as we were trapped in that mass of people. But as those ahead of us fell away, we were shoved forward until we found ourselves face to face with those two big men. Fortune once again smiled on me because one of them recognized me and waved us through. A great cry rose up behind us that this was not fair. Truthfully, I was so relieved, I put those still ashore out of my mind. Perhaps it was shameful, but I cannot find it in myself to regret that I never looked back. There was nothing I could do to help them. The young woman and I were safe, for the moment anyway. It occurred to me that a few days before, I'd served the man who'd allowed us to board a little extra meat with his meal. Perhaps that small action, which cost me nothing, was his reason for allowing us to board the ship. I never even knew his name, and I could not know his reasons because, shortly after, as we began to move into the harbor, we were struck very hard by another boat. The man who surely saved our lives was knocked overboard never to be seen again.

Not knowing what else to do, I took the woman with me to a small space I knew of, off the engine room, where no one else would go. It was noisy, but it was warm and dry, and there was at least a place where she could lie down to recover. Her leg was beginning to swell. She slumped on the edge of a plank laid across two five-gallon buckets. She was exhausted and still very frightened. I turned to the hatchway with the idea of finding us some help and a bit of food, but she grasped my sleeve and would not let me leave. I sat next to her hoping to assure her that everything would be okay. She leaned into me and began to weep miserably in my arms. She told me through her sobs that her entire family had been killed. They were inside the pulverized building where I had found her. She had only been spared by the fact that she, in those moments, had been returning from the market, and had not yet entered the building. Her parents, her sister, and her brother had all been killed. She pulled at her hair and began to wail that it was her fault. I felt helpless and assured her there was nothing she or anyone could have done. We were victims of a world cracked in two—powerless in the face of nature. She seemed to understand the sense of my words, but everything was still so fresh in her mind. Nothing I could say would make any difference, but still, I wanted to try. I did not want to think about what had become of my family, only praying that, where they live in the countryside, the earthquake was not as terrible. Maybe since they live in a simple wooden house, if it collapsed while they were inside, they wouldn't have been killed. Anyway, at the time the quake took place, I think they would have been in the fields, tending their crops.

Finally, exhausted, the young woman fell asleep. I went above deck to see what was happening. It was chaos! People were pushing through hordes of others huddled in every corner. There, doctors were attending to a few people who looked to be in worse shape than the rest. Some of them would not make it. The sounds of horror continued to fill the air even as the ship carefully navigated its way out into the harbor. Smoke was rising over the city that was no more. The wails of those left behind, though far from us now, were deafening to my ears. Where I had blocked the sound before, it became now the most terrible thing I have ever heard.

Elton held Cassandra in his arms as she cried. Her clothing smelled of earth, grass, and cedar. Her linen blouse was coarse against his skin. He carefully placed his hands on her upper arm, gently resting his head against hers as he cradled her. Her auburn hair fell in ringlets across her face. The first thing he had thought when she emerged from the portal chamber was that she looked like a da Vinci painting…or a Botticelli. She had never been so beautiful, distraught as she was.

"How could I have left him, Elton, how?" she sobbed. "I should never have gone. I should never have put us through it."

"Shhh," he whispered, not able to think of anything particularly helpful to say, other than, "it will be all right."

"I love him, Elton, I love him!"

Why did her saying so cause an ache in his chest?

"I know."

She continued to cry without ceasing for several more minutes. He was helpless to truly comfort her. At least he'd been the only one in the lab when she returned through the portal.

Finally, her sobs relented. She lifted her head from his shoulder and applied the handkerchief he'd given her to dry her tears. "I'm sorry," she said, her voice hoarse.

"Don't be silly," he replied gently. "This is what I'm here for."

She smiled a little. "You shouldn't have to deal with my drama, Elton. I made the choice to go be with Lauro and I made the choice to come back. I tell you, it was one of the most difficult decisions I've ever made."

This confession resulted in another stab of emotional pain. "You came back early. You could have stayed another month. I thought you'd stay out the year."

"I was worried," she said, dabbing at her eyes with the handkerchief, "that you and James would start to wonder if I might decide to stay for good. As the one-year mark grew closer, I felt I had better not prolong my time there. Leaving Lauro was the hardest thing I've ever had to do, but I left before it became impossible. He didn't want me to go, but he understood that that our time together was never meant to be anything more than temporary."

"I'm so sorry. It must have been very hard."

Tears pooled in her luminous eyes again. She sighed, mopped away the tears, and looked around the room. She delicately blew her nose. "Tell me about you," she finally said, fixing her gaze on him again. "Distract me. What has happened since I've been gone?" She blinked. "Oh dear, it feels strange to speak English again."

"Well, I hired another team member. Alex. He's British. Helping me and Yoshi out here has been a kind of apprenticeship for him."

"Oh, that's right," she said a little vaguely. "He applied right after my trip to Regency England. Poor guy's been waiting a long time."

"Well, I finally had a place for him. And James has been coming by for a week or two at a time."

"I can't wait to see him." Her smile lit up her face. "Your son has been an amazing help to me this year."

"I'll call him tomorrow. And what about you?" She laid her hand on his.

He took a deep breath. "Well, there's a lot to tell, actually, but we can talk about it another time."

"No tell me," she said.

"Don't you want to at least go to the house so you can change your clothes?"

"No," Cassandra replied. "Let's stay here awhile. I'm not ready to see anyone else. Or modern-day Florence. It will be a shock."

"I wish we could have arranged more of a buffer for you. Anyway, we can be comfortable here for a bit."

He went to the mini-fridge and took out a bottle of fine Pinot Grigio from Orvieto. He poured two glasses and handed one to her.

She sipped it. "Mmm, that's good. Wine has come

a long way in five hundred years."

They shared a moment of laughter.

She then said, "You mentioned lots has happened. Like what?"

He took a deep breath. "Jeannine and I got divorced."

"What?" Her eyes grew wide. "Elton, you're kidding me. What happened?"

He sighed. "It had been coming for a long time. She had been unhappy about my spending so much time away from home."

She started to speak but he silenced her with a gesture of his hand. "No, it wasn't because of this trip of yours. She had been dissatisfied for a while now. She just didn't understand my passion for this work. She tried, Lord knows she tried. You know that too."

Cassandra nodded.

"But she had her own life and her own interests. We just grew apart. And then she met someone else."

"Oh, no!"

"No, it's okay. I completely understand. She deserved better."

"She is a wonderful woman and she deserves the best, I agree, but, in my opinion, you are the best."

He searched her grey-blue eyes, the color of the sky just after a storm. Did she really mean that? He couldn't tell her that his heart hadn't really been in his marriage for years. That he

had suffered through the time-journeys Cassandra had made, in which she'd fallen in love more than once, including the months, just a few years back, that she'd spent with that reprobate, Nick Stockard. It had really been since her husband had died, ten years ago now, that his feelings had begun to grow from that of mentor, to colleague, to friend…to love. "Thank you, Cassie," he finally said, "but you know what I mean. She deserves someone that can be with her emotionally and physically all the time, and I wasn't that person. I wish her the very best. We are, and will remain, friends. She will always be dear to me."
"I'm glad, but still. That's so hard."
"I'm okay."
She pressed her palm into his and gave it a squeeze. Her warmth radiated through him. "Where is James right now?"
"He's back in Boston. He's holding down the fort at MIT. Your son has really become my right-hand man. I'm very proud of him."
"Have the Elizabeth letters been published yet?"
"Yes, but only the MIT academic community has seen them so far because they have to be thoroughly analyzed for their authenticity."
"Their authenticity! He practically got them from Queen Elizabeth herself!"
"I know, but technically that's only James's word until they can be one hundred percent authenticated, and that takes time."
"I suppose."

"Cassie, I feel like we need to get you someplace more comfortable. You'll need to change clothes and have a bath..."

"Do I reek?" she said with a laugh.

"On the contrary," he replied more emphatically than he'd meant to.

"Thank you, though I doubt that's true. Yes, I guess I'd better get on with it."

"The car can come right to the door here and we'll whisk you to the entrance of the house. You won't have to deal with the city at all."

"That's fine. I'll be okay."

"May I tell you how wonderful it is to see you again? To have you back here safe and sound?"

"Yes, Elton, you can, and I appreciate it." Her eyes began to fill with tears again.

He took both her hands in his.

"It will just take me some time, that's all."

"I know."

"Thank you for being here for me."

"I'm here every step of the way. Anything you need."

She threw her arms around him and hugged him tight. He closed his eyes and let himself melt, just for a moment, into her embrace.

Chapter Three

From the memoir of Akito Wakai

In the midst of the chaos on the ship, a man ran into me and knocked me off my feet. He looked down at me and, in spite of being white, offered his hand. I took it and he helped me up. He was a doctor, and asked me to come assist him with an injured child. There was no way to say no, though I was still concerned about the woman in my charge. I felt an almost desperate need to return to her side before she awakened. Perhaps I might provide a bit of normalcy in a world gone insane. At that time, I did not realize she was providing me with the same, but there was no time for thinking. I followed the doctor, Thomas Reynolds, into the ship's commissary. The space had been divided in two with sheets. The dining tables on one side had been set up as beds and operating tables. Clustered around the worst of the worst were doctors, nurses, and anyone who had a pair of helping hands who would not falter at the sight of blood. Dr. Reynolds led me to one group surrounding a boy of about twelve. He had a large wound on his head, and a long piece of metal protruding from his lower stomach. The team around him was working to remove the metal bar and halt the blood flowing freely. At last the pipe came out with a loud sucking sound, the child screamed, and, mercifully, passed out. Dr. Reynolds grabbed my hands, poured alcohol on them and thrust them directly into the gaping hole. "Press hard and don't stop until I tell you," he said. I nodded that I understood and tried not to feel what was beneath my hands. It took perhaps ten minutes for the repair to be made and the blood staunched. It felt like as many hours. When he was done working, the doctor gently pulled my hand from the wound and thanked me. Sweat ran down his face and into his eyes as he nodded at the boy on the table. "That's my little brother," he said. "I owe you one." The face of the woman below came to my mind and I turned to leave. The doctor caught me with a look that asked where I was going. He waved me back to him; there was more to do. I shook my head no several times. My English was not good enough to explain but somehow with motions and looks I managed to get him to follow me. We wound our way through the tumult and I led him to the little room. The woman thankfully had not died, nor had she awakened to find herself alone. My heart stopped beating so fast. We went to her and I pulled back the crude bandage I had fashioned across her leg. I could hear the other man suck air across his teeth as he saw that the bone of her leg was exposed. Had she been awake, she would have been in terrible pain. Without a word, the doctor removed the dressing and pulled the shirt he was wearing off over his head. He pulled hard at the fabric until the material ripped. He glimpsed a bottle of whisky someone had squirreled away on a high shelf and grabbed it. He tore his shirt into strips and soaked them in the liquor. He motioned for me to hold her down and placed the strips across the gash in her leg. Even in her unconscious state a deep groan escaped her lips and filled the small space. She tried to fight, to sit up, to get away. Her eyes flickered open for a moment and were filled with horror. She shrieked at the pain and then collapsed back against me, silent. Once again the scent of flowers filled the air. This time I knew the flower: night blooming jasmine. I wondered if the doctor could smell it too, but he gave no indication. Instead he smiled grimly and nodded to her. He said something like, "She'll have a terrible scar but she'll heal. Make sure to keep it clean." He pointed to the rest of the strips of his shirt and the whisky. I bowed very deeply to him as he left the room.

The modern city of Florence was a strange thing to behold after living on the outskirts of the seventeenth century version for nearly a year. From Cassandra's room in the three-story house Elton had rented in the center of the city for the team members to stay in while they were in Florence, she had a view that took in the red, white, and green marbled Duomo, the Campanile di Giotto, and the Baptistery. These iconic sights and many others throughout Florence never changed, but so much else had. Whereas, in 1605, the year she'd just returned from, horses and mules plodded through the streets leaving their dung and urine everywhere to be splashed through by the carriages of the aristocrats, now, the city was shining clean, devoid of the smells of waste of all kinds that used to pervade it, and which would surely have even made their way to her balcony on the third floor. Now, the only thing one smelled was delicious food from restaurants or homes, or the flowers, fresh vegetables, and fruits in the markets. There were people alive today who still remembered Florence as once being noisy with traffic and choked with exhaust. Now, driverless cars moved silently through the streets and all one heard was the chatter of residents and tourists, music floating on the air from street musicians, or the hawkers who still sold artisanal goods in the town squares. Florence was in its second Renaissance. Not only did people still come from far and wide to see the works of the great artists like da Vinci, Michelangelo, Botticelli, and Rafael in museums like the Uffizi and the Galleria dell'Accademia, and in the great churches and palaces, but new museums had been constructed in renovated ancient buildings that showed works of modern Italian artists: painters and sculptors, photographers, animators, mixed media creators, and virtual reality architects.

Cassandra took a sip of her sparkling water and watched a man and a woman walking along the street below holding hands: a beautiful Italian couple who seemed very much in love. Her thoughts inevitably returned to Lauro. She had originally met him in Siena, Florence's rival city, two years before. A disruption in the timeline had started it all. People all over the world had started dreaming of a woman's face in a painting as if it existed in a collective subconscious. This indicated a timeline shift, which was what Cassandra and her colleague Jake had gone back in time to investigate. They had gone to Siena of 1506, looking for Francesco Marino, the artist identified as the painter of the dream image, an artist who was a member of an art studio belonging to Lauro Sampieri. From there, the situation had become complicated. The painting had turned out to be of Giuliana Guerrini, the woman Jake had fallen in love with during his initial journey to Renaissance Italy, five years before. Jake's re-involvement with her sparked the ire of her jealous husband, and Lauro had gotten in the way of the skirmish. Cassandra and Jake had to flee to the future with Lauro to save his life.

Cassandra needed something stronger. She went into her room and looked over some of the bottles of liquor there. She didn't usually drink, but she needed something to fortify herself with. Anyway, she'd be having dinner soon. She selected a quality vodka, poured a little into her mineral water, added a hefty squeeze of lime, then returned to her seat on the balcony. She took a deep breath. When she was with Lauro in Florence…was it just a week ago that she had left him? Five days, actually. Well, they had barely spoken about Nick and all that had transpired in the Siena that had been Lauro's future and Cassandra's present. It had turned out that one of those Marino descendants was responsible for stealing Giuliana's portrait from the past and making it disappear from the present. It was Nick, Nick Stockard, a man who Cassandra had actually thought was a good man once, and had very nearly loved, who had been behind it all. He had caused innocent people to die to further his agenda and that of Marino.

Nick was dead now. There was no point even thinking about him, yet doing so gave Cassandra a stab of trauma that felt fresh, like he was still there, lurking somewhere around the corner, in the shadows. Because that's how he was: surreptitious, sneaky, insidious. Cassandra shook the thoughts away and called Elton on her palm link. Most people communicated these days by sending virtual texts that would appear in the air before the receiver, but Cassandra still preferred to actually talk. Besides, it comforted her to hear Elton's voice and he rarely neglected to answer when she called. They agreed on a place to meet for dinner and she went inside to change.

She stayed in Florence another week to help oversee the dismantling of the portal lab. Standing near the little alcove in the gardens of the church of Santa Maria Novella, it wrenched her heart to see the last of the temporary structure come down and get hauled away. There was now no chance to return to Lauro. It was final. He was gone forever, only to live on in her heart. Elton stood next to her, a sympathetic arm around her shoulder as they watched. He had been so kind to her these last couple of weeks. Not that he hadn't always been, but there had been a tenderness in his dealing with her since she'd returned that touched her. Her broken heart would need time to heal, and it was good to know she could rely on him when she needed someone to talk to. His palm link vibrated against her shoulder, and he took his hand away, glancing up at the message, invisible to Cassandra. "It's Suhan," he said with surprise.

"Suhan?"

"Calling from the rehabilitation center. We're in touch every now and then." He gave his index finger a flick. "Hello, Suhan," he said, speaking into the air.

Cassandra couldn't hear Suhan's side of the conversation, as the young scientist's voice was relayed directly into Elton's ear.

Their conversation was punctuated by exclamations of surprise on the part of Elton, and finally the word, "Nick," which made Cassandra's stomach churn.

"We'll be back in Boston tomorrow," he finally said, "Cassandra and I will come see you the day after. Bye. Take care."

Cassandra raised her eyebrows. "What on earth?"

"She says she thinks she spotted Nick's picture in a newspaper."

Cassandra's mind folded laboriously around those words. None of them seemed to make sense together. "Um, Nick is dead."

"Are you sure?"

"Am I sure? I left him on the ground in London, bleeding from a knife wound to his gut."

"That doesn't mean he died."

"He was dying, Elton; I felt his pulse."

"But did he die in front of your eyes?"

"Well, no. We had to leave him there, but I was sure he was dying."

"Maybe someone found him and nursed him back to health."

"Well, maybe. I mean, I suppose it's possible. What did she mean about seeing his picture in a newspaper? What newspaper?"

"A newspaper from the 1940s."

"She has to be imagining it. I'm sure it's someone who just looks like him. It can't be Nick."

"I'm sure you're right."

"Is she doing okay…mentally I mean? Maybe she's cracking up."

"I will tell you this," he took her by the arm and they began walking back to the house where they would finish packing up their things. "She was never convinced he was dead."

"She's just in denial."

"Maybe so, but you have to admit, she knows him better than anyone. In previous conversations we've had since she entered the rehabilitation center, she said she had a feeling he was still alive. And if he were still alive, he would be time traveling, staying undercover."

A chill ran down Cassandra's spine. If nothing else jolted her back to reality, this did. All thoughts of Nick while she'd been with Lauro were like recalling a vague nightmare that she could simply brush away. What she did often think about were the heroes who had rescued her the night she thought Nick had died: William Shakespeare, Edward de Vere, and Robert Cecil. Those three men had grown so dear to her while she and her son had been in Elizabethan London. She missed them, but she was able to think of them now almost like characters in a play she loved. Nick, on the other hand, had been an evil presence in her life for nearly five years and she'd thought she was finally done with him. Surely Suhan was mistaken. "No," Cassandra said. "I can't believe it. It just can't be true."

"Well, after we get to back Boston, we'll go see her and take a look at what she found. We've got to be certain she's wrong."

Cassandra's head was beginning to spin.

"She's in a facility about an hour outside the city."

"I'm willing to go but I have serious doubts."

He gave her hand a reassuring squeeze and she held on to it. His presence made her feel safe. If she was with him, everything would be all right.

"Goddammit, goddammit, goddammit!" Nick screamed inside the driverless car that propelled him from the small portal lab in Los Angeles to his hotel in Beverly Hills. He'd wounded Akito Wakai, but the man's stupid wife had appeared just before Nick had fired. She'd screamed when she saw Nick with the gun, causing Akito to jump out of the way. Then neighbors started poking their heads out of doors and Nick had fled. He should have known it wouldn't be that easy. Now what? He could have stayed and tried again, but, not only would Akito be on the alert now, but the 1920s in Los Angeles was not the magical era it was in Paris, or London, or even New York and he didn't want to linger there. It was congested and ugly and crass. He'd never had to worry about getting around by car in the other cities he'd visited in the twenties because he'd mostly been there for pleasure and had hired a car with a driver. In the short time he had been in 1920 Los Angeles, it hadn't been worth it to buy a car, and he couldn't very well hire a driver to help him get away after making a hit. Another way to get around the city was by cab, which is what he'd used, but those were few and far between. Street cars were the other option, but not for him. They were efficient, but Nick had an aversion to public transportation. Being from one of the wealthiest families in the world, he viewed it as something for common people; not for the likes of him. No, 1920, the year before Akito Wakai had produced an offspring, was not the right time to carry out his plan. Offspring… the word chimed in his head. Maybe, just maybe, there was something to that.

Chapter Four

From the memoir of Akito Wakai

Once the ship was underway, I reported for duty. I was immediately put to work making sure everyone onboard was sufficiently fed. This was no small task for there were several hundred more people who were in need than when we had docked. The cook and I used all our knowledge and skill to create dishes that would sustain us through a long journey, me working in a much greater capacity than just chopping, fetching, and serving.

The days dragged and the heat of the sun beat upon us without mercy. People were kind to one another at first, but, after more than a week, nerves began to fray and fights broke out. One man was caught stealing food from the larder and the captain was forced to declare a punishment—the man was made to keep the heads clean.

Day after day, sweat poured from all of us and the decks were very crowded as everyone sought out solace in the scant patches of shade available. The doldrums were upon us: no wind and very little movement of the water. It made it seem that the ship was barely moving though it was steaming along as usual. One afternoon, clouds poured over the horizon and a huge storm suddenly blasted us with its terrible wrath. Lightning filled the air and spikes of electric fire drove the crowds into the lower decks. The sea, quiet moments before, was now wild and raging. Giant swells rocked us like so much flotsam. The boat was tossed like a twig and many people were knocked from their feet. Two people, unable to escape below decks, were swept overboard. Then, as suddenly as it began, the storm abated and disappeared as though it had never been. The sun once again reminded us of its power. The air became even more humid than before. Nearly everyone reappeared on deck to get some relief from the stagnant, dank, and thick air below. It was one of the strangest days we experienced, especially with so many people packing the deck in absolute silence after the storm.

The woman, whose name was Mai, was mending well, but she was still terribly sad. I spent all the time I could steal away from work with her. I had found a little nook for her in one of the kitchen storerooms which was better than the engine room, as it was actually fairly cool and quiet. There, I could make sure she was safe. No one cared anyway. People had carved out spaces for themselves wherever they could find them on the boat. I tried to cheer her whenever I could, but my rate of success was slow. After a couple weeks, I began to see some improvement in her demeanor. One evening, when I brought her a meal, she reached out, took my hand in both of hers and kissed it. She looked up at me with bright eyes full of tears and thanked me. She said she felt very grateful and wished to repay me. She subtly let me know that if I wished it, I could join her in the bed. I didn't know what to say. Though I already had strong feelings for her, I would never want to take advantage of her situation. I smiled and told her as gently as I could that she was welcome, and that she owed me nothing. She immediately collapsed in tears and pressed her lips to my hand once again. Keeping her eyes lowered she said almost too

*quietly to hear, "but you see...I have come to love you."
My heart nearly burst with happiness but I felt I should
not allow her to love me because of gratitude. My pride
was in the way, and I did not know how to respond. I
was fearful of hurting this gentle, beautiful woman and
afraid to hear something other than words of love from
her. I was very confused. However, fate stepped into our
little space in that awkward moment and saved me. The
fire alarm began to wail throughout the ship. People were
screaming and we could hear them running outside in the
passageway. I opened the hatch and took her hand. She
was able to walk now, but still had to move slowly. Together we finally reached the stairwell to the upper deck.
Everyone was laughing and hugging one another. The
alarm had gone off to call attention to the fact that we
were approaching the western islands of British Columbia, and would soon be arriving at the Port of Vancouver.*

It was unsettling to be back in Boston again. How long had it been? A year? More? Boston was still Boston. Cassandra's beautiful, three-hundred-year old townhome was in perfect shape, kept that way by cleaning 'bots. They dusted, swept, vacuumed, watered the plants... they would even feed and play with pets if programmed to do so, but it had been a long time since she had kept a cat, as much as she loved them. The time traveling she'd done over the last five years, though only the first and last of those trips had been of her own design and desire, made it impractical.

She only had a day to enjoy the feeling of being at home before being whisked off by Elton Carver to Worcester, where Suhan was serving her sentence. The poor girl, she hadn't meant to do wrong. She had been seduced by Nick Stockard into doing his bidding, her love for him driving her to go against her conscience. As a result, people had died, and, for this, Suhan had to pay the consequences. Yet the Turkish scientist was not a bad person, Cassandra was convinced. If there were any truth to Suhan's conviction that Nick was running around free while she was paying for his crimes, she would probably be all the more willing to help them find him.

They pulled up to the facility, a compound of modern wooden buildings lined with windows from the ground to the second story peaked roofs, something resembling more of a spa than a space to house prisoners. The buildings were surrounded by forest, and a gentle stream babbled under a small bridge, which they crossed to get to the parking area. Their driverless car hummed along until it found a niche to fit into, then turned itself off.

Cassandra and Elton entered the main building without ceremony, passed through an eye scanner, and were admitted into a room where several women, dressed casually in the clothing of their choice, were engaged in various activities from working on VR computer stations to painting the old-fashioned way with paint and canvas. Suhan looked up from her VR terminal and waved at them. She stood to greet them, her dark eyes intense.

Cassandra had a moment of hesitation. Did Suhan resent that it was Cassandra who had turned her in? But then Suhan grasped her in an embrace and Cassandra breathed a sigh of relief. Suhan stood back from her for a moment, looking her over.

"You look wonderful, Cassie."

Her tone was hard to read. Was there a hint of sarcasm or even jealousy in it? "Thank you. You, too."

Suhan laughed loudly. "Oh, I doubt that."

"She's right," Elton said to her. "You look rested. You look good." They exchanged a gentle hug.

"Come here," Suhan said. "Let me show you what I found."

Cassandra and Elton joined her at the terminal. Suhan called up an old newspaper article onto the holographic screen for them to view.

"Look at this!" Suhan said, gesturing with a flourish of her hand.

Cassandra peered with interest at the photo of old movie stars, some of whom she recognized: Clark Gable, Bette Davis, Katherine Hepburn... the others she wasn't sure of. Only film buffs such as she knew these icons from the early days of the art form. And there, glancing out from behind the shoulder of Bette Davis was, undeniably, the face of Nick Stockard. He looked as though he'd been caught unawares and was trying to hide before the camera snapped his image.

"That's him!" Elton exclaimed. "You're right,

Suhan, that's definitely him."

"I'd know that face anywhere," Cassandra said as a shiver went down her spine.

"I've studied it and analyzed it in every way possible," Suhan said, "trying to convince myself it was just someone that looked like him, but the computer can't be wrong. I ran Nick's photo through a recognition program and, among the many recent images of him, as well as those from earlier in his lifetime, this one came up."

"What made you think to look for him?" Cassandra asked.

"I had to be sure he was dead. Or not dead, as the case seems to be."

"Is there any way this photo could have been taken before he, supposedly, died? After all, he had access to a time machine, he could have gone anywhere in history during the time he was avoiding us in the present," Cassandra observed.

"I thought of that," Suhan began, a note of impatience edging into her voice, "though I don't know why he would have gone to the 1940s. He told me the time periods he had visited, and was planning to visit. When he wasn't involved in his schemes in Italy or Elizabethan England, he stuck to Britain or France of the 1920s. It was his favorite era. He had no reason to visit the 1940s —especially Hollywood. However, to be sure, I did an age analysis. This photo shows him to be about a year older than the last time I saw him, which means he doesn't look much different, other than his hairstyle and clothes. So that's the proof he didn't die that night in London when you thought he did."

"You were right, Elton, someone must have come to his aid," Cassandra said with a sinking in her chest. "Maybe he was carrying some nano-healers with him. Otherwise, there would have been very little chance of his surviving infection."

"I guess I'm glad he's not dead," Suhan said, looking up with her large dark eyes into Elton's face. "Not that I have any feelings for him anymore at all. I've come to see I was being brainwashed by him in a sense. I just wish he could be brought to justice once and for all."

Cassandra hated to admit she'd thought his death had done just that. Now, it seemed she'd been mistaken. She glanced at Elton, trying to read his thoughts.

"The question remains," he said, "why would he choose Hollywood in the 1940s? There must be a reason for it."

"What's the exact date of the newspaper photo?" Cassandra asked.

"June twenty-third, 1942."

"1942," Elton mused. "Early in the war—for the U.S., at least."

"And June," Cassandra continued, "which means he somehow healed from his knife wound, got himself back to his portal exit in Southwark, returned to our time, and the team who was working for him must have come to the States and arranged to build another portal in Hollywood, or thereabouts. Though I suppose he could have built the portal anywhere in the U.S. and traveled from there to Los Angeles, it would make the most sense to build it right there."

"Yes," the professor went on, "the whole process, from the time he was stabbed in London until time traveling again, only took him a couple of months."

"And here he is hobnobbing with movie stars," Cassandra observed. "He had to have had some time to worm his way into their circle. That couldn't have been easy."

"Well, as I found when I went to 1920s Harlem," Elton said, leaning back in his chair, "it's not hard to meet who you want to meet when you have a lot of money. And he does. You dress a certain way, drive a certain kind of car, pay your way into the best clubs, send an expensive bottle of champagne the way of some big shot, and, if you're charming enough, you're in." He shot her a smile.

"And of course you were charming enough," Cassandra said with a sidelong glance and a smile to match his.

"Thank you, my dear." He tipped an imaginary hat.

"And Nick could be too when he wanted to be," Suhan interjected.

"I'm afraid that's true," Cassandra said with a

sigh.

"Is there any other information with this picture, Suhan?" Elton wanted to know. "Does it say his name?"

"There's a short article with the picture. It was taken at a gala at the Brown Derby Restaurant to benefit the Hollywood Canteen, which was a type of club the celebrities ran. The servicemen would come in and meet them. It was a kind of morale booster. I did some research on it. Bette Davis was president at the time. All kinds of film stars worked there, volunteer, of course, just to give the servicemen a chance to have some fun. This is Hedy Lamarr, Betty Grable, Gene Tierney and Davis in the picture," Suhan said, pointing them out, "along with Clark Gable, William Holden and Lana Turner. And then there's Nick behind Davis."

"I've heard of some of these people," said Professor Carver, "but I've never heard of the Hollywood Canteen."

"Yeah, it was a big deal apparently," said Suhan. "You had people like Clark Gable and Errol Flynn washing dishes, Betty Grable and other sexy actresses waiting tables, others working a phone desk to raise money for the war effort. Some of the stars would dance with the servicemen too, and sell kisses for a buck."

"Interesting," Cassandra murmured. "But why was Nick at the gala? It doesn't make any sense."

"I have no idea," Suhan replied.

Cassandra felt Elton's eyes on her and turned to look at him. "We're going to go find out, aren't we?"

"I don't know how else we'll get our hands on him. We'll have to go just before June twenty-third and be ready to nab him." He appeared deep in thought.

"But nab him how?" Cassandra wanted to know. "Walk into the Brown Derby with a gun, which would ultimately involve the police? Get him to quietly go with us? That's not going to happen."

"And there's another problem," Elton remarked, "I'm black. L.A. at that time was almost as segregated as the south. If there's any kind of altercation, I'll end up being the suspect instead of Nick."

"Then maybe you shouldn't go with me," Cassandra reluctantly proposed.

His dark brown eyes penetrated her gaze. "You're not going alone. No way."

"Well, who else is available to go? Not Yoshi, for god's sake. He's the worst possible choice for that era."

"And not James," Elton added. "He's got to stay here and work with the Chronology Board on the Elizabeth letters."

"He's too hot-headed anyway," Cassandra admitted. "We need someone steady."

"Alex isn't ready," Elton said. "It's too bad Jake isn't on the team anymore."

"He and Giulia have a new baby anyway," Cassandra said, smiling at the thought of her former colleague being so happy.

"You could do it, Dr. Carver," Suhan cut in. "But you would have to go in a capacity that makes sense for your race at that time. Maybe as Cassandra's bodyguard, or chauffeur."

"No, no, no, no," Cassandra exclaimed, horrified at the thought of her boss having to pose as her servant. "That's unacceptable."

"Alright, Cassie, now let's think," Elton said, laying a hand over hers. "Maybe I could pretend to be your bodyguard."

"And who would I be?"

"I don't know, but we'll figure it out. This is how I see it though: I should go first. I should go a week or two in advance, buy a car, and maybe rent a house or an apartment for you..."

"Wait a minute, how long do you think we'll have to be there? If we catch Nick while he's at the Brown Derby, and we know he will be, we may be able to grab him and get him back to the portal in a day."

"And if we don't succeed?" Carver said. "We'll need to regroup. It could take a while. Also, the one thing we can't do is make him aware of our presence because, if he gets away, he'll know we've come after him, and he'll escape back through his own portal. It may make more sense to stalk him, if you know what I mean, and grab him when he least expects it. There will be no second chances, Cassandra. If we lose him, we lose him for good."

"That true," Suhan piped up.

She seemed all too in favor of this plan. So did Elton, as a matter of fact.

He went on, "Right, so I'll go in advance, like I said. I'd better allow at least a couple of weeks."

"Well then, I guess we're setting up a lab in Hollywood," Cassandra relented. She still wasn't convinced. "I haven't even unpacked yet."

"I'll send the team to California to start scouting a location for a portal. Go ahead and unpack, Cassie," he said. "You know it will take a few weeks to find the right spot and at least another month after that to get the lab built, which is just about all the time we have. Anyway, there's no reason you should have to go out there yet."

"I would give anything to be on that team," Suhan cut in, her eyes still shining with that intense glow.

Cassandra gazed at her. Her going was not a possibility, as she still had a year to go on her sentence. Anyway, could she really be trusted when it came to Nick? "I'm sorry, Suhan," she said.

"There can be no delay in getting everything ready for the journey," Suhan rushed to say. "You've got to get there by June twenty-third, by the time this picture was taken. We don't know what Nick's up to there. I just have a feeling that whatever he's doing, it's not good."

"I agree," said Cassandra. "I don't think he just went there on a lark. There's got to be a reason he chose that time and place. He's got a motive, and it probably has something to do with me."

"Or me," Suhan added.

"Why would it have to do with you?" Cassandra asked as gently as possible.

"I mean, I don't know. I was his...I don't know what to call it."

"His lover," Cassandra offered.

"And his right hand," Suhan added, looking sharply at Cassandra.

The redhead felt a stab of anger as she remembered again how Suhan's helping Nick had caused innocent people to die.

"It could be he wants revenge in general," Elton added, "against the whole team."

"Right," Cassandra agreed. "But what do any of us have to do with Hollywood of that time period? Or the war?"

"I don't know," the professor replied, "but we'd better get to figuring it out. We won't know anything more until we actually go."

He stood and Cassandra rose with him. "Suhan, thank you so much for bringing this to our attention. I'll make sure the parole board knows how helpful you've been."

"Thank you, Dr. Carver," she jumped to her feet and went to give him a tentative hug.

He wrapped her in a fatherly embrace. "Take care of yourself."

Cassandra didn't want to hug her again. She held out a hand and Suhan took it with a shake.

"Be careful," Suhan warned, "I wouldn't underestimate Nick.
"Trust me," Cassandra replied, "I've learned that lesson the hard way."

Chapter Five

From the memoir of Akito Wakai

Mai and I now had a decision to make. Going back to our country was out of the question. Though we knew the island had not been entirely devastated by the earthquake, we were too traumatized to think of ever returning there. Her family was gone, and, even if mine was not, there was nothing there for me but my parents' farm. Remaining on the Empress of Australia with Mai was not an option either. Besides, neither of us ever wanted to be on a boat again after that experience. By this time, it was clear our destiny was to be together. I now knew she loved me, not out of gratitude, but for the man I am. We had gotten to know each other well. We had talked about our families and childhoods. We'd spoken of what we thought the future might hold for us though it was impossible to picture at that point.

As the ship pulled into the port, I asked her to marry me, and she said yes. We ran to the bridge and asked the captain to perform the ceremony. He did so hurriedly, not having the time or patience to make a fuss over it. Then, we went to the bursar, and I asked him to pay me what I was owed. He wasn't able to give me all of it, but enough for us to make our way in the new world. Then, our heads spinning, we made our way off the ship with the others.

Vancouver was a poor city, dangerous and rough. Many people lived on the streets. We spent our wedding night in a cheap motel on the edge of town. All of this was a far cry from the Shinto wedding we would have had in Japan, with all the traditions and ceremony. But then, in Japan, our marriages would have been arranged and we would never have found our way to each other. So we were happy—blissfully happy—to now be man and wife, regardless of what happened next.

The next morning, we bought passage on a train to Seattle. I had a passport, and Mai was my wife, made official with the stamped document the bursar had given us, so we were able to cross into the United States. It was my hope we would be able to become U.S. citizens eventually. As I mentioned, I spoke little English, and Mai none, but we were determined to learn.

Suhan Bostan needed to talk to her counselor. She was losing her grip on reality. While she wanted Nick to pay for what he'd done—to her and to others—she'd begun to have that fluttery feeling in her stomach that still crept up on her when she thought of him. It was the feeling that had made her do anything he'd asked her to and, even now, she wasn't sure she was free of his spell.

She made an appointment and the next day at one o'clock walked into the serene office decorated with simple wood furniture and muted colors. Karina, the woman who had been her counselor since she'd been sent to the facility a year earlier, gazed at her with a kind but detached expression as she motioned for Suhan to be seated. "Tell me what's going on," she said.

"There's something I've been keeping from you." Karina tilted her head but didn't seem surprised. Suhan went on. "It's about Nick."

"I'm listening."

Suhan explained her discovery of him visiting the 1940s. She then continued. "There's a lot I haven't told you, actually. I told you he tricked me into helping him break the law. Obviously, that's why I'm in here. But I didn't tell you everything."

"I know you were indicted as an accomplice to murder."

"Yes." Suhan looked down at her hands.

"You pled not guilty to that charge."

"Because I didn't know he was going to murder anyone!"

"You've told me that much."

"I don't know where to start."

"Where did it start? Your obsession with Nick Stockard."

Suhan took a deep breath. "It started almost as soon as I met him. When he returned from England of 1820."

"Hold on," said Karina, running a hand through her short, grey hair. "If you're going to start talking about time travel, you're going to have to give me a lot more detail. I don't understand any of that stuff and we've barely touched on it in our sessions. If you're going to tell me the whole story, then I need everything."

"Okay. It started when Nick was a student of Professor Carver's, my former boss, about twenty years ago. You know that much."

"Yes."

"That was before Cassandra Reilly joined the team."

"Your rival for his affection."

"Um, yes. Anyway, Nick told me he left Carver's team early on because he felt Carver wasn't moving fast enough toward a breakthrough. I think I've mentioned that Nick comes from one of the wealthiest families in the world, right?"

"We've all heard of the Stockards," Karina replied.

"So Nick was able to build his own lab, attract other brilliant scientists, and work toward a breakthrough of his own. It always irked him that Carver got there first."

Karina nodded and tapped her pencil against her chin.

It had always amused Suhan that the woman still took notes on paper with a pencil. She focused her thoughts and went on. "Nick wasn't far behind though his method was just different enough not to infringe on Carver's patent. So, while Carver proceeded to move forward with great caution, Nick plunged ahead, sending himself on short trips to test the functionality, all with great success. But when his wife, one of the scientists on his team, went on a longer trip— to ancient Egypt in fact—something went terribly wrong and she died there. Something Nick never forgave himself for." Suhan took a deep breath. "After that, he decided to go live in England, circa 1810 and was never going to come back. He brought a ton of money in replicated pounds sterling and his 18th century cello. He bought himself a nice townhouse in London and opened a music shop. That's how he planned to live out his days. Until, one day in 1820, Cassandra walked into his shop."

"She had time traveled there?"

"Yes. Anyway, I won't go into all the details of how they developed a friendship back then, but he helped her out of a very sticky situation. Once they disclosed to each other that they were both time travelers, he decided to hitch a ride back to the present day via her portal. Professor Carver and the MIT chronology team were so grateful to him for helping Cassandra they offered him a position on the team. He accepted, and worked side by side with Cassandra, Carver, and the team for the next year—a very valuable addition at MIT. He fell in love with Cassandra, and they dated, but I don't think she ever really loved him. When Carver asked Cassandra to take another time journey, this time to pre-Civil War New York, Nick started to freak out. He didn't want her to go without him. He started to become irrationally possessive of her and, so, just before she left, she dumped him."

"I remember reading about that trip," Karina exclaimed. "The artist Evie Johnston traveled back in time to meet Caleb Stone, famous for one painting he did, but whom nobody knew anything about."

"Right. She was also the descendant of the man Cassandra had been involved with in Regency England, another long story. Anyway, in 1853 New York, Evie and Cassandra got involved with the Underground Railroad and nearly got themselves killed. When they didn't return to the future at the appointed time, Nick convinced Carver to let him go look for them. Carver agreed, something he's always regretted doing, and with good reason because Nick hired some goons to kill this abolitionist that Cassandra had gotten involved with. Nick was driven by pure jealousy. No one knew he had done it though, until they all returned to the future and historical documents brought it to light."

"Why didn't they arrest Nick then?"

"They tried to but he escaped—then managed to get his own portal built and disappear into the past."

"Wow." Karina let out a long exhale.

Suhan went on. "Turns out he'd gone to Paris in the 1920s for a few months, then came back to Boston. That's when he contacted me."

"How did he know he could trust you not to turn him in?"

Suhan could feel the heat rise to her cheeks. "He knew I cared about him. While Cassandra was in

1853 with Evie, I spent a lot of time with him. I told you I'd been attracted to him since he came back from Regency England, but he never really paid attention to me. But, while she was in New York, he started being extra nice to me, and I fell for him."

"Even though you knew he loved Cassandra. Even though you knew how jealous he could be."

"I didn't see him that way. I saw him as a passionate man—a man who would do anything for the woman he loved. I wanted him to feel that way about me."

Karina nodded slowly. The pencil was tapping again. "This brings us back to your issues with your father. How he abandoned your family."

"I guess," Suhan said softly.

"What happened after Nick contacted you?"

"He wanted to know what Carver's team was up to, so I told him. They were planning to go to Italy—Siena, 1506. They had to fix a timeline that had been altered by something one of the team had done on a previous trip there."

"I read about this too. They went to find out why a famous painting had disappeared from the collective consciousness."

"Right. Well, Nick saw this as his chance to screw things up for them. He was operating in the past and in the present. He got involved in a political situation in Siena in the present, made the time machine available to a crooked politician so he could steal the painting from the past, and provided weapons that the guy used to kill some innocent people in the here and now, trying to blame it on his political rival. Through it all, I was Nick's contact. I told him what Cassandra, Carver, and the team were doing, and when. That's how I was involved. I didn't know what he was doing with the information I gave him, but, yeah, in the end, I was his accomplice."

"But Carver's team didn't know that then, did they?"

"No. I managed to keep it a secret because, by this time, I was so in love with Nick that I would do anything for him. After that, he took me with him, back to Paris in the twenties. We lived la vie bohème," she giggled, "even though he was so rich that we hardly lived like Bohemians. We went to the cafés, and the salons, we met famous artists and writers...it was so romantic!"

Karina studied her, pale blue eyes narrowed. "This worries me, Suhan. You obviously are still enthralled with the relationship you shared with Nick."

"No," Suhan insisted, shaking her head, "those memories are good, but I'm not under any illusions any more. He broke my heart. We came back to the present together after a couple of months, and I rejoined Carver's team so I could tell Nick everything they were doing. They thought I'd just been visiting my family in Turkey. I told Nick that Cassandra's son, James, had gone to Elizabethan England but there had been trouble there, and Cassandra had to go and help James out. Nick basically shut me out then, as he feverishly revised his portal lab in London so he could go to 1598. He had so much money that he had scientists and engineers at his disposal, people to whom he would pay huge sums to do his bidding and keep quiet about it. But again, he wouldn't tell me why he was doing any of this. Ultimately, it was his plan to kidnap Cassandra and take her to the 1920s—to our era! And that's exactly what he did."

"Again, Suhan, it seems like you have a lot of emotion going on that."

Suhan felt tears sting her eyes. "It's just that he hurt me so badly. Don't you see? That's why I told Cassandra and Dr. Carver that I found out he'd traveled to 1942. This is their chance to catch him once and for all and make him pay for what he did!"

"What he did to you?" Karina softly asked.

"What he did to everyone. For hurting me...for hurting so many people."

Karina was silent for a moment, then she spoke, "I'm so glad you told me all of this, Suhan. You've been holding it back for a long time. I have to tell you, though, I'm concerned about your stability."

"I'll do whatever I have to," Suhan said, resigned, "stay here as long as they think I should. I won't apply for early parole if you don't think I should. Honestly, you're right. I don't entirely trust myself. If they don't catch Nick, or if they do, and they bring him back alive, I don't know what I might be responsible for."

"Thank you for saying that, Suhan," Karina replied. "It's very brave."

Chapter Six

From the memoir of Akito Wakai

We stayed in Seattle for six months. There, we found a room in a boarding house, run by a Japanese family, and I found a job as a cook in a Japanese restaurant. The owner of the boarding house connected Mai with families who needed sewing and mending done, which she took in as often as possible. She began to embroider designs on special costumes, wedding dresses, etc. Her work was exquisite and became much sought after.

It was in Seattle that I finally figured out what was the source of the night-blooming jasmine smell that had surrounded Mai when we first met, but which had disappeared over time. Since we were staying in a mostly Japanese neighborhood, we had access to some of the products we were familiar with in Japan. One of these was a soap which Mai was thrilled to find in a store one day. As soon as I smelled it, I knew it was the source of that bewitching scent. We bought it, of course, and she uses it on her hair and skin. She doesn't need any scent to be bewitching. She mesmerizes me with her grace and beauty every day. The smell of her skin, without any fragrance at all, is like the smell of sunshine, but if I could provide her with this one little luxury, I was happy to do it.

Unlike Japan's, America's economy was booming in those years and Seattle along with it. We were saving money, hoping to buy a small house of our own in that same neighborhood. Then Mai had a miscarriage. We were so excited when we learned she was pregnant, and thought Seattle would be the perfect place to raise a child. But after the miscarriage, she was so depressed I thought it would be better to get her away from the place where it happened—where everything reminded her of it. I didn't know where we would go, but then I remembered that a cousin of mine had settled in Los Angeles several years before. This was someone I never knew but I remembered my parents remarking upon. All I knew was their name. I called the operator and asked for the address in Los Angeles. I then wrote my cousin a letter. A couple of weeks later, I received a reply. Though they didn't have a place for us to stay for more than a few nights, nor a job they could offer me, they said they could help me find a place to rent and that they knew of a few restaurants where I could apply for a job. That settled it for me. I told Mai my plan, and she agreed. The rain and cold in Seattle was making her even more depressed. She had heard that Los Angeles was sunny and warm. So we packed up our few belongings, bought tickets on the Shasta Daylight, and headed south.

Elton was excited about time traveling again. Though the most fruitful time journeys were those that sprang from something organic, usually a scientist's deep interest in the era, this journey would be out of necessity, as all but the first and last of Cassandra's had been. Still, he couldn't deny he was fascinated by the 1940s—as much as he'd been by New York of the 1920s, his first journey. Ten years had passed since then, during which he'd watched Cassandra travel again and again, going with others or because of others. He hadn't been able to go along...until now. So, yes, maybe he was more enthusiastic about the project than he should be, but he was still laser-focused on the objective: to catch Nick.

He found himself wishing, not for the first time, that it was possible to set the date to which a person was traveling to a specific day of the year. If he could, there would be no pressure to get the portal set up by early June. Unfortunately, there wasn't. The portal corresponded to the same day of the year in which one existed in the present to the day of the year to which one was going in the past, though if one left on a Friday, for instance, one might actually arrive on a Sunday, given how the days of the week changed dates from year to year. This time, if he wanted to arrive in the past on June eighth, he had to leave the present on the sixth. The idea that H.G. Wells had imagined, which was to set the date of your time machine to any you wanted, and to any place you wanted to go to, was not how the process actually worked. You had to be travelling from one location in the present to that same location in the past to use the wormhole that the time portal created. Too bad, Elton thought. H.G.'s concept would have been so much more convenient.

The team assembling the portal lab was comprised of Yoshi, who was taking a break from the preparations for his own trip in order to help out; James, who had also taken time from preparing to meet with the board at MIT about his Elizabeth letters to assist with the set-up of the lab; Alex Goodman, the Brit; and another intern, Sara Gonzalez, a gifted scientist who had been part of the team for just a few months. Being from Los Angeles, and a historical expert on the area, she was especially helpful on this project. It was Sara who'd pointed out that South Central Avenue was the hub of African American life in the 1940s, so it was there the team had begun their search for a portal location.

After thorough research, Sara actually found a location in Long Beach in which to build the portal lab: a house where the corresponding wormhole exit would allow the time travelers to emerge into a warehouse in 1942. Long Beach was not as heavily populated as it was farther north, and it was mostly industrial, which meant it would be quiet in the evenings, the warehouse closed, allowing for Elton to arrive there with less chance of being noticed.

Around mid-May, Sara flew out to Boston to meet Cassandra and Elton at the main lab at MIT in Cambridge. Joining them in Elton's spacious office, she described the area: "There were seaside attractions right at the shore, a rollercoaster and stuff like that, but farther inland were warehouses and factories, so a black man wouldn't seem totally out of place there." She hurried on in her enthusiasm for the history as they studied a holographic map that floated in the air above Elton's desk. "There was one warehouse on the corner of Watson Avenue and East I Street that was torn down after the war, when the area became more mixed residential and industrial. A group of bungalows was built in its place," she pointed out. "Those houses were recently replaced with more upscale homes, and there's one on this corner, where the warehouse was in 1942, that is for sale. I talked to the owners, and they said they'd be happy to rent it to us at the hefty price we're offering so we can build a temporary portal lab there. It was a warehouse that used to store equipment needed for building war machinery. I have no way of knowing how many people worked there, but certainly there won't be anyone there late at night, so it might be a good place for the portal exit."

'I'm going to want to find a hotel, or a boarding house or whatever," said Elton, "up here in Central L.A., right? You're saying that north of Compton, along South Central Avenue, was where the black population was most concentrated?"

"Yeah," she replied. "There were some nice hotels there. You aren't going to have to stay in a dump. As a matter of fact, some of the top black entertainers of the day stayed at the Dunbar. You should probably aim for that."

"We'll have to time it just right," he said. "And the place I find for you, Cassie, can't be a hotel because we'll have to be able to stay together after you arrive."

"How are we going to find a neighborhood that will accept a white woman and a black man living together?" Cassandra wanted to know.

"It'll be tricky. I'm thinking though, if I'm posing as your bodyguard, maybe I can rent you a home with a guest house where I can stay."

"Will they even let you rent the place?"

"Where there's a will there's a way. There's no one else who can do this. It has to be me. I'll figure it out."

By the end of the first week in June, the portal in Long Beach was assembled and ready for the travelers. The entire team gathered in the lab for Elton's send off. It would be nine PM on a Saturday night in 1942. They had been observing the warehouse for a week and had seen no activity at that time of night on weekends in the tucked away corner where Elton would emerge from the portal. He was dressed simply, in the kind of coveralls a janitor might wear, and he carried a satchel of personal necessities that might be taken for a tool bag, with a change of clothes inside as well. Shannon had had a driver's license made up for him that was an exact replica of a California license of the time. It had his description on it, but no picture, and was tucked into the authentic-looking wallet he had stashed in the satchel with a large amount of reproduced money.

With Alex in charge of the computer console, which was set for the correct year and time of day, Elton stepped into the portal chamber without ceremony. His heart beat fast. How many times had he said good-bye to Cassandra as she'd been whisked away from him into uncertain situations and unstable times? It hadn't been easy to send Jake or James off the three times each they had traveled either, but sending Cassandra—every time (though he had not let himself admit it in those early years)—felt like a piece of himself was being wrenched away. He had been married during those years, of course, so he'd tried hard not to think about it. However, given how beautiful Cassandra was, and that she'd fallen in love during that first trip to Regency England, it made the possibility that she'd become romantically involved with some compelling character on subsequent trips likely, and made each time he'd said good-bye to her harder and harder.

His mind flashed back to Harlem. During that trip, which had lasted no more than a handful of weeks, he'd very nearly fallen for the indescribable Josephine Baker—he, a married man, and she, a few decades his junior. That experience at least helped him understand how alluring the spell of the past could be, and how hard it could be to resist. He was glad this time he was going as Cassandra's steward, essentially, and that, after he returned to the present, with their housing and transportation arranged, they would be traveling back together.

The feeling of hurtling through time and space via the wormhole was no more pleasant now than it had been those ten years ago, but it was over soon enough, and in just moments he was standing on a concrete floor in a dark and out of the way corner of the immense military warehouse. He took a moment to let his eyes adjust to the dark then glanced around and listened for any human sounds: voices or footsteps. All was quiet. He located the front exit by the streetlights streaming in from high windows, not daring to use the flashlight he had stashed in his bag for fear of attracting attention. He found the door locked with a key bolt, and a dead bolt that could only be locked from the inside, meaning there had to be a security guard in there somewhere. Well, the dead bolt would have to remain unsecured. Once outside, he was able to re-lock the key bolt with a transforming key he kept on his key ring, one that looked like a normal key of that era, but which could mold to fit any lock.

Now, he was out on the sidewalk, looking like a humble worker. They'd planned his arrival for ten minutes before a scheduled stop of the Red Line trolley on Alameda. He was on East I Street, just two blocks from there. He hurried along the dark and deserted street to the well-lit boulevard. There, finely dressed people, mostly white, were going to and from the amusement park in Long Beach. Just as Sara had predicted, the trolley came lumbering along not long after he reached Alameda. He followed the lead of others boarding the car and jumped on when the trolley slowed. He knew what the fare would be and already had the coin in hand. He paid the driver and moved toward the rear of the car just to be safe, where other people of color were situated, and took a seat on one of the front-facing, padded benches. The trolley was abuzz with people from all walks of life enjoying their Saturday night out, but he couldn't help resenting the white people who took for granted their right to the front two-thirds of the car. As a well-learned historian, he knew about the harshness of discrimination during this era, and Los Angeles was not much better than the segregated American south. Understanding the historical reality didn't make it sting any less.

He took a deep breath. The first of the obstacles had been easily overcome; he could afford to relax a little. He gazed out the window in fascination at the early city. Enormous automobiles rumbled along the streets: Fords, Plymouths, Pontiacs, Chevys, Oldsmobiles, Hudsons. Soon the mighty freeways of Los Angeles, only one of which existed in this time, the Pasadena, would replace the Red Line entirely. Humankind during this era had been so short sighted, or ignorant, he supposed, of the damage the fossil-fuel driven culture would wreak upon the environment. We came so close, he thought, so close to losing it all.

The antique car-lover in him soon took over. He nearly drooled seeing all those gorgeous vehicles, so completely impractical and unsustainable, and fantasized about what kind he would buy for himself and Cassandra to use.

The ride into Compton was a long one but he had a lot to look at, a lot to think about, and much to be fascinated by. Not long after they left the environs of Long Beach, the area deteriorated. The homes along the avenue were little more than shacks, and there were many deserted fields, while in places the road was pitted and muddy. As the trolley rolled closer to Compton, the neighborhood began to improve again and the avenue now was lined with shops, taverns, and modest hotels. More and more black people got on and filled in the seats. They were so well-dressed Elton began to feel self-conscious about his work clothes.

Finally, the trolley approached Vernon Avenue. Carver hopped off along with many others and grabbed another trolley west toward S. Central. In a few minutes he was there. He stepped off into an explosion of nightlife. Saturday night at ten o'clock, and the scene was at its peak along the boulevard. Fancy cars rolled by and from them emerged the African American elite: musicians, singers, dancers, entrepreneurs. Hollywood may not yet have been employing black actors in anything but the most stereotypical roles, but, just like Harlem of the 1920s, Los Angeles of the 1940s was ruled by jazz, in particular swing music, and everyone who was part of the scene was getting rich off it, from the musicians themselves to the club owners to the doormen.

Elton struck off northward, his goal 42nd Street and the Dunbar Hotel. He ducked into a seedy looking bar, ordered a whiskey, slapped fifty cents onto the counter, and headed toward the bathroom. It was a filthy, cramped space. As quickly as possible, he shed his overalls and donned the zootsuit he'd brought along. Shannon had made it especially for him at his request and folded it carefully so it wouldn't get wrinkled along the way. It consisted of a white shirt, a short striped tie, a long blazer in royal blue that came down to mid-thigh with wide shoulders and lapels, and high-waisted, full-legged trousers of the same color, held up by suspenders. He replaced his work boots with two-toned Oxfords of black and white, and popped the royal blue fedora on his head that had been held in shape by paper stuffed into it. It was tricky keeping everything clean in the dank bathroom, but he managed to dress quickly, stuffing his boots and coveralls back in the satchel. He sauntered out to the bar under the surprised gaze of the bartender and other patrons. He downed the whiskey in one swallow, trying hard not to cough over the low-quality liquor, and hurried out of the tavern.

Now as sharp as any other character on the street, he approached the Dunbar Hotel, where all the staff and guests were black, and was cordially greeted by a doorman who directed him to the front desk. There, he was informed that one of their best rooms was available, which he booked for two weeks at a premium rate. He ordered a steak and a beer to be delivered to his room and took a gleaming elevator, manned by an operator, to the sixth floor, where he found a spotless and elegantly appointed room awaiting him. Sara had told him that later in 1942, meat, oil, butter, cheese, wheat, and many other foods would be rationed with the use of coupon books issued to every family. For now, though, he could enjoy his steak, something he rarely ate in his own era.

After he finished eating, he had a decision to make. He could either go to bed, or check out the nightlife. The second choice was too tempting. And so, out he went onto S. Central toward Club Alabam, another iconic locale of black life in L.A., directly next door to the hotel. Swinging jazz blared from inside, and women in long dresses and men in tuxes, or fashionable suits like the one he wore, lined up outside to get in.

Elton sauntered to the front of the line and laid a ten-dollar bill on the bouncer. The man's mouth fell open. He unlatched the velvet rope and gestured for Elton to enter. For Elton Carver, money was no issue. Technically, what he had was counterfeit, but so well reproduced that no one, not the banks or even the federal treasury would be able to tell the difference. He didn't feel great about using it since it could undermine the economy if too much were thrown around, but what he would spend, even what he and Cassandra might spend during the time it took to accomplish their mission, wouldn't make much of an impact. He had brought ten thousand in cash with him, about five hundred of which he had on his person at the moment. The rest was locked in the safe the hotel provided in his room. Even if he got robbed of every cent, he could make his way back to the portal exit, return to the future, and get more.

Now, here he was in the famed Club Alabam, and Duke Ellington and his band were burning it up on stage. Elegantly dressed couples were dancing on the floor or sitting around at tables, eating and drinking. He stood there stunned for a moment, unbelieving of the scene unfolding before him, especially that he was listening to some of the greatest music of all time played live by its composer. The approach of the Maître d' broke his reverie.

"May I help you, sir?"

"Do you have a table?"

"Is anyone joining you?"

"No, it's just me tonight."

"Very well. Follow me."

The tuxedo-clad man led Elton to a small table set for two, a couple of rows back from the dance floor, but not without a decent view of the band.

"Will you require a menu, sir, or will you be having only cocktails?"

"Champagne, your finest."

"Would you care to see the wine list?"

"No. The best champagne you have will do."

The man raised an eyebrow just the slightest bit and floated away. Before long, a waiter returned with a bucket of ice, a champagne glass, and a bottle. He showed the label to Elton: Moet et Chandon.

Carver nodded. The man poured the bubbling liquid into the glass and discreetly laid a black folder on the table. Carver peeked at it. The cost of the champagne was twenty-two dollars plus the cover charge of the club, which was three. He slipped a twenty and a ten out of his wallet and placed it in the folder.

People at some of the tables near him started to glance in his direction. He hoped he provided some mystery. Who was this confident, zoot-suited man, ordering expensive champagne all by himself?

As a couple skimmed by, the lady shot him a coy look. He couldn't help noticing that she was stunning, with a body to match, curvaceous yet sleek in a satiny, form-fitting gown, and sparkling with jewels. When had people lost the habit of dressing so finely when going out? He supposed when there stopped being clubs of the caliber of places like the Alabam, the Savoy, or the Cotton Club. And, he supposed, it was rather elitist to expect people to be able to afford that level of attire. Certainly the folks enjoying the music and atmosphere here tonight were not your average man and woman off the street. He'd better enjoy it now, because, when Cassandra came, he wouldn't be able to bring her here, nor would he be able to accompany her to the places the rich and famous white people frequented.

A slim lady wearing a white-sequined gown approached him. Her hair had been straightened, as was the style of the day among black women, and it was rolled up and back away from her face. She wore shimmery eyeshadow and bright red lipstick. She was a stunner.

"May I join you?" she asked in a sultry voice.

"It would be my pleasure," he replied, not sure what was in store for him.

"Do you like the band?" she purred.

"They're the cat's meow," he said, hoping that was the right expression. He and Cassandra hadn't had a lot of time to review the vernacular of the time. He raised a hand to call the waiter and gestured for another glass.

She smiled, revealing pearly teeth. "Yes, there's

no one like Ellington."

"I couldn't agree more."

"I'm Sarah."

He suddenly recognized her face. "Vaughn?"

Her sultry attitude evaporated as she broke into a wide smile. "You've heard of me?"

He realized how young she had to be. Nineteen at the most. "Yes," he laughed. "I have. Are you here singing with Earl Hines?"

"We go on at midnight. Will you stay?"

"Nothing could drag me away."

The waiter arrived with a glass and poured champagne for Sarah. She sipped it nervously. "I don't like to drink much before I go on."

"I don't blame you," he said.

"Do you play?"

"A little." He grinned.

She raised her eyebrows but didn't press him. "Where are you from? I've never seen you around here..."

"Elton. Elton Carver."

"That's an unusual name."

"Yes," he laughed again. "I'm from New York."

"We just came from back east. I never saw you in any of the clubs and I'm sure I would have noticed you."

"I get around."

"I see. Well, the set ends at one if you'd like to buy me a cocktail then."

"It would be my pleasure."

She took another sip of her champagne and

stood to go. He rose with her. She offered her hand and he kissed it lightly. She grinned and sauntered away.

He doubted the wisdom of buying the young Sarah Vaughn an after-show cocktail. He might not look it, but he was old enough to be her grandfather.

Ellington's band finished their set on fire, and then a filler act of scantily clad chorus girls went on, dancing to a ditty sung by some lesser-known talent. All the while, women and men strode by Elton's table, casting him curious glances. Finally, Earl Hines' band and Sarah went on and Elton watched, enraptured. Before long, another gorgeous woman sallied up to him and asked if he wanted to dance. He hesitated. It had been awhile since he'd brushed up on his swing moves, but he was itching to cut a rug, as they said, to the ultra-hot music. He rose and offered the woman his arm, moving her to the dance floor. She felt just right in his arms and everything came back to him as the music inspired him to let go. They partnered for a few songs, then he thanked her without asking her name and excused himself. It was time to go. He did not need to get distracted.

He went to the bar and bought another bottle of champagne, asking it to be delivered to Miss Vaughn at the close of her set, with the note: "From Elton. You're already a legend. I hope we meet again."

Chapter Seven

From the memoir of Akito Wakai

My cousin, Haruki Wakai, let us stay with him and his family on the floor of his extremely cramped apartment in Los Angeles. Like we did in Seattle, he also lived in a mostly Japanese area that the locals refer to as Little Tokyo, just north of Compton. I've never been to Tokyo, but I doubt it is anything like this. Little Tokyo was no more than a cluster of restaurants and shops catering to the twenty or so families that had staked out a claim in this area. With the money we'd saved in Seattle, it wasn't difficult to find an apartment of our own. It was also very tiny, but it was the first time we'd had a whole place to ourselves. No more sharing a bathroom with five other tenants in a boarding house. Our little place had one small bedroom, just big enough for the pallet and mat we were able to purchase for our bed. It had an equally small parlor, a kitchen, and a bathroom with hot and cold running water and a tub. We felt like royalty. In Japan, we'd had no running water at all where I'd lived in the countryside, and, of course, our only commode was an outhouse. Mai's family's situation had been the same, as was the way most people in our area of Japan lived. I don't know if it was different in Tokyo.

We quickly obtained a simple table, low to the ground as

we were used to before we came to the U.S. We bought pillows for the floor, a rush mat for a carpet, some simple shelves for our belongings, a narrow armoire and trunk for our clothing and bedding, cooking pots, utensils, and dishes. Now, we were set up for our brand new life, still newlyweds in many ways.

Then something happened that threw our life into a spin. I was leaving the apartment on my way to look for a job just a few days after we'd moved in, when a white man approached me in the hallway. He said only my name: "Akito Wakai?" I answered him pleasantly. "Yes." I couldn't imagine what he wanted with me. Then, just as he drew a gun from his pocket, Mai emerged from our doorway, my hat in her hand. "Aki, you forgot..." But her words turned to a scream when she saw the gun. I lunged to protect her. The man fired. I felt a searing pain in my shoulder. Other doors in the hallway flew open and neighbors peered out, terrified. The man turned and ran as blood flowed down my arm. Then, everything faded away.

Cassandra and James sat nervously together at the conference table in the MIT chronology lab. Around them were gathered the board members who made the decisions about which scientist on the team would be next to time travel, and whether the project merited their funding. She and Professor Carver had quickly obtained approval to go to 1942 because the board was gravely aware of the importance of finding and stopping Nick Stockard once and for all. When Cassandra had gone to Italy to spend the last year with Lauro though, she hadn't needed their approval since she had funded the trip herself.

It was also the board's job to have relics and documents that had been brought from the past authenticated and, if necessary, rule on improprieties that might have been committed by the time traveling team members. This had been necessary when Cassandra and Evie Johnston had returned from 1853 New York because Evie had smuggled back eighteen canvases in her suitcase, paintings that had been done by Caleb Stone, the man she had fallen in love with there. The board had decided that Evie's actions had ultimately been warranted—that the paintings would otherwise have been lost to perpetuity and that her saving them was a major contribution to the art world. If the ruling had gone the other way, she could have been severely penalized for her actions. She had been lucky. She had taken a huge risk, but it had paid off.

Now, the board was about to not only announce the findings of the authenticity of the letters "supposedly" written by Elizabeth the First, which James had brought back with him from 1598 England, but whether or not he had been right to do so.

Cassandra was nervous. They were not likely to issue James the harshest possible punishment for taking the letters because Professor Carver had been advocating fiercely in his favor. However, it was possible they would not only forbid him from ever time traveling again (something he probably wasn't likely to do anyway, given the Elizabethan experience) but they could remove him forever from the chronology team and destroy the letters altogether.

James looked at his mother. There was a sheen of sweat on his brow. Cassandra squeezed his hand. Any of the punitive actions the board might decide to take would be dire, but Cassandra knew James would be most devastated by having the letters destroyed. They were a valuable insight to Queen Elizabeth's life and loves.

The president of the board, Dr. Sandra Vingh, cleared her throat. There were eight board members present, plus Cassandra and James, at the table. Cassandra wished Elton were there too.

"The first issue to address," Dr. Vingh began, "is the authentication of the letters that James Reilly brought back with him from London, 1598. Our team of historical experts have examined them carefully, and have concluded that they were indeed written by Queen Elizabeth the First."

"No kidding," James mumbled.

Cassandra kicked him under the table.

"Now we come to the decision about whether it was ethical for Mr. Reilly to remove those letters, which, as he related to us, would have otherwise been burned in 1598."

A tense silence ensued.

"We have determined there is more value in having the letters with the information they give us on the woman and her time than there was harm in taking documents which otherwise would not have survived."

Cassandra and James exhaled simultaneously.

"Therefore, there is to be no punitive action," Dr. Vingh continued.

"Thank you," James said, looking about at each member of the board in turn.

"Now, we begin the process of deciding how to present the letters to the public," Dr. Vingh said. "Mr. Reilly, we know that your purpose in traveling to England of 1598 was to do research for your doctoral thesis: that Shakespeare was not the true author of the works attributed to him. However, since you were not able to make a final determination on that issue…"

Cassandra and James looked at each other. Only they knew the truth.

"…We would like to propose that the curating of a public exhibit displaying the letters, accompanied by visual aids on the time, as well as your interpretation of the contents of the letters, be part of your research focus for your dissertation. After all, you are now the ultimate expert on the Elizabethan era, being the only person who has traveled there for the express purpose of studying the main players in the Shakespeare authorship question. Are you willing to take on this task?"

"I am," James replied, his voice quivering with excitement.

Cassandra knew this was the result he had hoped for.

After the meeting, mother and son went together to a nearby restaurant for brunch to celebrate. She'd seen him a few times since she'd been back from Italy, but they hadn't had much time to really sit down and catch up.

"This is the start of a whole new direction for you," she said to him, savoring the taste of the excellent coffee she had missed while in Italy. By 1605, the year she had spent with Lauro, coffee, or espresso, was still not a common thing in the Italian states.

"Who knew that when I set out to disprove the Shakespearean authorship, I would end up with Elizabeth as my focus instead," he said.

"She sure was a monster to you though…to us."

"I will never forget those days I spent in the Tower." He shuddered. "The bugs, the rats, the nasty food, the cold…"

"What an experience."

"But you, kidnapped by Nick to the 1920s. I'll never get over what a miracle it was that you made it back to Elizabethan times."

"He's got to be stopped. Once and for all," she said, taking another sip of coffee for fortification.

"I wish I could go. I'd be a better choice than Professor Carver."

"In some ways, yes. But I know I'll be in the

best hands with him. Anyway, there's no way I'd let you go. Not with this new opportunity in front of you. You'll be doing work toward earning your PhD while participating in something incredibly important. It will be a great creative endeavor as well."

James nodded. "Nothing makes me happier than to know that I'll be in charge of the letters. That I'll be the one to introduce them to the world."

"People will see a whole new side of Queen Elizabeth. Not that they didn't already know she was a bawdy woman. Now, though, the whole debate about whether or not she was 'The Virgin Queen,' will be settled. You swapped one debate for another, and this one, you've already won."

"Not that I ever cared. The subject has taken on a whole new level of interest to me now though, having met her…" he paused.

"And almost having to be the proof yourself she wasn't a virgin." She laughed loudly.

"Mom!" he objected as a couple of diners looked their way.

"Sorry," she giggled, "it's just that she was so into you. She looked at you like a fresh cut of prime beef."

"Mom, please. The thought is just as repulsive now as it was then."

"Well, you're tall, good-looking: straight teeth, clear skin—those things were not taken for granted back then." She chuckled again. "You sure did dodge a bullet."

"Ok, let's talk about something else," he said as his waffles arrived. He took a big bite while she started on her omelet.

Finally, he said, "So, did you ever consider the possibility of not returning to the future when you were with Lauro? As long as we're talking about sex."

She felt her cheeks begin to glow.

"Oh, please, Mom," he said. "I think we're past the blushing stage on this topic."

"I can't control it, you know. It doesn't necessarily mean I'm embarrassed. It's just a reflex."

"Sure."

"Anyway, I think you know that with Lauro it wasn't only about the sex."

"Well, I wouldn't want the details anyway."

"Oh, now who's squeamish?"

"You're my mom!"

She laughed. "I know, I know."

"Do you miss him?"

"Of course. But there was never any way I wasn't going to come back here to you and everyone else I love."

"I have to admit; I did feel a little nervous about that. Especially since there was no way to communicate with you over the course of the year. As time went on, I really started to worry about it."

"I appreciate that, James," she said softly. "I actually did consider that maybe I could keep the portal open indefinitely...pop back and forth in time…but, not only would that have cost a literal fortune, but my life needs to be where my work and my family is. Living in 1605 was a fantasy. It was, I would say though, one of the very best years of my life. Lauro was…incredible…in every way. He is my soulmate." Her voice broke.

"I'm so sorry," James uttered.

She dabbed at her eyes with her napkin. "Nothing to be done about it." She suddenly had less appetite for her omelet. "But I've got to get past it and focus on this next trip." She shook her head as if to dispel the sadness.

"Do you not want to go?"

"I mean, as a scientist, yes, I do. I'm always interested in visiting another time period though that was not so much the case with Elizabethan England."

"Yeah," he added with a humorless chuckle.

"I'm very interested in seeing Los Angeles of the 1940s. I love that time period. It's one of my favorites, and of course, I never thought I'd have the chance to go there. But I'm really the only person for this job. I know Nick and his ways. I know how he thinks, and I have the most experience. Having Elton come with me makes me feel safer though. I wouldn't try to deal with Nick by myself."

"I'm a little worried about this one too," James said.

Cassandra picked at her omelet. "Yeah. It could be dangerous."

He sighed.

She looked up at her son and smiled. "We've been in really tight spots before James, you and me both. And we've come out of them just fine. I'm going to be okay."

"I know you will, Mom," he said without much conviction in his voice. "I know."

Chapter Eight

From the memoir of Akito Wakai

I was not injured gravely. I lost a lot of blood, but I recovered after a week in the hospital. The police questioned me about why someone would want to kill me. They questioned Mai with a translator. They questioned my cousin too, but no one had a clue, least of all me. Mai was traumatized and wanted to move out of our apartment, but we couldn't afford to after just having paid a security deposit to move in. We were both jumpy, looking for attackers around every corner. Slowly though, as the weeks passed, the fear subsided, and we distracted ourselves by talking about again trying to have a baby.

I found a job as a cook in one of the neighborhood restaurants. More and more Japanese were moving into the area every day, thanks to California's booming economy. We would even find that an occasional gaijin would wander in, curious about our strange food and foreign ways.

Once again, Mai enquired among the ladies in the neighborhood, and was soon doing all kinds of sewing: simple mending and complicated embroidery both, as the job required. She was also a wonderful cook. Every day when I finished my shift, she would have some lovely meal prepared for us—delicious and beautiful to behold. As the shock of the attack faded into the background, our days became filled with more and more happiness. Each morning Mai would make us a breakfast of porridge with rice, pickled plums and dried fish. Then, I would go with her on her rounds to deliver work she had finished, and pick up more work for the day, collecting the money as she went. I was hesitant to let her go anywhere by herself. Then, I would go to the restaurant around 11:00 AM to begin preparing for the lunch shift. I would stay until the dinner shift ended, around 8:00 PM. We would have a meal together, and maybe go to a movie or listen to the radio. This, we considered our English practice, and though we were speaking Japanese all day, by doing this, our English was improving little by little, mine more than hers, since I could at least practice speaking with our occasional American customers.

I had Sundays and Mondays off, as the restaurant was closed those days. On Sundays we would often take the Red Line to the beach for American food, go to a matinee, or visit with my cousin or other families we had become friendly with in the neighborhood. We loved our life. We only wanted one thing to make it complete, a baby. After a year in Los Angeles, it happened. Mai was pregnant.

Suhan had been at her computer station all day with only a break for the meals they were required to eat—hungry or not. She now grabbed the holographic message out of the air and crunched it down to a small version she could read in her hand. She didn't want any of her nosy fellow inmates getting a glance at it. It was from Mark Stein, a former Navy Seal from what remained of the U.S. military. Though their numbers had been pared way down from what used to be by far the biggest military power in the world, those who remained among their ranks were fervently devoted to their vocation—the elite, like the Navy Seals, in particular. This guy, Mark Stein, was beyond fervent—perfect for what she had in mind.

Stein's message read, "Stockard went on a trip and came back a few days later, mad as hell. Left again June 3rd. You are right about his destination. I only reveal this information having just received the much appreciated sum you sent. Why did he go? I don't know."

What did he mean? That Nick had gone on two separate time journeys? That made no sense. Suhan checked Nick's bank account. There was a dip in the total from the last time she'd looked, but nothing made much of an impact in that immense sum. The fact was, Nick had made a grave error when it came to her loyalty. He had once entrusted her with his bank account information, since she was the one authorized to make payments to his various employees. After he'd made it back from London, as bad a shape as he was in, he had obviously been in such a hurry to build the new portal he hadn't bothered to take her off his account. As a matter of fact, Suhan hadn't even heard from him since she'd ended up in prison. He'd deserted her without even a second glance. Probably assumed she was still his faithful follower. Well, maybe she had been, but no more. It hadn't occurred to her to access his account until just a few weeks ago; after all, she didn't want another strike against her. Still, once she'd gotten the idea to hire someone to look in on Nick's activities, and figured out that Mark Stein was still on his team (if you could call it that), she realized she could use Nick's own money against him. There was only one thing that kept his people loyal and that was money.

She typed out a reply to Stein instead of speaking it into the computer like she normally would have. She didn't want anyone to overhear: "I think all the time he's spent in Europe in the 1920s may have turned him to the other side. Do you know what I mean by that? Nazis."

That ought to rev him up. If Stein thought Nick was going back in time to somehow disrupt the outcome of the war, he might even be willing to do what Suhan hoped to inspire him to, which was to kill Nick, end him, once and for all. It wouldn't be that hard either. She knew exactly where he would be on June 23rd, though maybe not exactly the time. All Stein would have to do is stake him out, take one good shot, and that would be that. What Carver and Cassandra were planning was too complicated. They wouldn't be in favor of just doing him in and leaving it at that. They would opt for bringing him home to face justice in the courts, and the reprobate didn't deserve that. For what he did to her...for what he did to others, he deserved to die.

After a few minutes, a message pinged and she opened it.

"We should meet in person. I'm in L.A. I know you're detained outside of Boston. Rajesh can man the portal if I fly out for a day or so. Ok?"

Her heart beat fast. She hadn't anticipated actually meeting with him. He was right; they shouldn't talk about this on the net. She typed back, "Yes. I'll be here :)." She then permanently deleted all messages between them.

It being Sunday, Elton was not going to be able to buy a car or new clothes, which he was definitely going to need, and soon. No, Sunday was the day to stroll the avenue. It was the time to show off one's finery. The bars were closed, as were the shops, though restaurants and food markets were open and busy. He ate breakfast in his room, and then, zootsuit donned, joined the citizens for a promenade up and down S. Central Avenue to enjoy the beautiful L.A. weather. As people strolled, they stopped and visited with each other. And though everyone noticed the tall, handsome gentleman in the ultra-stylish blue suit with the black and white shoes and blue fedora, no one approached him. He was a stranger on the avenue. This was the perfect chance for Elton to see what Compton had to offer. There were several boutiques, some for ladies' clothes and some for men's. He scoped out a place that had several stylish suits in the window and made a mental note. He was heading north, toward Twelfth Street, the heart of the avenue. Vegetable stands were selling their wares, as were butchers and bakers; and the soda fountains and diners were hopping.

The fashions people wore were stunning and he wondered how the average folks afforded them though he realized the women probably made a lot of their own clothes. They strolled by in their broad-shouldered, slim-waisted dresses and strappy high-heels, twitching their skirts for optimum effect. The men that accompanied them wore everything from proper wool suits in grays and tans to the most outrageous zootsuits with long jackets almost to the knee, trouser waists approaching their armpits with legs so wide they looked like they could use them for parachutes. The colors were bright yellow, red, green, black and white checks—the flashier the better.

Elton stopped into a soda fountain for a root beer and started chatting with the guy behind the counter.

"Where's the best place to buy a car around here?" he asked.

The man assessed Elton's expensive looking suit. "You new in town?"

"Sure am. Just came out from New York. Need to get me a ride."

"What kind you interested in?"

"I'm thinkin' a Hudson."

The man nodded his head in appreciation. "That's gonna cost ya."

"That's ok. I work for a lady that's got plenty to throw around. Elton Carver," he said, holding out his hand for the man to shake.

"Joe McGee," the man said, pumping Elton's hand up and down.

"You the owner?"

"Sure am," Joe said proudly.

"It's a nice place you got here."

"Thanks." Joe polished the counter with a towel.

"Yeah, so, anyway," Elton continued "my boss wants a nice ride. Doesn't care about the cost."

Joe nodded again, knowingly. "You can take the Red Line out to Whittier tomorrow. Go see Sam Jones, corner of Whittier Boulevard and Calmada. He's one of us. He'll have something you like."

Elton glanced up at the lettered menu on the wall above the soda machine. The place only served drinks, ice cream, and dessert. "Hey," he said. "Where can I get a really good meal?"

"What d'ya got a hankering for?" Joe replied.

"Something…different."

"You like Japanese? We used to have a lot o' good places just up the avenue a bit, in Little Tokyo, but most places closed down after, you know, Pearl Harbor."

Elton nodded.

"Look for a place called Rakuzen on Second Street. They're still there and they're the best."

"Thanks." Elton finished his soda and left Joe a good sized tip.

He walked to the northern end of S. Central Avenue, now curious to see what had become of Little Tokyo since the war started. He had once read that African Americans had moved into houses and business vacated when the Japanese were sent to internment camps. Sure enough, the racial landscape of Compton now extended into the Japanese style buildings of the former Little Tokyo. He also knew that, eventually, most of it would be reclaimed by the Japanese. There had been some racial tension between two groups as a result, but for the most part, the black community had turned out to be sympathetic to a race of people who also were treated badly by American society.

He wandered through the partially abandoned neighborhood, sadness for the displaced people overwhelming him. Eventually, he came across the small restaurant called Rakuzen. He opened the door and inhaled the steamy wonder of broth boiling and vegetables simmering. He was greeted by an attractive, middle-aged Japanese woman who modestly kept her gaze toward the ground. The place was empty other than for him. The woman led him to a low table where he sat upon a tatami mat. She handed him a menu then left and returned a moment later with a pot of tea and a cup. She poured it for him, and as she leaned toward him, a lovely scent of flowers wafted toward him. She left, and with her the scent. He fell to studying the menu. The names of the dishes were in Japanese with rough translations next to them. When she returned, he ordered his favorite, beef sukiyaki, and a Sapporo beer.

The woman looked at him oddly. "Sapporo?"

"Yeah. Sapporo. The beer."

"Sapporo only in Nippon. We have Eastside or Maier."

That was definitely a flub on his part. "Eastside," he said, though he'd never heard of either of them.

She bowed and disappeared into the kitchen. He looked around. On the walls were traditional Japanese paintings of Mt. Fuji, cherry blossoms, and cranes, accompanied by beautifully painted calligraphy. Prominent among these decorations was a photograph in the style of a celebrity headshot of a handsome, young Japanese man. The photo was signed with an autograph.

When the woman returned with his beer, he pointed to the picture and asked, "Who is that?"

She replied in her heavily accented English with a broad smile, "Hiro Wakai. My son."

After that, a labored conversation ensued in which Elton enquired if he were an actor, and she replied in her broken English that he was: in Hollywood. She then proceeded to proudly list several films he had been in though the few names Elton understood he did not recognize. The man was probably one of those rare, minority-race actors who had been lucky enough to get some bit parts, probably playing every nationality from Chinese to Native American since the woman's son did not have strong Japanese facial characteristics, and given the disregard that Hollywood had in those days for ethnic correctness.

The woman, obviously glad to have someone to spill her thoughts to, finally confessed that the only reason their restaurant had been allowed to stay open, and they hadn't been shipped off to an internment camp, was her son's friendship with a prominent Hollywood actor. She said his name, but Elton didn't understand. Seeing his frown, she tried again and again to make him comprehend.

Finally, he exclaimed, "Oh, Humphrey Bogart!"

"Yes, yes!" the woman declared as if Elton were lacking in intelligence, "Bogaht!"

He nodded appreciatively, and the woman, beaming with pride, went off to retrieve his food. She delivered it to him with a bow and left him to enjoy it. It was one of the most delicious meals he had ever eaten. When he'd finished, rather than subjecting the woman to any embarrassment, he extracted a five-dollar bill from his wallet, a sum five times the amount of the food and drink, left it on the table, and hurried from the restaurant.

As he wandered back toward his hotel, inspired by thoughts of Bogart playing the famous Dashiell Hammett gumshoe in The Maltese Falcon, he stopped at a newsstand and picked up a couple of paperback detective novels that were on a rack. He also grabbed a newspaper. He was going to need some diversion. There was a console radio in his room, but no other form of entertainment available to him unless he decided to take in a movie. The radio, at least, served to remind him of what was going on in the world at this time, and, of course, the war news dominated everything. He found himself wondering where Nick Stockard was at the moment. He had two weeks until June 23rd.

Chapter Nine

From the memoir of Akito Wakai

There was a Japanese doctor in the neighborhood who practiced western medicine. We went to him to make sure Mai was healthy and the pregnancy sound. We were determined to do everything the western way now. After all, we considered ourselves Americans though we were not yet citizens. The doctor assured us all was well with Mai's pregnancy, though urged her not to strain herself. The walking she did each morning on her rounds was good exercise, he said, but I carried all the loads. I also insisted she let me bring home food from the restaurant at night instead of her cooking.

This baby was what we needed to complete our happiness. Now, we spent our weekends gathering the odds and ends we would need: cloth for diapers and rubber pants, and a big pot for boiling them clean. We already had a small clothesline on our fire escape where we dried our clothes in the warm California sunshine. Mai was making clothes for the baby and many of our neighbors had given us baby items they no longer needed. We even went to an American department store to buy outfits because we wanted the baby to look like an American child. That was a problem though. Whereas in Japan, we do not differentiate baby clothes by boys or girls, here they do, so we had to choose between pink and blue. We chose blue because we thought that a girl can wear blue, according to American standards, but a boy cannot wear pink.

We also learned that American babies sleep in a bed called a crib, often in a separate room from their parents. This is where we would not veer from our traditions. Our baby would sleep with us, as Japanese babies have done for generations, until he or she is old enough for their own mat. This presented us with a problem. Our apartment was barely big enough for two, much less three as the baby grew. We could not afford a bigger apartment on my salary, so we had to figure out how to make more money. I decided I needed to find a job in a different restaurant where they could pay me more. Mai could not work more —certainly not after the baby was born.

The other thing we decided to do before the baby came was enroll in a citizenship class and take the test. It was crucial to us that we both be American citizens before the baby was born. Though, apparently, a child born in the U.S. is automatically an American citizen, we would take no chances. We wanted our baby to be as American as any white baby in this country.

Come Monday morning, Elton headed out to Whittier on the Red Line, as the man at the soda fountain had suggested, and found Sam Jones's auto lot. Letting the car salesman know he had cash to spend resulted in his test-driving a shiny, deep red Hudson four-door Deluxe, built in 1940. Since the U.S. had entered the war, car manufacturers had ceased making new cars as all factories were now devoted to making military machinery, but this Hudson was still brand new and smelled of rich leather.

The dashboard and fixtures were real wood, the accents polished chrome—every detail made for luxury. Cars of Elton's time were no longer designed this way, and it was rare that someone actually owned one. They were utilitarian vehicles that drove themselves and were always handily available on demand. It was mostly only collectors who owned cars anymore, and, though he loved them, Elton had other priorities in life than collecting automobiles.

As a matter of fact, he hadn't been in the driver's seat since his journey to the 1920s and that had been ten years ago. Sam looked at him strangely as he sat in the passenger seat and Elton struggled with the clutch and gear shift while jolting along the side streets.

"Never driven one of these before," Elton said apologetically.

Sam shrugged. "If you want her, I'll throw in a spare tire."

Why would a spare tire be considered extra, Elton wondered? But then he realized rubber was a very precious commodity during war time. "Thanks," he replied.

By the time they returned to the lot, he had gotten the hang of it. He handed Sam the money, and the salesman slapped a sticker on the windshield with the letter A emblazoned on it.

"What's that for?"

"Are you kidding me, Mr. Carver? You from outer space or something? It's a ration sticker, what d'ya think?"

"Oh, yeah, yeah," Elton replied. "They do things a little differently back east."

"They do?"

"Yeah. So how much do I get?"

"No more than 4 gallons a week."

Elton nearly choked. Driving this gas guzzler would eat up that much in no time.

"You're lucky though," Sam said, patting the hood of the car. "She's got a full tank now. You can go a long ways on that before you'll need to get more."

Elton breathed a sigh of relief. If he was careful, that should last him until he went back to get Cassandra. Then he had an idea. "Which sticker will give me the most gallons?"

"That's an X, my friend, but no one gets those but cops, preachers, firefighters, the civil defense, and some government folks. Unless you're one of those, you're out o' luck."

"Gotcha." Elton nodded his head. "Thanks, Sam. You've done me real good today. I won't forget."

Sam grinned. "Thanks a lot! Hope your boss lady likes her."

"I'm sure she will."

After Sam loaded a spare tire into the trunk, Elton walked around the front of the car and noticed the headlights half painted black, like partially closed eyes. He pointed at them. "What's this?" he asked Sam.

Sam chuckled. "Maybe we do things differently out here 'cause we're a lot closer to Japan than you folks out east. But then, you're closer to Germany. It's to cut down on the light, Mr. Carver, so the enemy don't see you if they fly overhead."

"Oh. Oh yeah. I knew that." He grinned apologetically at Sam. He should, indeed, have known that. He waved at Sam, hopped into the driver's seat, and carefully maneuvered his way back to Compton, parking the Hudson in the small parking lot behind the hotel.

Now it was time to buy some more clothes. He walked up the avenue until he found the shop that had the sharp-looking suits in the window. He bought two pairs of ready-made trousers, several shirts and some ties, and ordered three suits made: a conservative grey in light wool, one of tan linen, and a slightly less flashy zoot-suit style in black. The man would have the grey suit finished in three days, he said, and the others a couple of days later. Elton also purchased undershirts, boxers, suspenders, and socks.

"Sorry about the prices," the store owner said to him as Elton handed him the cash for the clothes.

Elton raised an eyebrow.

"Well, if it doesn't bother you, you're a luckier man than I," the man went on. "Government's already rationing silk. The ladies can hardly get stockings any more. Soon it'll be cotton. It's getting harder and harder to keep stuff in stock."

"Oh, yeah," Elton stammered. "Yeah, I didn't want to say anything, but it's more than I thought I'd be paying."

"It costs me more so I have to pass it on to my customers. Like I said, I'm sorry about that."

"We all have to do our part, don't we," said Elton, hoping it was the right sentiment.

"Yes, sir," the man answered, wrapping up his purchases.

He gave the store owner a good tip and asked if he could deliver the clothes to him at the Dunbar. Then he went down the street to a shoe shop to get one pair of brown Oxfords, and one black, this time acting appropriately stunned at the "high prices" which to him were practically nothing, especially for such well-made shoes. He then visited the haberdashery and purchased a tan fedora and a black one, having everything delivered. After that he still had time to begin his enquiries into a real estate agent. The one he found on the avenue didn't have anything to do with houses in white neighborhoods. However, once the agent understood that Elton was looking to rent a house for his white boss, he called a friend who had a friend who knew one of the best agents in L.A., one who catered to white folks.

Elton made an appointment to see him the next day, and then, feeling like he'd accomplished everything on his agenda, decided to find another good place to eat. As he strolled along, he happened upon a music store that had several gleaming trumpets in the window. One was a Conn—the kind that Louie Armstrong played. Unable to resist, he went in and asked to try it out. He hadn't brought a mouthpiece with him, not expecting in the least to be playing, but the store owner had one that suited him. His embouchure was a little weak from not having played for a month or so, but the store had sound-proof booths for practicing so Elton went into one and tried it out. Its sound was absolutely golden—one of the best instruments he'd ever played, and every bit as good as his own at home in Boston. Without thinking twice, he purchased the trumpet and walked out of the store with it in its black leather case. He would not be able to practice in the hotel, but maybe, if he had some spare time, he'd come back to the store and practice there.

He felt a little frivolous. He was not in 1942 to play, but after hearing those bands the night before, something had stirred in him. It was one of his great secrets, from Cassandra and everyone on the team, that he played the horn. Not only did he play, but he was good—really good, and he knew it. If he could have been something in life other than a scientist and inventor, he would have been a professional musician. But time travel had proved to be the greater love, and, of course, he did not regret it. Whenever he could though, he took time away from his work to play, and had jammed with some amazing bands in his time. Even in 1920s Harlem, he'd soloed with some of the biggest bands of the nightclub scene on stage and had wowed the audience. Did he dare try his hand at it while he was here?

The next day he drove out to Hollywood to meet the real estate agent, wishing his suit had been ready. Confident he looked well enough in his crisp shirt, trousers, and tie—hat in place, he walked into the agent's office prepared to be met with suspicion. He was in luck. While the agent, a big-haired woman named Betsy with an ample figure and a mouth painted bright red, looked a little frightened when he walked in, once he explained his purpose in being there, she seemed eager enough for the commission.

"Listen Mr. Carver," she said to him, "I'm running the business while my husband is overseas, and I don't know everything about it that he does, but I'm not going to lie. I do know that not many owners are going to be willing to rent to a Negro. Even if they know it's going to be a white lady living there."

He didn't tell her he planned to stay there too. There was no way he was going to be separated from Cassandra. Not for an instant. If he could find a place with a guest house, he could sleep there, and Cassandra in the main house. As long as the neighbors thought he was a servant, they couldn't really complain. Still, he couldn't help feeling irked.

"Do they have to know?" he asked. "If you can show me properties without the owner being there, I'll pass the money through you and no one will have to know I'm the one making the transaction."

"It's possible," she said, "but it's not going to be easy."

"I've got less than two weeks," he said. "I've got to make it happen by then."

She clucked her tongue, but when he told her what his "boss" was willing to spend, she suddenly seemed all the more willing.

"I'll make some calls," she said, "and I'll have something for you to see tomorrow."

He told her he could be reached at the Dunbar Hotel and that he'd be waiting for her call.

Chapter Ten

From the memoir of Akito Wakai

The baby arrived, healthy and hearty—a boy! We named him Hiro. The birth was not too difficult, I was told, as births go. Mai is strong, and she persevered through the pain to bring our beautiful son into the world. Bringing him home to our little apartment was the happiest day of my life, other than the day I married Mai.

My boss at the restaurant knew, of course, about this addition to our family. A couple of weeks after Hiro was born, he sat me down for a talk. He told me he had been thinking of retiring for some time—that he was getting too old to keep running a restaurant. He asked me if I wanted to take it over. He said he and his wife would be moving out of the apartment over the restaurant, which had two bedrooms. They would buy a small house in Pasadena, nearer to their daughter and her family. He said I would keep all the profits for myself. I would pay him rent every month, for the restaurant and the apartment, until I reached the sum that would equal the cost of buying the place. Then he would turn over the deed to me.

I was overwhelmed. He had always been a great boss, but this was an extraordinary act of generosity. The payments we agreed upon were what I was sure I could handle, given that the restaurant was very popular and I knew it would continue to do well with me in charge. I was practically running it myself as it was.

And so, a few weeks later, we moved in. Now I could see Hiro all day, as Mai would often have him in the restaurant kitchen tied to her chest with a sash, or in a basket sleeping, and she would help me with little tasks. As he got older, we had him stay with some neighbors and their children for part of the day. We had a close community here in what is now a thriving Little Tokyo.

With life arranged so perfectly, we took our citizenship tests and passed. Now, we are Americans. We have pledged our allegiance to this country and will strive to be the best citizens possible. In this beautiful and prosperous country, we feel as though nothing could affect our happiness. We look forward to everything that life holds in the future.

Two days passed and Elton was getting anxious. Finally, he received a message at the front desk of the Dunbar that Betsy had called. He used the phone in his room to call her back and, at her request, went to Silver Lake to meet her at a house that was for rent. The landlord met them there but after taking one look at Elton, told him the place was no longer available.

Elton bit his tongue and walked back to his car as Betsy thanked the man.

"Did you tell him I was a Negro?" Elton asked, using the word uncomfortably as she approached him.

"Well, no."

"Why not?"

"Because I thought that if he met you face to face, he would see how..."

"How what?"

"How gentlemanly you are, and wouldn't mind that you're colored."

Another unpleasant word.

"But," she went on, "I've got another place for you to see tomorrow in Beverly Hills. It has a guest house, like you want."

"Don't you think it would save us time if you just told the owner I was 'colored?' Just explain to them that my boss is a white lady."

"Well, I'll try, Mr. Carver."

She called the hotel later that afternoon and left a message saying the appointment had been canceled. His temper was running short. To blow off steam, quite literally, he went to the music shop before they closed at the end of the day and spent an hour practicing his horn.

Another day went by, and then another, without a word from Betsy. He was beginning to panic. He wished he knew more people in town —someone else that might be able to get him a lead on a place. In just a few days he would have to be back in 2126. He supposed Cassandra could always stay at a hotel if she had to, but he wouldn't be able to stay with her, nor she at the Dunbar, and he didn't like the idea of being separated from her. He went back to the music shop to distract himself and practiced for a couple of hours.

Come Saturday night, just after another practice session, he hurried back down the avenue toward the hotel, trumpet case in hand. He ducked into the amazing Ivie's Chicken Shack for dinner, then back toward his hotel. As he passed Club Alabam, he heard the sounds of swing music coming from inside. It was too early for the place to be open, but he supposed the band was rehearsing for the night. He saw a man with a trombone case head down the alley next to the club and watched as he opened a side door and went in. Perhaps it was the artists' entrance. Feeling bold, Elton went to the door and eased it open, peering into a dark hallway. He went in and followed the corridor until he found himself looking out at the stage from the side curtains, straight at the profile of Duke Ellington as he led his band on the piano. Elton stood there awhile, taking in the wonder of it. When the song ended, Ellington looked around at his musicians, perturbed.

"Mr. Ellington," a voice called from the area of the bar.

"What!"

"Sammy Washington just called. He's not going to make it. Has a bad cold. Can't blow."

"Damn it!" the bandleader cursed.

Before he could stop himself, Elton stepped out onto the stage. "Mr. Ellington? Sammy sent me to take his place."

"What? Who the hell are you?"

"I'm Elton Carver, a friend of Sammy's. He sent me over. Just got back to the States from Paris."

Ellington glared at him. "You any good?"

"Yes, sir, I think so."

"Well let's see what you got. Play me something."

Elton opened his case, took out his horn, and inserted the mouthpiece. Taking a second to ready himself, he launched into Ellington's "Don't Get Around Much Anymore."

The bandleader let him play for a minute, then stopped him with a wave of his hand. "Yeah, you're good. You'll do. Jump on in here and let's do this one over now I have my lead player."

Lead player! Elton didn't know that was the role he'd be taking over for Sammy Washington. That Ellington thought he was good enough to take that esteemed position in the orchestra was a true testament to his playing.

The song was "It Don't Mean a Thing if it Ain't Got That Swing," one Elton knew well. His heart pounding, he went to take the first position in the horn section and was proud to find he was playing as well as he ever had. When the song finished, he got a nod and a smile from Ellington, and handshakes from the other band members.

One of them, an older gentleman who played the sax, approached him. "You look familiar," he said. "I played with a guy in Harlem back in the twenties looked and played just like you."

Elton faltered for a moment. "Oh, must have

been my old man. I picked up the horn from him."

The man peered at Elton then moved away. "Damn. The spittin' image," he mumbled.

Elton took a deep breath.

The band went on that night at ten. He happened to be wearing black trousers so only needed to change into a white tuxedo shirt, bow tie, and white jacket—apparently Sammy's, which fit him well enough—and then, there he was, as if in a dream, playing with one of the most legendary swing bands of all time at the height of the era. What would Cassandra think if she could see him? He wished she were there now, sitting in the audience, seeing the real Elton Carver, the man that, after fifteen years, she didn't even know completely.

The phone rang in his hotel room and woke him at eleven the next morning. It took him a moment to orient himself—the night before still swimming through his mind. The hotel operator patched through a call from Betsy. She said she had a property for him to look at, owned by out-of-town landlords.

Feeling optimistic after his triumph of the night before, Elton headed out in the Hudson to the Hollywood Hills. Following Betsy's instructions, he soon pulled up in front of a charming Spanish style bungalow on Hillside Avenue. He noticed a guest cottage on the property, which was just about enough to sell him without even looking at it. Betsy pulled up moments later and they went up the flower-lined walk together. She opened the front door of heavy carved wood with a key. The entryway was paved in reddish Saltillo tile. The interior featured accents like arched doorways, a fireplace, polished hardwood floors, and a wrought-iron chandelier. The kitchen was tiled in red and white and was as enchanting as could be. The yard was well-tended and there was even a clean, sparkling pool in the patio in the back. Though, hopefully, they wouldn't require the use of the place for long, he wanted the very best for Cassandra while they were there—and the home was tastefully furnished—icing on the cake. He took a peek into the guest cottage, which was just as nice as the main house, and the deal was done. He gave Betsy cash for six months' rent, the minimum the landlord required. She turned the keys over to him, just as simple as that. No contracts signed. No lease.

He left with a feeling of great relief and also resolve. The date was already the 22nd. He had no time to spare. He went back to the hotel, changed into his janitor's garb, gathered his things and checked out, the clerk more than a little confused at the sight of the normally well-dressed guest looking like the average workman. "I'm a well-paid plumber," he said to her with a wink.

He had bought a suitcase to hold his new clothes and he carried his trumpet with him. It would remain his treasured souvenir. He put them all in the trunk of the Hudson and now realized he had a new problem. What would he do with the car if he had to be gone overnight? He would need it when he and Cassandra returned. He remembered there was a parking lot adjacent to the warehouse where the portal exit was located. Taking a chance, he drove down to Long Beach and pulled up to the attendant's booth. Now that it was wartime, facilities like this had people working overtime so, though it was six PM on a Saturday, there were still people inside.

The man in the booth looked surprised to see someone of his own race dressed in workmen's coveralls, driving such an expensive car.

"I'm meeting my boss here," said Elton. "How long are you on duty tonight?"

"'Til midnight," the man replied.

"Perfect. Can I park?"

The man raised the gate and Elton drove through. He hoped and prayed Cassandra was in the portal lab and ready to go.

Now for the really tricky part. He grabbed his satchel and locked the car. He approached the side door of the warehouse and tried it. It was locked. He knocked loudly and, eventually, a worker came to open it.

"Yeah?" the man enquired.

"I'm here to take a look at the plumbing."

"The plumbing?"

"Yeah, I guess there's a broken-down toilet somewhere in here."

"I don't know." He was white and looked at Elton suspiciously.

Elton tried to assume an attitude of subservience though every bone in his body objected. "Well, you mind if I take a look? We got an emergency call and if I don't check into it, my boss is gonna be mad."

"Yeah, sure, okay." The man stood aside and let him enter. "Bathrooms are over there." He pointed toward the back of the facility.

Perfect. The portal exit was in that general direction. He made his way toward where the man had indicated, then, once out of his sight, veered toward his destination. It didn't matter if someone else happened to stand or pass through where the portal was located because whoever was at the helm at the lab, be it Yoshi, Alex, Sara, or Cassandra herself, they would only lock onto the exact coordinates of Elton's body size and shape which the computer had stored. Someone else could stand there all day and never be accidentally whisked into the future. However, the team wouldn't transfer Elton if there was someone else in the vicinity because that person would wonder how the man, who had just been standing there moments before, had somehow magically disappeared.

The warehouse wasn't as busy on a Sunday as

it surely was during the week, especially since it was nearing evening. Still, Elton had to look like he belonged until the coast was completely clear. He bent to tie his boot lace as a couple of workers walked by. He stood and looked around. No one else was near. He moved into the dark corner and held his breath. Hurry! he thought.

Sure enough, a second later he felt a lurch, and the transfer began.

Chapter Eleven

Hiro Wakai, December 7th, 1941

The world has come crashing down around us. Pearl Harbor in Hawaii has been bombed by the Japanese. I was at home in my apartment when I heard the news on the radio. I was alone. The first thing I thought of was my parents, who were sure to be in their restaurant in Little Tokyo. I picked up the phone and dialed the number there, but no one answered. I didn't expect them to. It was five o'clock in the afternoon, and they were certainly preparing for their dinner customers as usual. I wondered if they had even heard the news. Surely they had. Surely neighbors had come by to talk about it. Or maybe they were out in the street, talking it over as a community. Fear gripped me. The reporter on the radio was already vilifying the Japanese in the U.S., calling us spies and traitors.

I hopped in my car and sped along the Pasadena Freeway to the S. Central Avenue exit. I arrived at the restaurant right around six. When I walked into the small space, smelling just like home always smelled, my mother ran up to me and flung her arms around me, tears streaming down her face. "My boy, my boy!" she cried in Japanese. "What are we going to do?" I looked up to see my father, stoically stirring the pot of broth in the kitchen, his face just visible above the counter where he would put the food for my mother to deliver to the customers when it was ready. His eyes met mine. I had rarely known his expression to change in all my years growing up, but this time there was something on his face behind the stony gaze that I had never seen before: fear.

Mark Stein was more handsome than Suhan remembered. Maybe he had lost some weight. He had definitely let his military buzz cut grow out some which made him look less hard-core. He had a sexy mouth too, which she hadn't remembered. They sat in a quiet corner in the recreation room, the same place she had met with Cassandra and Dr. Carver.

"What did you mean when you said Nick took two trips?" She asked him, leaving out the pleasantries.

"He made a short one a couple of weeks before he went to 1942. Also to Los Angeles. 1920 to be exact."

Suhan's brain went into a whirl. "What?"

"I thought you knew."

"No. I—I don't have any way of knowing what he's up to. I only know about the 1942 trip because I found his picture in a newspaper from that year."

"Oh. I didn't realize…"

"I'm not in touch with him." Suhan thought she'd made that clear. "Do you know why he went to 1920?"

"He doesn't tell us the reasons for his journeys."

"What on earth?" she whispered to herself.

"Maybe it has to do with Nazis too," Mark said in reply.

He clearly didn't have much of a grasp on history. "Maybe," she said. The Nazi party was formed in 1920 in Germany, not Los Angeles!

"He's up to something about the war and the Nazis for sure," Mark theorized. "And I want to stop him. I don't want to wake up someday and find the world run by Nazis."

He also didn't have a solid grasp on the effect of one's actions on the historical timeline, but that was okay. He didn't need to. She explained in detail what she wanted him to do, though he was clearly already on board.

His eyes widened at the mention of the sum she was willing to pay for it.

"I'm listening," he said.

She went on. "I know of a clothing designer who used to work for Carver's team. She's working in the VR industry now. She's a good friend. She'll get you set up with some period clothing, no problem. I'll just say you're auditioning for a part or something—want to look authentic."

He laughed and she appreciated his mouth again. "I never thought I'd pass for an actor."

"She won't have to meet you. We'll just send her your measurements. Do you know them?"

"All military personnel know their measurements. As a matter of fact, I'd actually prefer a military uniform. Maybe army. I can do things and get into places I couldn't do otherwise if I'm in uniform. Can you arrange for that?"

"Absolutely. No problem."

"Wait a minute. If Nick spots me while I'm tracking him, he might recognize me. We can't exactly change my face."

Well we could, she thought, and pretty simply. But that was too complicated for her to arrange from prison. "My designer friend can give you dental prosthetics that you can take in and out easily, which will change your appearance some," she said, "plus, we'll have her give you some glasses, and you'll be wearing a military cap. That should be enough. He won't be expecting you to be there. He won't be looking for you."

"Got it. That makes sense."

"You'll need an authentic weapon too. There, I can't help you."

"Don't worry. I know someone in L.A. that can set me up. I'm a collector, you know."

She didn't know, but it didn't surprise her. "So you'll do it then?"

"Keep talking." He smiled and sat back in his chair.

"One thing is," she went on, "you've got to go before June twenty-third. Even just the day before so you can be ready to intercept him at this gala he'll be at. Brown Derby restaurant. I'm not sure what time, but probably in the evening."

"I can find out," he said.

"Once it's done, you come right back. Don't linger. The more time you spend there, the more you could do something to impact the timeline."

"I know how it works."

"You've never time traveled before though, right?"

"No," he replied, "but I'll be fine. I've been in extreme situations before."

"And what about Rajesh. He's manning the portal with you?"

"Yeah. He's gonna have to be the one to send me back." Mark frowned. "I hadn't thought of that. He's gonna want to know why I'm going. It's not like Nick can communicate with us. I can't tell him that Nick needs my help or anything like that. There would be no way to know that."

"Then we're going to have to make something up."

"Or maybe you could just buy him off. It sounds like you have that kind of money"

Suhan smiled. "I do. So, you're saying he doesn't have any more loyalty to Nick than you do?"

"Not at all. He could work anywhere with his skills but he's working for Nick because he pays him a ton. Same as me. Raj would do anything for a buck to tell you the truth. But let me say this: Nick is a source of ongoing income for us. If he's dead, that will stop. So even with this money you're paying us, it won't be as much as we could continue to make with Nick alive."

Suhan had already thought of that. In going

through Nick's bank statements, she'd found that Mark Stein was on his payroll, as well as Rajesh Bhau, his engineer. Mark was no scientist, not even the sharpest tool in the shed, but Nick had taught him enough so that he could do what he needed him to do, and she knew Stockard appreciated having his muscle and his military training, just in case. Several years ago, Nick had gotten rid of all his lawyers, accountants, and trustees, plus he didn't have any beneficiaries. Even after he was dead, Suhan could do what she wanted with his money. She explained this to Mark and then said, "So, not only will you both get this large extra bonus, but you'll keep getting paid, same as always."

He nodded slowly. "I'm liking this."

She then took a chance, reached out, and touched his hand. "Listen, I can't be certain why Nick's gone back there, but you know him, and you know he can't be up to any good. He may have figured out how to impact the outcome of the war just by having a conversation with the right person, or killing someone, or...I don't even know. I don't know what he's after."

He looked down at her hand, still touching his. "I wish we could go somewhere where we could have more privacy."

She raised an eyebrow. It had been a long time since she had been with a man. "I could arrange for that."

Chapter Twelve

Hiro Wakai - December 8th, 1941

I walked onto the set this morning to find the other actors, people I had always considered if not good friends, at least companionable colleagues, regarding me warily. No one said hello in the usual, easy fashion. From the stars down to the grips, no one spoke to me. No one except for one person: Bogart.

He walked up to me, patted me on the shoulder, and said, "How you doin', chum?"

I appreciated the gesture more than I can say. "I've been better, Mr. Bogart," I replied.

"We all have, my boy, we all have." He rested his hand on my shoulder for a moment, then turned away to light a cigarette.

This brief exchange lightened the mood on set, at least for the moment. Ronnie Lake, a young actress who's always sweet to everyone, smiled at me sympathetically. Then people went back to their work, and the day went on as usual. I'm a bit player, nothing more, but my parents are so proud of what I've achieved. I work steadily in Hollywood, playing everything from a Chinese laundry man to an Indian. but everyone on the set, everyone at any of the studios I've worked for, knows I'm Japanese. I wonder now if my work will dry up. Things haven't been great for the Japanese in America since Japan signed the Tripartite Pact with Germany and Italy a few years back, and even worse since they invaded China, but it's been pretty clear to me that one reason I'm still working is because of Bogart himself. I seem to be mysteriously cast in movies that he's in, even if it's just the smallest of bit parts. Heck, maybe I'll get even better roles now. There will be plenty more war movies, that's for sure, probably a lot of them about America fighting Japan. Though they'll put some big-name actors in the main roles, making them up with slanted eyes and yellowish skin in the typical Hollywood way, they're sure to want other "Oriental-looking" men in the smaller parts. I'm not saying I want to benefit from this terrible war, or the horror of the Pearl Harbor bombing, but we all have to look out for ourselves in the end.

"He's here!" Cassandra called out to Yoshi, who was lounging nearby as she manned the console. She ordered the computer to begin the transfer as Yoshi ran to her side. A minute later the portal chamber door slid open and there was her boss, dressed just as he had been when he left. She jumped up and threw her arms around him as he stepped out of the chamber.

"I'm so glad to see you! I was beginning to worry!"

"I wouldn't let you down." He hugged her tight then held her at arms' length, smiling broadly.

Yoshi took his satchel while Cassandra marveled at how handsome Elton Carver looked. The past had done him good. He looked younger, more relaxed, and with a fresh sparkle in his eye.

"How was it?" she wanted to know.

"Incredible. Amazing. It's...it's surreal being there. I'm so grateful I had the time I did to enjoy it because we've got a hard job ahead of us. Anyway, I bought a car and rented us a house. We'll wait a couple more hours until the warehouse clears out, then we'd better go."

"I just need to change clothes."

Shannon, the team's clothing designer, had come into the room. The fact that the portal lab was in a house meant the whole team could stay there and be on hand at all times. "It's great to see you, Professor Carver," she said, giving him a hug. Then she turned to Cassandra. "Let's get you dressed."

It didn't take long to slip into the undergarments, since she and Shannon had agreed she could forego the type of girdle most women of the 1940s wore. Cassandra was trim and fit, and could wear the pretty green dress Shannon had designed for her without being gusseted. The bra was certainly more heavy-duty than Cassandra's modest décolletage required, and the garter belt seemed cumbersome, but the panties were silky and loose fitting, more like shorts than underwear. She rolled silk stockings up her legs and hooked them onto the clasps of the garter belt, aware that the stockings were a luxury that few women of the time could afford. Silk had been allocated for parachutes for the war and, by 1942, stockings were generally made of rayon.

She and Elton had decided that Cassandra would be passing as some kind of textiles heiress from back east—a woman like that would probably be able to get a hold of silk stockings.

The dress was summery, with puffed sleeves that hit her upper arm midway, v-necked with wide lapels, a slim waist, cloth buttons up the front, and a swingy skirt that fell to her knees. On her feet she wore brown, high-heeled Mary Janes which matched her bag. Once Cassandra was dressed, Shannon straightened her normally curly hair, then parted it on the side and re-curled the front in large waves so that it flowed over the right side of her face seductively. She did her makeup in pale eyes, arced brows and deep red lipstick. Looking in the mirror, Cassandra liked the effect: like a glamorous, old-time movie star.

For the first time since she'd started time traveling, she was setting off on her journey in clothes she could almost have worn in the present. Since the styles of the various decades of recent centuries had gone in and out of fashion so many times, it was almost time for the padded shoulders and platform shoes of the 1940s, the 1980s, the 2040s and the 2080s to come back around again.

When she walked into the main room of the lab to join the others, she was gratified by the appreciative look Elton gave her. He then turned his attention to the monitor, which showed a kind of night-vision image of the exact spot from which they would be emerging at the other end of the portal.

"The exit looks clear," said Alex, who was manning the console.

"Let's go," Elton said. With one hand he picked up Cassandra's suitcase, which contained some changes of clothes that Shannon had made, plus her toilette articles. He offered her the other. "Is the sleep elixir in here?"

"Sure is," Cassandra replied. She placed her hand in his, appreciating the warmth and strength of it. "It seems strange not to have James here," she remarked. "He's been in the portal lab every time I've gone on a journey."

"He's with us in spirit, for sure," Elton replied.

Cassandra smiled. As long as she was with Elton Carver, she knew she was safe.

They stepped into the chamber together and waved to the rest of the team. The door slid shut and a humming sound filled her ears. The floor seemed to fall away. She clutched Elton's hand as she closed her eyes. She felt as if she were spinning, plummeting through space. There was nothing solid to stand on or hold on to. Just as she thought she would be sick, the floor seemed to rise up beneath her and the spinning stopped. She took a deep breath and opened her eyes, still holding on to Elton's hand. He squeezed it.

"You ok?"

"Yeah," she gasped.

It was very dark. As her eyes adjusted, she could see light from streetlamps outside filtering through high windows in the warehouse walls. The air was cool, but musty, and smelled like metal.

"This way," said Elton. He led her through the cavernous building, looming with the shapes of boxes and crates.

Suddenly the beam of a flashlight blinded them. Elton let go of her hand.

"Who's there?" a voice called out.

"Shit," Elton hissed. "Must be a security guard."

"Hello!" Cassandra called out. "Glad to see you're doing your job! Can I ask your name?"

"I'm Bob. Who wants to know?"

"Mrs. Cassandra Reilly. I'm the landlord's daughter. I was just passing through to make sure everything was secure. Dad asked me to do it since I was in the neighborhood tonight."

"Who's this?" the man asked, indicating Elton with his light.

"He's my bodyguard. You don't think I'd wander around in a place like this by myself, do you?"

"Nooo..." the man sounded confused.

She extracted a well-replicated five-dollar bill from her purse.

"Here you go, Bob, thanks for doing your job so well." She handed it to him.

"Well, th-thanks," he stammered. "Can I show you out?"

"Sure," she said, "and lock the door behind us."

They quickly walked to the entrance of the building, and Bob undid the bolt that was secured from within.

"By the way, my key let us in," she said, "but this wasn't locked on the inside, which it should be when you're the only one here. We bolted it after we came in."

"What?" Bob said. "I was sure I locked it!"

"Well, double check next time."

"Wait a minute, you're…Mr. Chen's daughter?"

"Um, it's complicated. Thanks again, Bob."

Cassandra and Elton hurried out the door and around to the parking lot where the Hudson sat gleaming in the lamplight.

"She's beautiful!" Cassandra whispered.

Elton smiled and opened the back door for her.

"What do you think you're doing?" she said. "I'm not getting in the back."

"Yes, you are. You can't ride in the front with me?"

"Why not?"

"You know why not."

"Elton, I'm not comfortable with this."

His gentle brown eyes looked into hers. "Cassie, it's for my safety as much as yours."

Understanding his meaning, she sighed. "I won't be able to get used to this."

"No. It's awful. But it's the way it has to be."

She got in and he closed the door, then went to put her suitcase in the trunk. The car smelled of leather. She breathed in deeply. The back seat was huge—like sitting on a sofa.

Elton walked to the front of the car, took something from his pocket, then slapped a sticker with a big X on it over the A sticker on the windshield.

As he let himself into the driver's seat she asked, "What's that?"

"It's a gas ration sticker. I had Yoshi replicate one for me while you were getting dressed. It means we can get unlimited gas rather than the 3-4 gallons a week allotted to civilians. It means we're bigwigs."

"What if someone asks us about it?"

"Maybe it means you're more than a 'textiles heiress.' Maybe it will mean your father is in the government. I don't know. We'll think of something. Hopefully, no one will ask."

"Well, okay. Hey, aren't there seatbelts?" she asked, searching around for them.

He chuckled. "This was before they invented seatbelts. But don't worry, I'm a good driver and this thing is a tank."

He drove to the exit gate and handed the guard a bill as they left. Cassandra waved to him while a perplexed look came over the man's face.

"We've got a ways to go, so settle back and relax." He turned on the radio, which emanated the very best swing music.

She sat forward and rested her chin on her hands on the back of the front seat. "No. I haven't seen you in two weeks and I want to know all about your time here!"

And so, as they drove to Hollywood, he told her about his experience of being in Compton, and the challenges of being a black man in the white man's world outside of the African American neighborhood. She was fascinated to hear about the avenue, though saddened by the racism he'd encountered. As he talked, she gazed in wonder at the world as it sailed by, and, before she knew it, they were in the Hollywood Hills. Elton led her to the bungalow, unlocked it, and showed her in.

"It's adorable," she cried with delight.

He set her suitcase down.

"Where is your stuff?"

"I'm staying in the guesthouse."

"What?"

"Cassie..."

"Yeah, I get it," she said, suddenly realizing how complicated this was going to be. "I get it."

"Let's get some rest," he said. "Tomorrow we'll stake out the Brown Derby in the afternoon, and work out a plan to ambush Nick in the evening."

"Okay."

He came to her and took her in his arms for a moment, kissing her on the cheek. He smelled like himself—a wonderful, undefinable fragrance that she had always loved, and also of the wool and cotton of his clothes, which somehow had a smell that must be particular to this time because it was completely foreign to her.

"Goodnight," he said, smiling. He handed her a key to the front door.

"Goodnight, Elton, sleep well."

He let himself out and locked the door, leaving her to wonder at being, once again, in a time and place she never imagined she would be.

Chapter Thirteen

Hiro Wakai - February 1st, 1942

I was dismissed from the film so I went to enlist today. I wanted to show my country that I love it as much as any other American. After all, the USA has done so much for me and my parents. Just the fact that they could run their own restaurant and be successful at it is something they could have never done in Japan. I, however, am running out of options. I've been offered no parts, and my savings is dwindling. That's just one reason I decided to enlist. I want to serve this country and pay it back for all the good it's done for me and my parents. Mom and Pop weren't happy about the decision. They were upset that I would want to go and fight what they consider their own countrymen (the Nipponese as they still call them), but those people are not my countrymen. I'm an American, through and through, and I was determined to go fight against Japan and Germany, standing with my true countrymen. I was ready to give 'em hell!

But the military didn't take me. Turns out I have a slight curvature of the spine which I didn't even know I had, but I guess it's enough to keep me from serving. And that was that. I did have a moment of wondering if it was because I'm Japanese, but other Japanese men I know, sons of my parents' friends for instance, were snapped right up. So now what?

The following morning Cassandra awoke from a wonderful dream, her entire body tingling. She had been with Lauro. They were at Bellosguardo, Galileo's home where Lauro lived in the year she'd gone to be with him. Galileo had never come home the whole time Cassandra had been there, busy as he was in Paris, so they'd had the whole villa to themselves with the exception of the servants. In the dream, it was as she had lived a whole day in much the same way she and Lauro had lived their quotidian life, but, in the dream, that day had lasted only a few moments. It had started with them waking together. They were in the beautiful bed they'd shared of heavy carved wood, nestled in the down mattress, fine silk sheets covering them. Their bodies were pressed close together, her legs wrapped around his firm butt. They were making love, and he was kissing her over and over. The next moment they were at breakfast, eating the coarse brown bread she loved, dipped in oil from the olives of Galileo's orchard. Then they were strolling through a field. The Tuscan sunlight lit up Lauro's dark eyes, just a little more crinkled around the edges than when she'd met him in Siena. That had been one hundred years before, though he had only aged three. He took her in his arms and they melted into the tall grass, where he lifted her skirts and they enjoyed each other again. Then, once more, they were at the table, being served a meal of roast pheasant, gnocchi with garden tomatoes and basil, summer fruits, and a rich, red wine. The next moment they were on the rooftop of the villa, looking into a telescope at the stars. It was Galileo's telescope, but Lauro had invented it. History had not given him credit for his inventions and discoveries, but she knew, and he knew, the truth. The dream ended with them there, under the glistening night sky, Lauro loosening the ties of her blouse so it fell off her shoulders to her waist, pulling down the chemise she wore under, and caressing and kissing her bare breasts. They continued to undress each other and then lay down on a divan and made intense love under a sea of stars.

She sat up, hoping to hold onto the dream as long as possible. As she gazed out her bedroom window, the sparkling pool caught her attention. She had not brought a bathing suit, but she could never pass up an opportunity for a swim—besides, it would help cool her down. It was early and Elton would probably not be up for a while. She grabbed a towel from the bathroom and slipped out of her light cotton PJs. She wrapped the towel around her and opened the glass door to the backyard. Growing there were orange and lemon trees, and a few low palms. There was lovely green grass surrounding the flagstone patio, and it was all surrounded by a high wooden fence and shrubs. She dipped a toe in the pool. It was cool but not cold. Flinging the towel aside, she dove into the deep end, shocked at first by the contrast of the temperature of the water to her skin, but a few quick laps warmed her up nicely and she continued back and forth several times. As she was about to finish up and had turned her head to the side for a breath under her raised arm, she caught a glimpse of movement and stopped abruptly, treading water.

"Oh!" cried Elton, who must have just stepped into the yard from the gate along the side of the house. "I'm sorry!" He quickly turned around.

"I didn't think you'd be up!" she said, gasping for breath.

"I wondered if I should go pick something up for breakfast," he said, his back still turned to her. "I heard you in the water, but didn't realize you'd be..."

She swam to the edge of the pool, clambered out, and grabbed for her towel. She wrapped it around herself. "Okay, I'm decent now. Sort of."

He turned to face her. "I'm really sorry." His face had turned a shade of deep brownish-red, and she could feel the inevitable blush creeping over her own skin.

"It's okay," she said, trying to brush it off. She and her boss had never found themselves in such an intimate setting before. "Um, where will you go to get food?" It was clear they could not go into a restaurant together, which frustrated her to no end.

"I noticed a market down the street."

"You don't think there will be a problem? This seems like a pretty white neighborhood."

"They're either black or white. There's no in-between. I may as well give it a try."

She noticed he was dressed well, in a tan linen suit.

"Pulling up in the car may help," he added.

"Okay. I'll jump in the shower," she said.

He smiled at her and went back through the gate. She supposed he'd been dealing with this world for a couple of weeks now and must know what he was doing.

By the time she had showered and dressed, he was in the kitchen making an omelet, his jacket draped over a kitchen chair, swing music playing on the radio in the living room.

"Mmm, that smells good. So, no trouble?"

"Well, the store lady didn't seem all that glad to see me, but she didn't refuse me service."

"A lady running the store? Is that common?"

"Normally it wouldn't be, but it's war time. The women have taken over their husbands' businesses because there's no one else to do it while the men are overseas. I suspect if it had been a man, he might have given me a hard time."

"Small blessings," she said sarcastically.

He glanced at her. "You look nice," he offered, then turned his attention back to the stove.

She suddenly wondered how much of her naked body he had seen before. "Thanks. It's great to be able to wear pants. The first time ever on one of these trips, if you don't count when I had to dress like a man back in England."

"I forgot about that," he laughed. "Well, that style really suits you."

It was a style she loved: High-waisted, wide-legged pants and a trim blouse tucked in, low-heeled Oxford shoes on her feet. She felt dapper.

He took the pan off the stove, took a step toward her and held a hand out. She took it with a questioning look. Moving to the music, he took her in his arms and did a quick six-count step which she fell into without thinking. She had mastered swing dancing several years ago, and the steps were second nature. He sent her out with a turn under his arm and she spun effortlessly. He then pulled her back into a lindy-hop, eight-count swing-out, and she followed like she'd been dancing with him forever. They both laughed and finished off with a few more snappy moves before he dipped her, spun her out, squeezed her hand, and bowed to her.

"Whoa! Elton! I didn't know you could dance like that!"

"I'm full of surprises," he said with a wink. "I knew you took lessons. You're good."

"We'll have to do that again," she said, breathless. There was nothing more attractive than a man who could dance.

"You're on," he said. "And now, breakfast is served." He cut the omelet in half and slid it onto two plates, snapped some toast out of the old-timey toaster and gestured toward the table where butter, jam, coffee, and juice awaited.

"You're spoiling me," she said as she took a seat.

"Feel free to get used to it," he replied.

Whatever he meant by that, she liked it.

After breakfast, they decided they should call the Brown Derby restaurant to find out what time the gala would take place. Cassandra approached the heavy-looking, black apparatus and picked up the receiver. Its heft and smooth texture felt good in her hand.

"Okay," she said to Elton, looking at the little round holes surrounded by numbers and letters on the base of the phone, "how do you work this thing?"

He chuckled. "Dial O for operator." He put his finger in the hole and swung it around until it hit a little metal barrier. It swung back around of its own accord to the original position.

She listened as it made a ringing sound, and finally a woman's voice answered. "Operator, may I help you?"

"Um, yes, can you please connect me with the Brown Derby Restaurant?"

"One moment, please."

There was a long pause, and then the sound of ringing again.

Another female voice answered. "Brown Derby, how may I help you?"

"I'm calling to find out what time the gala is taking place today."

"The gala is a private event and it is sold out," the woman said rather snootily.

"Oh, I see. Well, would you mind telling me what time it starts?"

"Eight PM," the woman said, and hung up.

"So much for courtesy," Cassandra remarked. She placed the receiver back on the hook.

"Hmm. Eight is good. It will be almost dark. We can wait in the car across the street, or as close as we can."

"But it may make it harder to spot Nick."

"True. And we have to make sure he doesn't see us."

"Maybe we should use binoculars," she suggested.

"We could, though anyone seeing us spying on the event with binoculars might think we're up to no good."

"Maybe if I do it from the back seat..."

"Yeah, okay. We need to get some binoculars, and I know where."

"So, here's what I'm thinking," she said. "We wait outside and watch him go in. We don't act then. We wait until he comes out again when it will be really dark. Then, if he's alone, I follow him by foot, you in the car. I'll get up as close behind him as I can, then I'll tap him on the neck, or hand maybe, with the wand of the sleep elixir. He won't get very far before he passes out. You'll pull up in the car and we'll put him in."

"Then we've got to get him straight to the portal exit. It will be late, there shouldn't be anyone around."

"But someone will be there. The guard at least. We'll have to drag a sleeping man past him, or whoever, and to that corner of the warehouse."

"Yeah, that's tricky," he said, mulling it over.

"We can't let him regain consciousness. He's too dangerous."

"We'll need some kind of trunk, or better yet, a shipping crate, and a dolly. We'll put him in it."

"This is starting to feel like a gangster movie."

"I don't see any other option. I'll bring him in, and if I get stopped, I'll say I'm making a delivery. I can let myself in with my transforming key. You'll wait with the car in the parking lot. I'll take him through the portal, turn him over to Alex and Yoshi, then come back to get you."

"Then what?"

"I don't know. We'll come back here. Tomorrow morning we'll call Betsy, my real estate agent, and tell her we're leaving town. We'll tell her the owner can keep the six month's rent. We'll drive back to the warehouse late tomorrow night. I guess we'll just leave the car in the parking lot with the keys in it. Someone will be thrilled to have it."

"Somehow I doubt it's going to go that smoothly."

"Yeah, but at least we have a plan. It's a start."

They went outside to the car parked in the driveway just as a lady was walking by with a dog on a leash. Cassandra smiled at her but she frowned back. Elton opened the back door of the car for

Cassandra and made a gesture for her to enter.

The woman's face took on a friendlier expression. "Hello!" she said, pausing in front of the driveway. "I'm Mrs. Jane Watson. I live two doors down. You must have just moved in."

"Cassandra Reilly." She went to her and offered her hand to shake.

Mrs. Watson grasped it lightly for a moment, then let it go. "Nice to meet you."

"I'm just in town for a few weeks," Cassandra said, making it up as she went along, "and this place was available. So much nicer than a hotel. I love the neighborhood."

"Yes, it's lovely," the woman said, glancing at Elton with trepidation.

"This is my driver, Mr. Carver," said Cassandra, motioning toward Elton.

Mrs. Watson merely nodded. "Well, I hope to see you again," she said to Cassandra.

"Have a nice day," Cassandra responded, going back to the car. She and Elton both got in as she huffed, "Bitch..."

"You gotta let it go, Cassie," he said. "It does no good to judge people. It's how they were raised. It's what society has led them to believe is acceptable."

"Well, I hated it in 1853 New York and I hate it now. It's appalling how little has changed in a hundred years."

"It's bad, I'll grant you that."

Her mood improved with the drive. Passing

beautiful homes, the streets lined with date palms, the sun shining brightly, all made Cassandra feel like she was in an old Hollywood movie. Everyone they passed on the street was well-dressed in the glamorous fashions of the times. Even nannies out walking with children were spiffily attired in their well-pressed uniforms and high-heeled Oxford shoes.

Before long, they were on Hollywood Boulevard, driving past Grauman's Chinese Theater and other classic buildings, most of which Cassandra didn't recognize. The theater was the only thing that still existed in the vicinity until her time. The boulevard was studded with other art deco buildings as well like the Pantages Theater and the Roosevelt Hotel. Shoppers strolled along, going in and out of the high end stores. The area reeked of the well-to-do. Elton took Normandie Avenue to Wilshire Boulevard and then they drove along Wilshire to the corner of Alexandria where the iconic Brown Derby restaurant, actually shaped like a big, brown hat, was situated.

"It's a good wide avenue," Elton commented. "If we can get a parking space just across the street, here, we can watch for Nick without being noticed."

The stake out location confirmed, they continued on Wilshire into downtown Los Angeles and on to S. Central Avenue.

"Don't sit forward, now, Cassie. Sit back so that

you're more or less out of sight," Elton said.

"Is it dangerous?"

"No, it's not that it's dangerous, it's just that there are literally no white people here. You'll be out of place."

She was fascinated by the avenue: so lively, so obviously thriving. She wanted to get out and walk to really experience it, but Elton seemed to know what he was talking about so she stayed seated with the rear side panel blocking her face, and looked out as best she could through the front windows.

He pulled up in front of a Sears & Roebuck department store, and told her to stay put and out of sight. He rolled the front windows down a little, then locked the doors and went in. It soon grew stifling in the car but she had no choice but to endure it. She fanned herself with the small notebook she had in her purse, and huddled in the corner.

After a few minutes he was out of the store and in the car. He handed her a shopping bag and she extracted the kind of binoculars one might use for birdwatching.

"It just so happens we might be able to find the crate here too," he said. "There's a loading dock in back and the saleslady said we might be able to buy one off the workers who unload the furniture."

He pulled the car through an alley to a large paved area behind the store. There, some men and a few sturdy-looking women were opening crates of sofas, tables, lamps and other large items. Elton went out to talk to them while Cassandra crouched low. After a few minutes, he returned and opened the trunk. She watched through the rear-view mirror as he handed one of the workers a bill, then took a medium-sized crate off a dolly and placed it inside.

"That wasn't too hard," she commented after he got in.

"They don't have as much merchandise as they did before the war. They aren't selling any appliances because the metal is all being used for machinery. People still gotta have furniture though I guess. I paid the guy a month's salary for the crate and the dolly, which obviously belongs to Sears. He didn't seem too concerned about it. I think the sticker on the windshield kept him from asking questions."

"Now what?" she wanted to know.

"We've got some time to kill."

"I'm hungry."

"Hmmm, let's see what we can do about that."

From S. Central, they took El Segundo Boulevard to the coast, then up the highway to Santa Monica Beach. Cassandra rolled down the window, sat back, and let the wind blow through her hair. It was around four by the time they reached the beach. Elton parked along Pico Boulevard and they walked to the sand, not exactly together, but not one behind the other either. Santa Monica was not a segregated beach, but one area of it was where mostly black people hung out. A white woman in company with a black man could feel reasonably comfortable there. While she waited on a bench on the boardwalk, he went to buy them food and came back with hotdogs, fried clams, chicken, and soda pop.

They strolled onto the sand and found a driftwood log to sit on. She dove into the food: all new flavors. She had never had a hotdog in her life. People in her time didn't eat much meat, and certainly nothing processed. It was delicious. She'd also not had fried clams, though she'd had fried chicken in New York in 1853, prepared by the gifted hands of the southern cook in the home she'd stayed in. This was not as good, but still strangely delicious. Soda pop was completely new to her. Some people in her world drank it if they could get their hands on it, but most people would never imbibe something so full of empty calories. It was sublime.

They sat and talked, mostly about what they might expect that night staking out Nick and the various scenarios that might befall them. Yet it was so relaxing just watching the waves crash on the shore, feeling the cool, ocean breeze, the sand between her toes. She and Elton had never shared such easy camaraderie. It felt good simply to be with him and watch the sunset.

They stayed until almost seven, then drove back

to Wilshire and Alexandria and found a space diagonally across the street for a good view. They were in place by seven-thirty. No one had gathered yet at the Brown Derby—certainly no one wanted to be unfashionably early—but the staff was busily cleaning the front sidewalk and laying out a red carpet. Though there were no searchlights crisscrossing the sky like she had seen in old movies announcing Hollywood premieres or fancy events, likely as a precaution in case of enemy aircraft, photographers began to assemble and passersby too, realizing something exciting was about to happen. Soon, a velvet-roped barrier was set up, and finally, a black Lincoln arrived. Out stepped a glamorous-looking lady in a slinky gown, accompanied by a tuxedoed gentleman. The people cheered, the flashbulbs popped, and the couple waved.

Cassandra had her binoculars at the ready. She peered at the couple. "Well, it's definitely not Nick. I don't know who it is."

Moments later, another long black sedan arrived, and another dazzling couple emerged. "Oh my god, I think that's Katherine Hepburn! And Spencer Tracy!" She took the binoculars away from her eyes for a moment. "Elton, I'm freaking out. She's one of my idols from old Hollywood! And I love him too!"

He laughed from the front seat. "Cassie! Look for Nick."

"I didn't think this would be so exciting!"

More black cars rumbled to the front of the restaurant, and one by one the stars emerged.

"It's Bette Davis! Gary Cooper! Rita Hayworth and Orson Wells! Elton, I'm dying."

"Keep calm," he chuckled.

"Wait a minute, wait a minute, there he is! Elton, there he is! He just got out of that car. He's with a lady but I don't know who she is." Her heart pounded. She thought she might be sick. "I'm so disgusted to see him again. I think I'm having a post-traumatic stress reaction."

"Deep breaths, Cassie, deep breaths."

She inhaled deeply and her heart rate began to slow. She watched Nick hand the car over to a valet, then he and his date walked up the red carpet, he slightly behind her. His date stopped to pose for a photographer, but he dodged the camera, ducking behind a pillar. The woman was blonde, wearing a red gown with a low-cut back. She was beautiful and looked familiar. Cassandra figured she must have seen a picture of her somewhere. Suddenly there was a tussle in the crowd near Nick, and the police who were keeping an eye on the scene moved in quickly, nudging the people backwards. Cassandra noticed a tall man among the fans who didn't look like he belonged, mostly because the majority of them were women. Then she noticed he was wearing an army uniform. He seemed stiff, uncomfortable. Suddenly, he turned around and shoved his way out of the crowd. Cassandra followed him with the binoculars for a moment. He quickly walked down the street to a battered old car, but did not drive away.

Nick's date, startled by the commotion, hurried toward the entrance of the restaurant and Nick joined her, still avoiding the photographers. He was wearing a black tuxedo and his hair was cut short in the style of the era. "That bastard," Cassandra grumbled, "what is he up to?"

Soon Nick disappeared into the restaurant. She took a deep breath and sat back in the seat. "Now what?"

"Now we wait." He passed her a thermos of water and she took a large swig.

The night was cool and the air refreshing. They rolled all the windows down and she tried to relax, both of them still keeping an eye on the door. It appeared that everyone who was attending the gala had now arrived. Eventually the crowd got bored and wandered away while the photographers sat here and there on curbs or benches and smoked.

A couple of hours passed, and one by one celebrity couples began to emerge as their cars pulled up and they were whisked away. Nick and his date finally came out as well. He spoke to a valet who ran to get his car and then he and the woman lingered in the front for a few minutes, chatting with other gala guests.

"There's no way to corner him alone," Cassandra said. "He's surrounded by people. What are we going to do?"

Out of the corner of her eye, Cassandra saw the man in uniform get out of his car and walk quickly toward the entrance of the Brown Derby. He seemed to be intent on Nick. He put his hand inside his breast pocket and Cassandra gasped. It was the kind of motion people used when reaching for a gun.

Just then, Nick's car pulled up in front of the restaurant, the valet handed him the keys, and he and the blond got in.

Elton started the engine. "I guess all we can do is follow them."

As Nick's car pulled away, the soldier hurried back to his car. Elton swung the Hudson around on the avenue and began trailing, keeping a stealthy distance behind. The army man's battered grey sedan pulled out onto the roadway and seemed to be following them too.

"That's a Daimler, I think," Elton commented, indicating Nick's car. "From the mid 30s. A model 15. I believe they call it a Daimler Light."

None of that meant anything to Cassandra.

"It's like what you see Bonnie and Clyde drive in the movies," he went on.

"Oh," she replied. "Fitting." But who was this person who now seemed to be following them? It was eerie being on the winding roads with the half headlights barely cutting through the darkness though Elton seemed to have a handle on it. At times she thought the man in the grey car had turned off, but then she'd see him again, keeping a good distance behind. They trailed the Daimler into Beverly Hills, but then it disappeared behind the gates of a mansion and they could follow no more.

"Now what, do we wait?"

"Yes, let's wait. Maybe he's just dropping her off."

Elton pulled the car up the road, pulled over, and cut the engine and lights. The grey car pulled over about a half a block behind them.

"Elton," she said. "I think someone else is stalking Nick. There's a grey car back there with a military guy in it. He was in the crowd of fans at the gala and he's been following us…or Nick."

Elton peered into the rear view mirror. "If anything, he's probably stalking Nick's date. History is full of crazed fans who would do anything to get closer to the object of their desire."

"I wish I knew who she was."

"She's famous enough for the photographers to be all over her. We'll keep an eye on the guy just in case though."

"Yeah, maybe he's her husband or boyfriend. I swear I thought he was going to pull a gun out back there at the gala."

"Really?"

"Yeah, but then I thought it was just my imagination. Until he started following us—or Nick."

After an hour, Nick still hadn't come out. The man in the grey car had stayed put.

"I don't think Nick's just dropping her off," Cassandra observed.

"What's this now?" Elton said, still staring the rear view mirror. "There's a cop back there. He's talking to the guy in the grey car." He paused a moment. "He's coming our way."

A moment later, a black and white police car came pulling up next to them. Cassandra poked her head out the window and smiled.

The officer rolled his window down. "Can I help you, ma'am?"

"Yes, I'm afraid my driver and I have gotten lost."

The officer glanced toward Elton and frowned. "Where are you trying to go?"

Elton whispered the address of the bungalow to her and she repeated it to the officer.

"You're a long ways from there," the man said.

"I'm new in town. We drove out from New York just last week and are still trying to find our way around."

"Well, come on, follow me."

"Oh, thank you so much!" Cassandra replied.

The officer drove ahead, and Elton started the car and began to follow him.

"Damn it!" Cassandra hissed. She glanced behind and noticed the grey car was staying put.

"I don't think there was much point hanging out there anyway," Elton said. "Nick could be there all night."

"Well, we know something at least," said Cassandra, "we know he's seeing this woman. And, maybe he's staying there permanently. So, we've at least got that much."

"Tomorrow let's pick up one of those fan magazines and maybe we can find a picture of her so we figure out who she is."

"Good idea. Well, I guess we're not returning to the future any time soon."

"As I suspected, this is going to be complicated."

"We've got our work cut out for us." Cassandra agreed. "I'm still wondering about the army guy though. I wonder why the officer didn't ask him to leave. Maybe it's because he's military. Maybe he's the woman's bodyguard."

"Or maybe it's because he's white and I'm not," Elton observed with a bitter edge to his voice.

Once the officer had shown them to their house, Cassandra reluctantly thanked him and, with a sigh, said goodnight to Elton as they both retired to their separate dwellings.

Chapter Fourteen

Hiro Wakai - March 6th, 1942

I've looked everywhere for work but no one will hire me. I've applied in factories, at grocery stores, as a cab driver, a waiter, a life guard, a bus driver, you name it, but I'm turned away with disgust every time. Life for the Japanese in this country is becoming a challenge bordering on dangerous. I've had bottles thrown at me from cars as I walk down the street. I've stopped going to bars for a drink because someone always wants to pick a fight. My landlord let me know he won't be renewing my lease when it's up next month. Not that it really matters because I won't have money to pay the rent.

Once nice thing was that Mr. Bogart called me the other day to find out how I'm doing. He says he's tried to get me parts but they aren't hiring anyone who even vaguely looks "Oriental" right now. I told him I appreciated him trying.

All I do these days is scan the classified ads in the newspaper, hoping to find a lead on a job though sometimes I spare a few cents to go to the movies. That's depressing though, seeing all those working actors. And then there are the newsreels—happy boys going off to fight the enemy, proud and strong. The radio isn't any better. When it isn't news of the war, it's patriotic messages, telling us to plant victory gardens and save our scrap metal. President Roosevelt continues to give his Fireside Chats to build the morale of the American people and if I weren't in the position I'm in, I'd be stirred by them. "We are fighting," he says, "as our fathers have fought, to uphold the doctrine that all men are equal in the sight of God. Those on the other side are striving to destroy this deep belief and to create a world in their own image— a world of tyranny and cruelty and serfdom. That is the conflict that day and night now pervades our lives. No compromise can end that conflict. There never has been— there never can be—successful compromise between good and evil. Only total victory can reward the champions of tolerance, and decency, and freedom, and faith."

Do these words apply to me? Am I equal in the sight of God? Do people see me as one of "those on the other side?" I am confused and disheartened. Where is my place in this war? In this country?

Nick had gotten just what he wanted from the blonde. Before leaving for this trip, he'd done his research well, and believed that Veronica Lake might know something about Hiro Wakai. Searching the information on the man, he hadn't been able to find an address, but was able to find out he had been an actor, working on the film To Have and Have Not in 1942 with Lake and Humphrey Bogart. It wasn't easy worming your way onto a movie set, so Nick decided that, since Veronica Lake was single at the time, she'd be vulnerable to his charms, and he could use her to get him on the set. Getting to know the Hollywood crowd was a simple matter of going to the the best clubs, talking like a big shot and throwing a little money around. The first time he'd met Lake, at a party he'd finagled an invitation to, he bought her several drinks and got her to take him home. Damn the fact that, when he'd gone with her to the set the next day where she was filming the movie, he'd found out they had let Hiro go several months ago. Nick hadn't even returned from his London fiasco until spring. If he had known, he could have set the trip for an earlier year—but then, the only information he had about Hiro Wakai was that he had worked on this film in 1942, and Nick couldn't have possibly arranged to get here any sooner in this particular year.

He was here now though, and Hiro had to be somewhere in L.A. So while he zeroed in on his prize, he may as well have a little fun gallivanting around with movie stars. Nick had always had a fondness for those old films and, as it turned out, the actresses all seemed to want a piece of him. At the clubs and parties he'd gone to, before he'd met Veronica, he wowed them one by one: Davis, Grable, Tierney, Horne...even Hepburn, who was rumored not to be particularly into men. They all swooned over him. If he knew anything, he knew how to charm. It wasn't until a week before the gala that he had finally met Lake. She took him home with her that very night. Oh, she was a sweet young thing— just twenty years old if he wasn't mistaken. She took him to her luxurious home in Beverly Hills and bedded him. It was definitely a side-perk of his mission, that was for sure. Her long, blonde hair was like silk, her skin like satin. She had full breasts, upright and at attention. Her butt was perky, her legs long, her waist slim, curving into her shapely hips. She was pure starlet, through and through. She was already well educated in sexual matters too—knew things that surprised him. But then, he could only imagine what a gal had to do back then to get cast by the big directors. Sure he took advantage of her, but she wanted it. He knew that for a guy his age (who looked a good twenty years younger than the average sixty-year old of 1942) he was still good-looking. He prided himself on his physique —took excellent care of himself and worked out like a maniac no matter what era he found himself in. It was all for one thing and one thing only though: Cassandra.

As he went to get into his Daimler, parked in the driveway of Lake's gated grounds, a searing pain shot through his side. He sat for a moment behind the steering wheel and took a few deep breaths. Goddamn that Robert Cecil! Though Nick was grateful the man had missed his vital organs with the dagger by a few inches, the pain of the wound was an unpleasant reminder of his failure. It irked him to no end that he hadn't gotten the better of that cripple Cecil, the old man Edward de Vere, and the idiotic William Shakespeare back in jolly old England, that seething pit of filth and disease. And damn the "good Samaritan," who'd come along and found him, bleeding out on the streets of London. If he had been left to his own devices, the wound would have healed before he bled to death. Before leaving for that particular trip, he had been injected with a dose of illegal nano-healers that only someone with his money and connections could secure. They had gone to work as soon as he'd been stabbed, staunching the wound and fighting infection, though he must have seemed on the verge of expiring to Cassandra, who had left him there for dead.

The Samaritan had hauled him off in a cart to Bethlehem Hospital, or "Bedlem" as they said, where the "care" nearly killed him in spite of the nano-healers. Dear god, no more foul or putrid place existed on the face of the earth, present or past, than that hell-hole of disease and insanity. They stuck him in a vermin-infested bed, washed his wound with soiled cloths steeped in dirty water where his blood had mixed with that of a thousand unfortunate souls who had had the horrid luck to end up in that place before him. They fed him spoiled food and attempted to treat him in the only way they knew how, with leeches, before he fought them off and escaped with the little strength that was left to him. He made his way, practically crawling each step, to his portal exit in the South Bank. He didn't even want to think about how many mishaps along the way almost prevented him from getting back to 2126, because, ultimately, he did, and his team nursed him back to health. That had been in March.

It had taken a Herculean effort not only to get his health back, but to form a plan, do the research, and get a new portal built in Los Angeles so he could first go to 1920 and attempt to kill the father, then regroup and come after the son. Now, finally, he was zeroing in on him. Lake had seemed upset at the gala, but Nick couldn't get her to tell him why until she had a few drinks in her. Finally, she whispered to him that a friend had been sent to an internment camp. "A fellow actor," she'd said. She wouldn't say how she knew. He got her to tell him the actor's name, and that cinched it for Nick. It was strange, actually, that in his search for the names Akito Wakai and then Hiro, neither came up in the databases of the War Relocation Authority, the government organization in charge of the internment camps. He shrugged. Those old databases were full of flaws and a simple misspelling by the camp authorities could result in someone being listed incorrectly. Anyway, at least he finally had the information he wanted. He'd need a few days, probably, to find the one other thing he needed to assure a successful outcome; then, he'd go after Hiro.

That morning, he'd tried creeping out of bed without waking Veronica, but she'd been wrapped around him like an octopus. "Where are you going, baby?" she'd sleepily queried.

He'd untangled himself from her lanky limbs, threw his clothes on, and said one thing to her in reply. He owed her nothing and didn't want her to know anything about his business. "The desert."

Chapter Fifteen

Hiro Wakai - May 7th, 1942

I've been too preoccupied to write here for the last several weeks but tonight I find myself in my old room in my parents' apartment with nothing else to do. I finally gave up my place and moved back into this small set of rooms above the restaurant where I grew up. I don't mind the lack of space but I don't want to be a burden on them. I'm helping out in the restaurant but will not take any money from them. They don't need another person to support, that's for sure, but at least I have a roof over my head and food to eat.

Sadly, the other restaurants in little Tokyo are mostly all closed up now because few people come to eat here anymore. What will become of these diligent people, the Issei, who worked so hard to carve out an honest existence for themselves in this country that, heretofore, had mostly welcomed them? We are being shunned by the white community, people who before were charmed by our quaint, "Oriental" ways, and who craved our "unusual" food. Our colored neighbors to the south, in Compton, still come. My parents' restaurant has always been a favorite so there's still that business, but it's dwindling.

We keep hearing about these relocation camps that are being set up around the country, and fear that soon we will be ordered to go, like criminals in our own land. What have we done? Worked hard to contribute to the economy, lived peaceable lives, been good citizens, paid our taxes... my parents sent me to school where I learned to speak English as well as any white kid. Why then, are we to be persecuted? Maybe it will come to nothing after all, but we cannot deny the fear that is creeping over us and this community like a disease.

Elton didn't want Cassandra to think he was trying to get a peek at her in the buff, but what he had glimpsed the day before, her sleek, slim body gliding under the water, her perky rear just visible below the surface, had unsettled him. He was not here to carry on an affair with her, that he was clear about, but he felt closer to her every minute he spent with her in this era, doing the work that was not only of dire importance to them, but possibly to the world too. God only knew what Nick was up to. Was he trying to change history in some way? Was he trying to affect the war? If so, why was he hanging out in Hollywood with celebrities? Obviously, whatever he had come to do, he had not had success with yet, because the device Elton had invented, which alerted the MIT team if an alternate timeline in the past had been created, had not sounded the alarm. That was good, but if Nick was here in 1942, he had to have some reason. Though the man had been known to choose time periods simply to escape to for pleasure's sake, this time, Elton could sense he was up to no good.

He had awoken early and felt like having another swim but didn't want to surprise Cassandra again. He kept his boxers on and threw a robe over them, grabbed a towel, then walked toward the backyard pool, listening for sounds of splashing as he approached. All was quiet. He slipped his robe off and threw it and the towel onto a chaise lounge, then eased into the water, being careful to be quiet. It was chilly, so he quickly swam underwater to one end and then the other. When he popped his head out to start another lap, he saw her out of the corner of his eye. He turned to look at her full on, standing on the patio, wearing her bra and underpants, one hand on hip.

"I couldn't resist," he said.

"I don't blame you. Mind if I join you?"

"Of course not!"

She dove into the deep end, and they both swam their laps. When he'd had enough, he got out and quickly wrapped the towel around his waist, aware of how clingy his wet shorts were.

She had stopped swimming, and was treading water.

"Can I get you a towel?" he asked.

"Please!"

When he returned, she took it from him as she emerged. He looked away. When he looked back, the towel was wrapped around her, but she was gazing at him.

"What?"

"Oh, nothing!" she exclaimed, while a blush

crept over her skin.

He smiled to himself as he put on his robe. He knew he was in excellent shape, especially for a guy that was no longer exactly young. He was glad she'd noticed.

"My turn to make breakfast," she said. "Meet you in the kitchen in a half hour?"

He agreed and went to shower and change. As the hot water poured over him, he thought about how his ex-wife, Jeannine, used to sing in the shower. Actually, she sang everywhere. She was a first-rate musician and singer, which was what had originally brought them together way back in the days before physics had won out for him over music. It was in their undergraduate days at MIT. She was majoring in music, he was minoring, though he was teetering on the brink of making it his focus instead of physics. She was classically trained—a true virtuoso. He was well-trained too, but his playing came more by instinct. When he saw the hours and hours of practice she put into perfecting her art, he knew he could never be a professional musician. Not because he wasn't good enough, or didn't have the discipline. He was, and he did, but he realized he couldn't do music full time and pursue his interest in time travel, which was where his studies were leading him. After they got accepted to their Masters' programs, she in music and he in physics, they decided to get married. He became a star in his field and went on to get his PhD. And while she grew into a celebrated performer, she was also deeply interested in his pursuit of unlocking the key to time travel—the basis of which was the Einstein-Rosen Bridge wormhole theory. When he finally made the breakthrough, though it took him a decade to do so, she was the first to celebrate with him. Then it took another decade or so to put time travel into actual practice. That was when Cassandra's husband, Franklin, joined him, and not long after, Cassandra herself, working on her PhD in chronology. Elton smiled to himself. He had been so in love with Jeannine that, at the time, it had been beautiful watching Franklin and Cassandra fall in love too, their work binding them to each other. And then James had come along and as soon as he was old enough, fell right in with his parents' interests. When James was around twenty, Franklin had died, risking a trip into the future before they knew everything about the process.

Elton turned off the water and began to dry off. It was wrenching to remember that time, but Cassandra had stayed strong through it all, even when Elton almost ditched his work, so devastated that it had cost his dear friend his life. It had been Jeannine who had held him up; persuaded him he couldn't give up. She insisted he take the first extended trip into the past although he'd warned her about the dangers. She was always stronger than he was—always had more faith in his work than he did. After that though, something seemed to change. As they began planning Cassandra's trip to England of 1820, Elton spending as much time with her as he did, Jeannine started to drift away into her own life and interests. She had had a lot of success as a musician and a singer...was popular within her genres which were jazz, blues, gospel, and classical; but once Elton was less available to her, she began to tour and was away more and more. It wasn't long before they saw each other only a few times a year for a couple of weeks, maybe a month or two, at a time. It wasn't enough to sustain a marriage. They tried, they really tried, Elton thought as he shaved, but both came to see it was no use. And then there was the fact that Elton had begun to have feelings for Cassandra that he couldn't deny. He never told Jeannine about them but he was sure she had begun to suspect. And then, last year, she finally told him it was over and he had felt—he couldn't deny it—relieved.

Thank god, good woman that she was, she had never resented him. That's what made them able to stay friends to this day. He dressed, smiling sadly to himself, then strolled across the front lawn to the bungalow. When he walked into the kitchen, Cassandra was standing at the stove wearing a white sundress with red piping. She was barefoot. Her hair curled naturally around her shoulders like she usually wore it and she had no makeup on. She looked about twenty years old, though, in reality, she could not really be considered young anymore either. He stood gazing at her as she went about her work.

Finally, she noticed him. "Oh!" she turned to face him and they stared at each other for a moment. He was wearing his tan suit, the jacket flung over one shoulder. "You look nice."

"So do you."

"Oh, I still have to do my hair and makeup."

"To fit in here you do. Otherwise, you look perfect."

"Why, thank you." The compliment seemed to disconcert her and she went back to what she was doing.

"I think we should drive back to that house this morning and see if we can spot Nick."

"Elton, I think we need a better plan."

She served them both a plate of scrambled eggs, bacon, and toast and they sat and ate.

"What do you have in mind?"

"I think we need to go at this from another angle. If we just try to follow Nick around," she said, "he's going to spot us, and then he'll escape for good. He'll probably go to his portal exit and head out of here altogether."

"Unless whatever he's doing is so important to him that he's determined to stay here and get it done."

"What do you think he's up to? I sort of assumed he had just chosen this era to escape to so he could have some fun."

"I had considered that too, but...the war era? Why? If he just wanted to mess around with movie stars, he could have chosen any time period...like the late forties—just after the war, or the 1950s when the U.S. was more or less at peace. Or the 1960s, which would be interesting, or the 1980s..."

"I see what you're getting at."

"Or anytime really, other than the pandemic years, up until the World Wide Crisis. And once that was resolved, I mean, he could have gone just a few decades back, like to the 2140s, to the Global Renaissance. It was twenty years or so before he was born. But why 1942? There's something special happening right here, and right now, and I really don't think it has to do with movie stars. I think that's just a distraction."

"Yeah, I think you must be right."

"So what are you thinking?" he asked her.

"Well, you were telling me about how you hobnobbed with musicians and such at the clubs in Compton."

"Yeah..." He hadn't told her he'd actually played with those musicians. He had surreptitiously taken his horn out of the trunk of the car and stowed it in the guest house.

"Well, maybe we should try to get to know some of those celebrities he's been hanging out with and find out what they know about him. You said it wasn't hard to do if you have the right clothes and enough money. I'll buy a couple of swanky gowns and we'll go hang out where the stars go. We'll pick up a couple of gossip rags liked we talked about and see where they go."

"Actually, you will do that. I will drive."

"You're my bodyguard. You'll go where I go. No one can object to that."

"They can and they will."

"Well, damn it!"

"Cassie, you're onto something here." He finished off his breakfast. "Come on, let's go shopping."

They headed to the heart of downtown Los Angeles: Seventh Avenue and Broadway. Cassandra leaned her chin on her arms on the back of the broad front seat.

"Will they let you in?" she worried.

"Yes, I think so. Though they might make it uncomfortable."

"I hate this."

"If I'm there as your driver, there to carry your parcels for you, they can't exactly object."

"Ugh, what a nightmare! Elton, I don't want to spend any longer in there than I have to. I never have liked to shop, you know."

He actually didn't know that about her. "Well, I think you could choose several gowns and bring them home to try on. Then we'll just return what you don't want."

"Perfect. Let's do that. Then you can help me choose."

Bullock's Department Store, on the corner of Seventh and Broadway, was their destination: the biggest and finest department store in L.A. Normally, the richest women of the era would have their gowns made for them by a haute couture designer, but the travelers didn't have time for that.

They found a place to park and waded through the throngs of shoppers on the avenue. The place was packed with people coming and going. Elton thought sadly about how downtown L.A. would decline considerably in the coming years as residents flocked to the suburbs after the war. This area would become a ghost town, mostly populated by drug addicts and vagrants until it began to revive again around the middle of the twenty-first century. At the moment, it resembled the bustling Broadway of New York more than anything.

He was careful to walk a few steps behind Cassandra, which he knew annoyed her, but it was not okay for them to be seen as companions. They didn't meet with any opposition upon entering the store, nor on the elevator ride to the ladies' department, but once there, the female clerk looked at him askance.

"He's my driver," Cassandra told her through clenched teeth.

Elton made himself comfortable in a chair while the lady helped Cassandra peruse the gowns. She selected several, including shoes, bags, hats, and some jewelry. She paid for it with the understanding that she would return at least some of it. The woman seemed to have no problem with the arrangement and began carefully packaging the items up in bags and boxes. She then called for a store porter to bring it downstairs while Elton went to get the car.

He was waiting in the car at the curb when Cassandra and the African American porter emerged, all her acquisitions piled on a brass cart. Elton immediately hopped out to help the porter load everything in the trunk. (He'd had the forethought to unload the crate and dolly they'd got at Sears, and left them in a shed at the bungalow.) Cassandra started to help but Elton subtly shook his head at her and she stepped away. She tipped the man and got in the back seat.

"Don't say it," Elton joked.

She sighed deeply. "Fine. But you know what I'm thinking."

On the way home they stopped at a Ralph's supermarket and Cassandra hurried in to buy some food to have in the house. They'd decided it would be easier to eat at home than to worry about how to navigate restaurants. Back in the car, she showed him a copy of the newspaper she'd picked up that had Nick's picture in it from the night before—the one Suhan had found.

That night after dinner, Cassandra began her fashion show. While Elton relaxed on the sofa, she modeled one gown after another, with various combinations of shoes, hats, and jewels. He felt guilty as he admired her. He was supposed to be an objective observer, helping to make practical decisions, not noticing the sensual curve of her hips, the way the small of her back flowed into the beautiful shape of her derriere, how her collarbone was so delicate, and her breasts small but sufficient to fill out the gowns. She was playful, pretending she was a movie star on the red carpet, but he was having trouble not feeling a bit aroused by the display.

They finally agreed on three dresses: a beige formal with capped sleeves, a sweetheart neckline, and a diagonal waistline that cut from one side of the waist to the opposite hip, from which a gauzy skirt flowed to the floor; a dark red gown with thin shoulder straps, cut square above the bust, fitting snugly all the way down along the legs with a slight flair at the bottom and a gathering of fabric just over one hip; and the last, black, which set off her pale skin and auburn hair beautifully, cut low down the back in a V-shape, and flowing over her figure to a slight train behind. She had chosen some long white gloves to wear with it, and a diamond bracelet to go over one glove, drop earrings to match. He sat there, gazing at her, speechless.

"So, this one too, yes?"

He cleared his throat. "Yes."

"What's the matter?"

"Nothing, nothing. You look...amazing."

"Thank you, Elton."

He stood and she looked at him for a moment. There was tension in the air; he could feel it.

"Do you need help wrapping up the stuff you don't want?"

"No, maybe I'll leave it 'til morning. I'm tired."

"Yes, then, I should go."

"I wish..." she began.

His heart beat faster. "Yes?"

She paused. "Nothing."

"Tomorrow night we'll go out to the best club. You'll be on your own, basically, Cass. But you'll create a stir in any one of those dresses. Especially that one. You'll be the beautiful mystery woman and everyone will want to know who you are."

"You think I'm beautiful?"

He took a step towards her. "Cassandra..." It was hard to know what to say. "I have always thought you are one of the most beautiful women I've ever known. You must know that."

She looked down. "Not really."

"Well now you do." With all his heart, he wanted to add, 'And I love you,' but there was no point in muddling things. This trip was going to be hard enough. Still, he couldn't resist going to her. He took one of her gloved hands in his, leaned in and kissed her on the cheek. Her smell was intoxicating.

When he stepped back, he noticed her eyes were

closed. Her lips tempted him beyond reason. But then she opened her eyes.
"Good night," he said.
"Good night," she whispered.

Chapter Sixteen

Hiro Wakai - May 8th, 1942

Today I was cleaning the apartment, beginning to organize my parents' belongings in case we are to be sent away next. None of us wants to believe it could happen to us, but, if it does, we'll have to be ready to pack up quickly and won't be able to bring everything. In doing so, I found a set of papers, old and yellowed, tied up with ribbon. They were in my father's handwriting. Before I could stop myself, I started reading what could only be described as a type of memoir—not exactly a journal like I've been writing because it's not in dated increments. It is the account of how he and my mom met, and their early life together. I was fascinated from the first few sentences and was soon lost in the story, but then I heard Mom coming upstairs and squirreled the papers away in my room. After the dinner service tonight, I finished reading them all, staying up late into the night. Then, I decided to start translating them into English, suddenly grateful for my mother's careful lessons in reading and writing in Japanese. This is a story that needs to be told and understood for the future.

Decked out in the dark red number, Cassandra stepped into the backseat of the Hudson while Elton held the door for her, an amused look on his face. He looked downright dashing. He was wearing his black zoot-suit, which he had apparently purchased while he'd been staying in Compton, black fedora on his head, black and white Oxfords on his feet. Cassandra was still a little foggy about what exactly he had been up to during the two weeks he had come here in preparation for her visit and he seemed somewhat cagey about it. He'd bought the car, he'd rented the bungalow, which she knew had taken quite a bit of doing, and he'd visited some nightclubs. There seemed to be something he wasn't telling her though.

They were headed to Club Mocambo on Sunset Boulevard. It was ten in the evening. Cassandra didn't know what to expect, but Elton told her she was going to have to brave it by herself. Well, she could do it. If her previous time journeys had taught her anything, it was that she was capable of feats of bravery far beyond what she'd thought possible. Surely, lounging in a club full of strangers couldn't be that hard.

They pulled up to the front where a doorman rushed over and opened the car door for her. She placed her gloved hand in his and let one leg, swathed in a sheer black silk stocking and adorned by a black high-heeled pump, slink out from the slit in her dress like she'd seen women do in the old movies. Elton stepped out too and motioned to the valet.

"Park it," he said with authority, handing the young man the keys. He then walked around the car to join Cassandra and they approached the entrance of the club together.

When the doorman began to object, Cassandra said, in the slightly upper class, New England accent she'd heard Katherine Hepburn and other stars of that era affect, "This is my bodyguard. I go nowhere without him." With those words, she handed him a twenty-dollar bill.

He stammered a moment then ushered them both forward. Inside the club, the Maître d' looked simultaneously dazzled by her presence, and shocked by his.

"Miss..." he began.

"Missus," she corrected him. "Mrs. Cassandra Reilly of New York. This is my bodyguard, Elton Carver. It is essential that he stay with me at all times. Surely you can arrange for that?"

"It is against our policy, Mrs. Reilly, to..."

She glared at him and produced another twenty. He eyed it eagerly. "But perhaps special arrangements can be made."

"See to it," she demanded.

"May I arrange to have Mr. Carver situated where he can see you at all times? Would that suit you? I am afraid it is the best we can do."

She and Elton exchanged glances and he nodded. "Very well," she said, resigned. Clutching her black beaded bag, she allowed herself to be escorted. She requested a table near the dance floor and, as Elton had advised, immediately ordered a bottle of champagne.

The table was covered with a white linen tablecloth. A candle glowed in the middle, and a slim vase held one red rose. A band was playing on the dais and she instantly recognized the band leader as Cab Calloway. She might not know jazz like Elton did, but there was no mistaking Calloway's theatrical style and the band's distinctive music. She looked around for Elton. He was standing across the dance floor from her, next to one side of the stage. He seemed mesmerized for a moment by the band, but then looked around to find her and smiled. The champagne arrived quickly with a crystal champagne glass. A menu was discreetly placed by her, but she ignored it for now.

She tapped her foot to the music, wishing she and Elton could dance again. As she looked around at the other impeccably attired guests seated at tables, a woman's beautiful face caught her eye. There was something familiar about her. She hadn't been in the photograph with Nick, but Cassandra had definitely seen her picture before. The woman was seated with two men and another lady. Even in the low light, something about the woman seemed different from everyone else, and then it struck her: the woman was light-skinned, but she was not white. Here was an African-American woman seated in the club where Elton had nearly been refused entrance. She must be famous. So famous, the club had made an exception for her, which, obviously, was rarely done.

The woman looked over at her, nodded, and smiled. Cassandra smiled back. Then she glanced at Elton, who was staring at her from his vantage point with recognition. Cassandra pretended to have nothing else on her mind but listening to the music and watching the couples dancing on the floor. Before long, one of the gentlemen sitting at the table with the tawny-skinned woman got up and walked over to her.

"Good evening," he said.

"Good evening," she replied.

"I'm Harry Salzburg."

"Mrs. Cassandra Reilly, very pleased to meet you." She shook his hand.

"Miss Horne was wondering if you'd like to join us."

Lena Horne! "I would be delighted. I have one problem though."

"Perhaps I can help you."

"Well, I don't know. My bodyguard is over there." She indicated where Elton stood.

He was watching the exchange.

"Actually," she confided, "he's my friend, though I say he's my bodyguard, you know..."

"Oh, yes, I understand," he said, nodding.

"I would love for him to join me, but the club's

policy..."

"Don't say another word." He marched off, and Cassandra watched him speak with the Maître d'. When he came back, he said to her, "I told him it was Miss Horne's express wish that your friend join us at the table. He objected, but I told him if he didn't allow it, we would leave and not come back, and part of the popularity of this club relies on their clientele getting to hobnob with celebrities. Miss Horne is very highly admired in Hollywood, regardless of her race, so he said he would make an exception."

Cassandra thanked him, trying to maintain her composure. This whole race thing was so absurd she could hardly believe it, but there was no changing history. It was the way things were in 1942. She knew it wouldn't be much more than a decade until the Civil Rights struggle would begin to gain momentum. She also knew that many black activists in L.A. at this time were starting to rise up, but the movement was small and contained for the time being. Anyway, she and Elton were not there to change things. It wasn't their job, nor their place.

She beckoned to Elton and he came. "We have been invited to join Miss Horne at her table," she said to him. "This is Mr. Harry Salzburg." The two men shook hands. Two waiters hurried over and brought extra chairs to the other table, moved the champagne bucket and Cassandra's glass, then hurried off to bring another.

Cassandra and Elton joined the celebrity and her friends, and introductions were made all around. It turned out the other lady at the table was Gene Tierney, the movie star Cassandra had thought she'd recognized the night before, going into the Brown Derby gala, and the man with her was her husband, the famous designer Oleg Cassini. They were both incredibly charming, she so young and so beautiful, her film career just beginning. Cassandra vaguely remembered that the actress would struggle with mental illness later in life and it made her sad to see her now so vibrant, yet know what was to come. Her husband was older: very handsome and debonair, with a distinguished accent, somewhere between Russian and Italian. He was dressed in an officer's uniform.

"Oleg is on a brief leave," Tierney told them. "He returns to duty in a week. We found out I'm expecting, and so he asked for a couple of weeks now, and a couple when the baby is born. That's all they can give him." She took a sip of champagne.

"Congratulations!" Cassandra said to the two of them. And then, knowing she probably shouldn't, leaned over to whisper to the young woman, "you know, I recently read there was some new research that relates alcohol to problems with a baby's health. Forgive me for butting in. I just thought you might like to know."

Gene looked in horror at her drink and pushed

it away. "Thank you!" She picked up a glass of water and sipped it instead.

Elton couldn't have heard her in the noisy club, but he must have suspected what she'd said because he shot her a look. In fact, it was too loud for much conversation, but this was their chance to find out if any of the people at the table knew Nick.

"We are visiting from New York," Cassandra said loudly to her new acquaintances. "We're looking for a friend of ours whom we've lost track of, but heard had moved out here. As a matter of fact, we saw his picture in a photo from last night's gala at the Brown Derby. You might have been there, Miss Tierney. I think I saw you in the same photo. His name is Nick Stockard, do you know him?"

"Nick!" both Lena and Gene declared, beaming at each other.

"Yes," Lena continued, "we met him just a couple of weeks ago. We were all at Ciro's together. He bought champagne for the entire club! He made quite a splash. He's been frequenting the better clubs since. I wasn't at the gala last night though." She made a face which might have indicated why she hadn't been included.

"Oh, he was there, yes," said Gene. "Everyone loves him. He's the life of the party."

"Of course he is," said Cassandra, doing everything in her power not to smirk in disgust. "Have you seen him tonight?" she said, looking around, suddenly realizing it would be bad if he spotted them there.

"No," Gene replied. "He said he had to go out of town for a couple of days."

"Oh," Cassandra said, acting disappointed. "Do you have any idea where he's going?"

"No, he didn't say. But he said he'd be back soon." Elton and Cassandra glanced at each other.

The music was heating up and further conversation would be difficult. Gene and her husband got up to dance, and Lena looked after them enviously. "They may let me in," she said loudly to Cassandra and Elton, "but god forbid I dance with my boyfriend."

"Or that we get at all chummy in public," Harry said. "Lena may get some special privileges, but it could end her career if she's seen fraternizing with a white man."

Cassandra nodded, taking her cue from them. She was longing to dance with Elton too but now realized what a mistake it would be.

"Say," Elton began, leaning in close so they could hear, "speaking of couples, do you happen to know if Nick is seeing anyone? He's such a dear friend; we're hoping he's met someone nice out here."

"Why, yes," Lena replied. "Last time I saw him, which was here, as a matter of fact, he was with Veronica Lake. You wear your hair rather like hers, Mrs. Reilly."

Cassandra now remembered seeing her picture

as she and Shannon had gone through old photos of movie stars and Cassandra had said she wanted her hair to look like Lake's. That's where she recognized the woman Nick had been with last night!

"It's hard not to be influenced by her. She's so beautiful," Cassandra said. "Well, good for Nick." Maybe this was a lead.

"Although," added Harry, "Nick does get around. I think he's seeing more than one gal."

"Well, yes," said Elton, laughing, "that does sound like Nick."

Cassandra nearly shuddered. She hated to think of some innocent young woman falling prey to Nick and whatever he had in mind. He could be very compelling when he wanted to be. But what, exactly, did he have in mind? She doubted it was just getting laid by Hollywood starlets. He always had a higher, and more diabolical, motive.

"You know," Lena declared, "you should talk to Bette. She's always in the know about who's dating who, what they're doing, and where they're off to."

"Betty?"

"Davis."

"Bette Davis? Would she talk to us?"

"Oh sure, if we made the introduction. She'll be at the Hollywood Canteen tomorrow. Negro servicemen are welcome if they're in uniform," Lena said, eyeing Elton, "but if Bette says it's okay," she added, "they'll let you in."

"Great!" Elton cried. "When should we go?"

"Let's see," the star continued, "I'll call her in the morning and ask what time she'll be there. She's always there on a Friday night. Then I'll give you a ring. Can I have your number?"

Cassandra borrowed a pen from Harry and jotted HO5-4125 on a napkin, glad she had taken the time to memorize the number that had been typed out and taped on the telephone at the bungalow.

"Perfect," Lena said.

"Well, maybe we should be going," said Elton.

"Really?" Cassandra questioned, "we just got here."

"Trust me." He gestured subtly with a jerk of his chin, and Cassandra looked around, realizing that people were staring at them, and not in a friendly manner.

Perhaps Lena Horne's presence wasn't as much of a buffer as she'd thought. They said goodnight and waved to Tierney and Cassini on the dance floor, then made their way out quickly, had the car brought, and headed back to the Hollywood Hills, pleased with their success.

Chapter Seventeen

Hiro Wakai – June 10th, 1942

We are to be sent away. We've been ordered to pack one suitcase apiece and appear, papers in hand, at the bus station in downtown Los Angeles at eight in the morning on Friday. That gives us less than a week to close up the restaurant and put whatever affairs we can in order by then. Mom has not stopped crying and Pop's face has become like stone. He stoically scrubs the pots and pans and every square surface, leaving it immaculate for when they return, which he thinks will be very soon. And what is this place where they're sending us? Manzanar, it's called, in the desert, between Death Valley and the base of the Sierra Nevadas. Surely it won't be too bad. After all, this is America. I'm trying to imagine it as something like the summer camp I was sent to as a child. Basic, yes, but clean and civilized. Still, it gnaws at me to think that we will be separated from the rest of the country because of suspicions that we might be spies or worse. It is an insult to the deepest core of my being and to that of all the other Japanese as well.

Pop says that, with the Americans now in the fight, it will all be over in a matter of a few months. I hope he's right and yet I doubt it. After all, no one knows better the fierce determination of the Japanese than he does, a man who served in the Imperial Navy during the Great War, even though, as I've now learned, he was nothing more than a cook. Until reading his diary, all that history was just that to me: history. I had no personal relationship to it, nor to the "homeland," as he calls Japan. I am an American. This is my country though I am clearly no better to my fellow citizens than a cur now—some base creature to be cast aside. And yet, while I still can, I continue to translate my father's story. The story of how we became Americans.

There were so many stars at the Hollywood Canteen Elton didn't know which way to look. He wasn't as familiar with the names and faces as Cassandra was, but he sure knew Bette Davis when he saw her...and Rita Hayworth, Humphrey Bogart, and Clark Gable. Though he and Cassandra lived in an era more than a hundred and eighty years beyond 1942, those big names and personalities, and their famous films, had endured. His head spun, but not only from the stars. Cassandra was looking as stunning as any movie star in the place. They had gone shopping again that day because she needed something in between the everyday clothes that Shannon had made her, lovely as they were, and the elegant evening gowns they had purchased at Bullocks. He had driven her to a local boutique they'd spotted in Hollywood, not far from their neighborhood, and waited in the car while she tried things on. The result was the floor length skirt in red and white checks she now wore which flowed around her legs most alluringly when she moved, and a crisp white blouse tucked in at the waist, very form fitting through the torso, with full transparent sleeves, showing off her toned arms. It was all very Hepburn-esque.

True to her word, Lena Horne had called and told them she'd phoned ahead to the canteen. She said Elton and Cassandra's names would be on the guest list so there would be no objections when they made their entrance. There were a few African-American servicemen in the room but they were sitting with their beers, watching the action. There were no black women to dance with and so they could not dance at all—not even with the celebrities since Lena Horne had not yet arrived.

With great pluck, Cassandra went directly up to Bette Davis, who was manning the bar.

"Hello, I'm Mrs. Cassandra Reilly," she said.

Davis turned from the cash register to face her. Elton almost gasped. To see that iconic face in person and close up was surreal.

Cassandra went on quickly, "Lena Horne said you'd put us on the guest list and that we should introduce ourselves to you." She held her hand out to the actress. "It's a thrill, Miss Davis."

Davis took it and gave it a solid shake. "It's nice to meet you." With one elegant eyebrow raised she then asked, "And who is this?" She looked Elton over with interest.

"Elton Carver," he said, though he didn't extend his hand. In this day and age, it was not considered polite for a man to offer to shake a lady's hand. She had to be the one to initiate it.

And so she did. "A pleasure," she said.

Davis then went to attend to a soldier but Cassandra and Elton remained at the bar so they could continue to talk to her in her spare moments. She wasn't actually mixing drinks. She would hand a serviceman a beer now and then, but it was Humphrey Bogart who was doing the bartending. Elton knew that the actor was too old to serve actively in the military now, but that he'd done his service in World War I. As a matter of fact, Elton was surprised at how star-struck he was over meeting him. He was a fan of all his films: Casablanca, The Maltese Falcon, The Big Sleep... He watched them for more than just historical context; he loved Bogart's swagger and his chemistry with Ingrid Bergman, Mary Astor, and Lauren Bacall. He tried now to remember at what point in Bogart's romantic life the actor would currently be, but couldn't recall which of his four wives he was married to at the moment. He watched as the star served drinks to the servicemen at the bar, chatting with them in such easy camaraderie. Needless to say, they all looked just as star-struck as Elton felt, and incredibly grateful for Bogart's attention.

Elton tapped his foot to the music emanating from the juke box until Davis came back around to talk to them.

"What brings you to town?" she said to Cassandra in her clipped, upper-crust accent. She had to be in her early thirties or so at this point in her life—very beautiful, more so than in her films because she looked more natural, more girlish than in the bitchy parts she was usually cast in. Her huge blue eyes had a kindness to them. Her skin was flawless, the lips of her bow-mouth full. She had an innocence about her that astonished him. He thought she was probably now the most attractive she had ever been, or would be in the years to come.

"Just in town on some business," Cassandra replied.

"What is your business?" Miss Davis said, sounding surprised. Cassandra, was, after all, a woman.

"I'm out here representing my family's company," Cassandra said without missing a beat. "We're in textiles, actually, working with the military now."

Miss Davis's eyes glazed over slightly. It was too boring an occupation to pursue. "How did you meet Lena?"

"Oh, we were at Club Mocambo last night. She invited us to sit with her."

Again, Davis raised one of her thin, arched brows and looked at Elton.

"She made sure we were accommodated," Cassandra said in answer to her unasked question.

"That sounds like Lena," Davis replied.

"Are you talking about Miss Horne?" Bogart cut in.

It was unbelievable hearing that inimitable

slurred cadence in person. "We met her last night," Elton replied, almost as a challenge. He would see what the famous star might have to say about the black actress, as well as his own presence in the canteen.

"She lives just across the street from me," Bogart said.

"She does?" Bette replied. "I didn't know that."

"She's a great gal," Bogart continued. "I'd do anything for her. When some neighbors complained about her moving in, if you know what I mean," he said, turning to Elton, "I told them they'd better take it up with me. That was the end of that." Elton grinned. His cinematic hero was, in real life, exactly what he thought he would be. "I'm glad to hear it, Mr. Bogart," he said.

"Call me Bogie; everyone does."

"I'm Elton Carver, and this is my friend Cassandra Reilly."

"The pleasure is all mine," Bogart said, lifting Cassandra's hand to his lips and placing a kiss upon it, his dark brown eyes gazing into hers.

Cassandra flushed pink and an irrational stab of jealousy shot through Elton's heart. Don't be ridiculous, he said to himself.

"We're hoping to connect with a friend of ours whom we heard is in town, and who was at the gala at the Brown Derby the other night. Miss Horne said you might know, Miss Davis," Cassandra said, turning, so it seemed to Elton, with reluctance from Bogart's gaze while leaving her hand in his. "His name is Nick Stockard."

"Oh, Nick!" Davis replied. "Yes, he's become a great favorite in our crowd. My goodness, but he's very generous. He gave a fortune at the gala toward the war effort."

"Yes, that sounds like Nick," Cassandra said, her voice slightly strained.

"Cigarette?" Bogart asked Cassandra, finally letting go of her hand to reach into his pocket and produce a silver cigarette case. He clicked it open.

She smiled sweetly and said, "No, thank you."

Bogart winked at her, took two out, put them in his mouth, lit them with a silver lighter, and handed one to Davis.

"Smoke?" he said, holding out the open case to Elton.

"I'm afraid I've never developed a taste," Elton replied.

Bogart shrugged and snapped the case shut. He held his cigarette with his index finger and his thumb, the lit end cupped in his hand like soldiers did on the battlefield to keep the enemy from spying the red ember.

"Miss Horne said you might know where we could find Nick," Cassandra pressed. "She said he went out of town for a few days; do you know where?"

"No, I'm afraid not," the actress replied. "He was a little secretive about it if you want to know the truth. But Ronnie will know."

"Ronnie?"

"Veronica. Lake. I'm sure she'll be at Miss Grable's party tomorrow night."

Before Elton could ponder what to do to get invited to this heralded event, Bogart spoke to Cassandra.

"I'll be sure to finagle an invitation out of her if it means seeing you again tomorrow night, doll," he purred.

"It very well might." She shot him a provocative side glance from under a perfectly waved lock of hair and smiled coyly.

Bogart grinned.

It was clear why women fell for this rather short and not particularly handsome fellow. He had a way, there was no doubt about that, and it was beginning to irritate Elton.

"I'll make sure you're on the guest list," Bogart said.

"The two of us," Cassandra said, and leaned in close to the star. "Elton's my bodyguard," she whispered. "I don't go anywhere without him."

Bogart raised his brows with a wry expression. "My, my, you must be very important."

"She is," Elton returned flatly.

As if to change the subject, Cassandra gestured over to where Clark Gable sat at a table, smoking, with a drink sitting in front of him as he signed autographs for the servicemen. He rarely smiled, and when he did, there was a great sadness in it.

"Is he okay?"

"Well, you know," Miss Davis began. "His wife, Carole..."

Cassandra looked back at her inquisitively.

"You'd have to be from another planet not to know that she died in a plane crash a few months ago."

"Oh, of course! How terrible," Cassandra replied. Elton searched his memory for knowledge of Clark Gable's biography. Ah yes, his wife had been Carole Lombard. Elton hadn't remembered when her tragic death had occurred. "Poor guy."

"Hasn't been the same since," Bogart remarked.

Just then, a young serviceman came over and tapped Cassandra on the soldier. She turned to face him.

"Care to dance, miss?"

Cassandra glanced at Elton who shrugged. The kid couldn't be more than eighteen.

"I'm no one famous, you know," Cassandra said to him.

"Ya coulda fooled me," the boy said, grinning and holding a hand out to her.

Cassandra smiled and put her hand in his. They sailed out across the dance floor. Elton was impressed. Cassandra followed the boy's two-step flawlessly. The kid wasn't a fantastic dancer, but good enough. As a matter of fact, it seemed everyone in this day and age had a few moves they could pull out if the occasion and the music required. It wasn't like that in Elton's own time.

Most people really didn't know how to dance with a partner any more. It was sad the art had been lost.

Another soldier, one who just had been dancing with Rita Hayworth, approached the bar and asked Davis, "Who is that?" He gestured toward Cassandra.

"A wealthy heiress," she replied mysteriously.

"Wow, she's a looker!" the man observed. He maneuvered over to Cassandra and her partner and tapped the boy on the shoulder. Elton couldn't hear what he said but he could read his lips. "Mind if I cut in?"

There was a bit of back and forth between him and the first boy, who looked miffed, but then Cassandra fell in with her new partner. Elton grew antsy. They didn't really have time for this, but he couldn't approach Cassandra on the floor. That would really stir things up.

The song ended, and Cassandra stepped away from her partner with a smile and a nod. Another record dropped in the juke box and another schmaltzy love song began. Cassandra turned to leave but was immediately asked to dance by another soldier. She looked over at Elton. It was clear she was done dancing but didn't want to disappoint the men.

"Mr. Bogart," Elton said when he could get the star's attention. "I have to get Mrs. Reilly downtown..."

"Don't say another word," the actor replied.

With alacrity, he leapt over the bar and went to the dancing couple. He said something to the soldier, who moved away from Cassandra, clearly awed to be spoken to by the star himself. Bogart then smiled at Cassandra and held his hand out to her. She took it and they moved back toward the bar.

"At your service," Bogart said with a slight bow to Elton.

"Thank you," both he and Cassandra said at the same time.

"My pleasure," Bogart said, still standing quite close to her. "Maybe you'll save a dance for me sometime."

"I hope we'll have the chance," Cassandra rejoined, aiming a high-wattage smile at him.

"Shall we?" Elton said to her. Enough was enough.

"Thank you so much your hospitality," Cassandra said to Davis and Bogart. "It's been a pleasure meeting you both."

"See you tomorrow," Bogart murmured, leaning closer and smiling seductively at Cassandra.

"Nine PM or after," Davis said, while she scratched an address on a scrap of paper. "I'll make sure you're on the guest list. You and your 'friend'."

"Oh, thank you! You are most kind," said Cassandra. She reached into her clutch purse and withdrew a pre-prepared envelope with five hundred dollars in cash inside, handing it to Miss Davis.

"For the cause."

"Why, thank you," the actress replied, taking the envelope, brows arched even higher than usual.

Cassandra smiled and nodded.

"It's been a pleasure," Elton managed, and with that, they made their way out of the club.

Silently, Elton guided Cassandra to the car and opened the door for her. He shut it harder than he intended, then went around and got into the front.

A few moments passed in which they did not speak as he started the car and pulled out of the parking lot.

"Elton, is something wrong?" Cassandra queried from the back seat.

"Nope."

"It seems like something is."

"It's just, you know. There's nothing you can do about it. I just feel like a second class citizen."

"Oh, Elton, I'm so sorry! Was it me telling Miss Davis you were my bodyguard?"

"Not exactly. I mean, that's what I'm supposed to be. I guess I just, you know, felt a little like chopped liver."

There was silence from the back seat for a moment.

Finally, Cassandra spoke. "Do you mean because Bogart was flirting with me?"

He didn't know how to respond. "It's fine. I'm fine," he finally muttered.

They rode quietly the rest of the way home. This

trip was turning into an exercise in restraint for Elton as the time he spent with Cassandra confirmed how much he was in love with her. But such feelings were not appropriate—at least not here, not now. They had to find Nick and that was all that mattered.

Chapter Eighteen

Hiro Wakai – June 19th, 1942

Summer camp this is not. Manzanar is a dried up, dusty, hole of a place with drafty barracks made of wood, surrounded by a high, chain-link fence—guard towers at each corner. It looks as much like a prison as anything I've ever seen. We were only allowed to bring one suitcase per person, and so I slipped my father's diary into mine, along with all the writing paper I had on hand so I can continue to translate it. He doesn't know I have it. He's probably not thinking about it at all.

Though families are mostly kept together in small rooms divided only by blankets, the young men are in a different building, me with them. I didn't want to be separated from Mom and Pop because they both looked so lost and helpless but I didn't have a choice. My barrack has no privacy at all. We each have a cot, all of them lined up in long rows, and a bench at the end of the cot that we can keep our trunk or suitcase on, plus a coarse wool blanket to keep us warm at night. Though the days are hot, the nights out here in the desert get really cold, and the winds blow down off the Sierra Nevadas. It's not that I'm uncomfortable—really, I don't care about my own comfort anyway. I can sleep anywhere—the snores, grunts, and groans of the other men don't bother me, but I'm constantly worried about my parents. I've been spending the majority of each day with them, helping them fix up their quarters as well as possible. I found some old newspapers and stuffed them into as many of the cracks and crevices in the walls as I could, but still, it drives them both crazy that the dust blows in all the time. My mother sweeps constantly and I fear she is exhausting herself. Besides that, the food they serve in the mess halls is terrible. The rice is runny and the vegetables are overcooked and tasteless. We get meat once a day, chicken, I suppose, though it's hard to tell, and it's always tough and stringy. For breakfast they serve us rice in milk, sweetened with molasses, and it's terrible. They've given no thought as to what Japanese are accustomed to eating, other than serving us rice three times a day. As a result, everyone's bowels are affected, but going to the latrines is a nightmare. Most of them are broken and overflowing much of the time, though some of us have figured out that the latrines at the farthest end of the camp from the barracks are generally less crowded and in better working order, so we make our way there whenever possible. The older people and the children can't go so far, and it's really hard on them to face that level of filth. Not only that, but there is absolutely no privacy for using the toilet. They are all lined up in rows, facing each other—men in one building, women in another. For a people who are very modest, this is hell. Personally, I just deal with it. I don't like doing my business in front of other people, but it's not like anyone is looking at you. Everyone is too embarrassed for themselves. For my mother, though, this is the worst possible thing. So, this afternoon, I saw some supplies being unpacked from large, cardboard boxes. I waited and watched what they did with the boxes, and saw that they folded them up and put them in the back of a truck to be re-used. The truck sat there some time, unattended, and so, when no one was around, I snuck over and grabbed one of the folded up boxes and ran off with it. I took it to my mother, and we fashioned it into a sort of booth, which she can fold up and hide under her shawl until she gets to the latrines, then unfold and place around her for privacy.

She told me it had worked well. So well, in fact, that other women asked to borrow it when she was done. This has led her to make a few friends so that makes me glad.

Word has gotten around the camp that I'm an actor and today one of the camp directors came to me and asked if I might want to run an acting class for the "evacuees" (a euphemism if there ever was one—like they were doing us a favor by "evacuating" us from our lives). He said they needed a distraction, and that people with various skills are starting different kinds of classes in order to keep the people busy and engaged. I said sure, why not. I asked if he could get a hold of some books like the plays of Shakespeare, maybe Moliere, or Shaw or other classics of that sort. He said he'd look into it. The camp has a small library so he said it might be a possibility to round up some volumes. So this is what I've been reduced to: teaching acting for prisoners in...let's just say it, a concentration camp.

Cassandra wore her slinky black evening gown for the party at Betty Grable's house while Elton sported his royal blue zoot-suit. Perhaps a tuxedo was more fitting for a party like this, but he was feeling rebellious. He was a black man in a world where he didn't belong, and he'd be damned if he was going to try to fit in with white people's expectations. Anyway, Cassandra said she loved his look and that was enough for him.

They pulled up in the Hudson to an elaborate

wrought-iron gate in Beverly Hills, where a man stood checking the names on the guest list. Finding Cassandra and Elton's there, he waved them on to the front of Grable's mansion, where a valet took over the parking, but not before Elton could hurry around to Cassandra's door and open it for her. In movie star style, she exited the car legs first, pulling back the form-fitting skirt of the dress to reveal her long, lovely limbs, swathed in nude-colored silk stockings. He tried not to think about the garter belt they must be attached to.

They stood for a moment in front of the pinkish, Spanish-style home, roofed in traditional terracotta tiles. From the arched entryway, light blazed into the warm, California night. The smell of orange blossoms and sage were in the air. Two tall thin cypress trees flanked the archway. A butler, standing just inside, beckoned them in, and a maid took the black, sheared lamb capelet Cassandra wore as a wrap. Every eye turned toward them as they entered the immense living room. There, the floor was of a similar reddish-brown Saltillo tile as in Cassandra's bungalow, covered with authentic Turkish carpets. The ceiling was crossed with thick beams of dark wood and the elegant but comfortable looking furniture was a mix of Art Deco and Spanish style. A large fireplace on one wall was tiled in a checkerboard pattern of Moorish influence, and everywhere in the detailing of the room could be found the same mix of Art Deco and Moorish flavor that was so popular during the era.

Bette Davis spotted them from across the room and swished over in her tight-fitting red gown with a wide flounce at the bottom. "Dah-lings!" she cried, "you are the most interesting couple here." She air-kissed Cassandra on both cheeks and held out her gloved hand, upon which Elton bestowed a kiss. "My, but you are charming," she said to him. "I adore your suit. Oooh, with you sporting that outrageous look, I feel like the party suddenly became a tad dangerous."

Elton wasn't sure how to take this and so he smiled.

"And you, my dearest Mrs. Reilly..."

"Please, call me Cassandra."

"Cass-ahn-dra!" The movie star declared. "How glamorous. You could put us all out of work!"

"Nonsense," Cassandra murmured. "No one could do what you do in the way you do it, Miss Davis. You are unparalleled."

The big-eyed actress rewarded Cassandra with a fetching smile. "And you must call me Bette as well. Come, let me introduce you to our hostess. Oh, Betty!"

A woman with bleached blond hair piled atop her head turned to them, displaying a figure that almost blurred Elton's vision. She was wearing a form-fitting gown of white sequins and she, literally, sparkled. The smile she threw their way was no less dazzling. This is what they meant by "movie star."

She slunk her way through her guests, all of whom were, by now, staring openly at Cassandra and Elton.

"This is the couple I told you about," Davis said to her as she approached. "They were at the canteen last night."

Grable held out her hand, gloved in elbow-length white satin as most of the ladies wore, including Cassandra. She barely brushed her hand along Cassandra and Elton's fingertips as they each extended their right hand.

"This is Mrs. Cassandra Reilly, a textiles heiress; and her beau, Mr. Carver," said Davis to Grable. "Aren't they divine?"

Elton opened his mouth to object to the work 'beau,' but Grable pounced in with her reply. "Oh, I'm just thrilled to have you here," she cooed, leaning in toward them slightly, revealing a staggering view of her impressive cleavage.

"Mrs. Reilly gave a most generous donation toward the war effort yesterday," Davis said.

"Why thank you!" Grable exclaimed.

"Mr. Carver poses as her bodyguard," Bette whispered to Betty. "Isn't that delicious?"

"Mmmm, you can guard my body any time," Grable murmured to Elton. "Come," she continued, taking him by the hand. "You are mine for now. I'm sorry, Mrs. Reilly, but you must share him. He is simply irresistible."

"As long as you return him in one piece," Cassandra returned with a sly smile.

She certainly is playing the part, Elton thought, a tad miffed at being thusly objectified. He strolled away with Grable, her arm firmly entwined in his, and heard Cassandra say to Davis, "Is Miss Lake here? I'm dying to meet her!"

A half an hour passed before he spotted Cassandra again, during which time he had been introduced to all manner of movie producers and directors, and had tried to avoid imbibing too much champagne. It was outside, by the long, rectangular pool, sparkling with turquoise light, that he finally spied his partner standing annoyingly close to Humphrey Bogart. Cassandra was leaning against a stucco column under the portico, and Bogart was leaning into her, one hand just above her shoulder on the column. They were both smiling as they chatted. Grable had yet to release Elton from her grasp and he couldn't think how to escape without being rude. Just then, on the other side of the pool, he saw a stunning young woman lounging on a chaise all alone.

"Excuse me, Miss Grable," he said to his hostess. "I see a young lady in distress. She has no drink and must be parched. Do you mind if I rescue her?"

Grable pouted, but granted him leave to go. He swung past a waiter with a tray, grabbed a glass of champagne off it, and made his way to the girl, whom he recognized without a doubt as a very young Lauren Bacall. He handed her the glass with a flourish. "You look thirsty," he said to her, flashing as charming a grin as he could muster.

"Thank you," she responded with a smile that nearly melted him into the pavement.

"Do you mind?" He asked as he went to pull up a chair.

"Of course not," she said.

She was so beautiful she was luminous. They introduced themselves and fell into a light conversation.

"I'm nervous being here," she confessed in her iconic low rumble of a voice. "My agent got me an invitation but I don't know anyone."

"I'm pretty new to the scene too," Elton said, "but I've gotten to know a few of the major players. As a matter of fact, I met Mr. Bogart yesterday." He gestured in the direction of the actor.

"Oh, I adore his films!" she declared.

"Would you like to meet him?"

"Really?"

"Come with me." He stood and offered her his arm.

Together they walked around the pool toward Bogart and Cassandra. The redhead turned to them, eyes growing wider as they approached, while Bogart kept his gaze fixed on Cassandra.

"Elton!" Cassandra exclaimed, and Bogart finally turned to look. His expression was of slight annoyance at first, and then, as he took in the striking young starlet, his face lit with wonder.

"Mr. Bogart, Cassandra, I'd like to introduce you to Miss Lauren Bacall, she's new to Hollywood, but will soon be a rising star, I have no doubt."

Suddenly it was if, to Bogart, no one else in the galaxy existed. "Well, hello," he said to the starlet, turning his full attention to her.

"Oh, Mr. Bogart," Bacall crooned, "I heard you just wrapped a new film. I'm so looking forward to it. I'm such a fan!"

"Yeah, doll, it's called Casablanca. Set to open in September. I'll make sure you get an invite to the premiere."

Elton and Cassandra moved away and Bogart didn't even notice.

"Do you think this party is where they actually met?" Cassandra whispered.

"No, I don't think they were supposed to meet for a couple of years from now, but, oh well. It had to happen eventually."

"He was just telling me about his marriage to a woman named Mayo Methot. He seemed to imply it was an open one."

"I bet he did," Elton replied, trying to keep his voice even.

"Don't worry, I was under no danger of falling for him," Cassandra teased.

"I just don't want you to get distracted from why we're here in the first place."

"I'm not distracted," she said defensively. "I've been asking about Veronica Lake since we got here, and no one has seen her."

"Well, I think our luck just changed," he said, gesturing toward the house.

A sultry blonde in a long green gown was emerging onto the patio. She was alone.

"Come on," Cassandra said, "before anyone scoops her up."

"Wait! We shouldn't go together. If she describes meeting us to Nick, he might suspect it's you and me. It's not often that a black man of my description would be with a redhead of yours in this day and age."

"I see what you mean. Okay, I'll go."

"Oh, Mr. Carver!" Grable beckoned from the door with a wave. He went to her while Cassandra made a beeline for the other blonde.

He was once again absorbed into Grable's orbit while he watched Cassandra from the corner of his eye. It wasn't long before the two women were laughing together like old girlfriends. He left her to it and let Grable continue to guide him around the party. It was obvious his hostess had been drinking to excess because her speech had become slow and deliberate, and she was leaning into him, her ample breasts pressed against his upper arm in a way that seemed most purposeful.

Thankfully, Cassandra rescued him just as the actress seemed to be trying to steer him to some secluded spot. "Elton," Cassandra said to him, taking in Grable's condition with a glance, "I'm afraid I have the most frightful headache. Do you mind if we skedaddle?"

"But you just got here!" Grable slurred, clutching Elton by the hand.

"I'm so sorry to steal him away from you," Cassandra said, smiling graciously, "but, you know, he is my ride." She peeled him out of Grable's grasp, while another drunken guest snuck up from behind and grabbed the actress around the waist.

Grable spun around and declared, "Errol! Where have you been hiding?"

A young attractive woman was just emerging from the same door where Flynn had, arranging her hair and dress. Elton could well guess where the swashbuckling actor had been and what he'd been doing.

Flynn and Grable smooched with abandon and Elton began to hurry away with Cassandra, placing a hand lightly on her back before realizing the impropriety of it and then letting it drop.

They were halfway across the floor, uttering their farewells to all they had met, when a voice called out from behind them, "Wait a minute!"

Elton turned to seen Flynn advancing on him menacingly.

"Errol, no!" Grable called out.

"What's the meaning of this?" Flynn demanded, his Australian accent muddied with drink. He gestured with a hand between Elton and Cassandra.

"I don't know what you mean," Elton replied indignantly.

"A boy like you sporting around with a dame like this?"

"How dare you speak to him like that!" Cassandra shouted, her face growing red.

"Stay out of it, baby," Errol said, pushing Cassandra aside. "He's obviously got you hoodwinked." Grable rushed up and tried to grab the actor by the arm as the other guests backed away. "He's her driver!" she cried.

Flynn shook her off. "They seem a little too chummy to me, and I don't take kindly to that sort of fraternizing," Flynn went on, eyeing Elton up and down. "Each to his own kind, if you know what I mean."

"First of all," Elton said, advancing on the man, pulling himself up to his full and impressive height. Though Flynn was quite tall, Elton had at least an inch on him. "It's none of your business what the lady and I do. Second of all, you will not lay hands on her."

"Elton," Cassandra began, but Flynn cut her off.

"What are you gonna do about it?" he spat, as he squared off to Elton.

"I'm going to behave like a gentleman, which is more than I can say for you, and depart."

"Oh yeah?" Flynn swung his fist toward Elton's face, but he was drunk and Elton was too quick. Elton grabbed the actor's fist in his own hand and twisted it around until Flynn cried out in pain.

"Somebody call the cops! Somebody call the cops!" Flynn screamed.

"If anyone picks up the phone you'll be answering to me," Grable shouted.

Elton let go of Flynn's arm and stepped away.

No one moved.

"And you," she said to Flynn. "Get out of here!"

"You're gonna side with him over me?" Flynn slobbered. "I never took you for a n—"

"Don't you dare." Grable growled.

"Alright, chum," Bogart strode to Flynn and grabbed him by the arm. "Let's go. My car will take you home." He maneuvered the man toward the door. Flynn deflated at Bogart's touch. Though the older actor was practically six inches shorter than Flynn, he was obviously the alpha male.

As Flynn stumbled away with Bogart, Grable grabbed Elton by the bicep. "I'm so sorry," she said to him, batting her eyelids. "That should never have happened. Errol gets so drunk that he's unpredictable."

"It's okay," Elton returned as politely as he could manage. He was about as fed up as he could be.

"You handled that so...impressively," she went on, running her hand up and down his arm.

"I think we need to be going," Cassandra cut in. "You've been most gracious, Miss Grable. Thank you."

"No," Grable murmured, still clutching at Elton.

"Let me make it up to you." She ignored Cassandra and stared into Elton's eyes.

She suddenly was less attractive to him. "I appreciate it," Elton said, "but we do need to call it a night." He removed her hand from his arm, giving it a light squeeze of friendship. "Good evening."

With that, he and Cassandra quickly moved toward the exit.

"Don't forget about midnight!" he heard Grable slur as the door closed behind him. He wondered what she meant.

They stood silently as they waited for the car to be brought. The scent of orange blossoms and jasmine was in the air and the headiness of it was making Elton nauseous. Once the car had been fetched and they were on the road, Cassandra leaned forward against the back of the front seat and said, "That was horrible. Are you all right?"

He let out a long exhale. "I will be."

"I see what you mean now. About the risk for you. Being here, with me."

"I chose it, Cassie. I knew what I was getting into. It's just that, I guess I was starting to think we were in a kind of a bubble. The movie stars all seemed so...accepting."

She was silent for a moment. "We need to be careful."

"Yeah."

Another pause. "Lake wasn't very helpful with information about Nick. She just said he'd gone to the desert."

"The desert? Well, that's vague," Elton said. "Maybe she meant he went to Palm Springs."

"I don't know. She was just as puzzled by it as I was, and miffed that he'd taken off without her. She also said he visited the set with her one day about a week and a half ago. She's making a movie with Bogart. She said he had insisted on going with her. When they got to the set, he asked about a Japanese actor who had been working on the film in a bit part. She said he was irritated to find out he wasn't there."

"What would he want with some minor actor?"

"I don't know, but then she said the actor had recently been sent to an internment camp. She said not to tell anyone. That she found out by eavesdropping on a conversation that she shouldn't have been between the director and a military official on the set."

"Why did she tell you?"

"I don't know. She was drunk. Upset about Nick having run out on her."

"Hm. Did she say the actor's name?"

"Yes, I asked, thinking it could be a lead. Hiro something. Wait, I'll remember..."

He racked his brain for a moment. "Was it Wakai? Hiro Wakai?"

"That's it!"

"We've got another stop to make." Elton whipped the car to the left and headed in the direction of Compton. He took a peek at the watch on his arm. "It's 11:00—probably too late."

"Too late for what?" Cassandra cried from where she'd tumbled into the depths of the back seat.

"For the restaurant that his parents own to be open."

"You know this guy?"

"No, but I met his parents. They'll know where to find him. This is a lead."

"Elton, I'm lost. Like you said, why would Nick be interested in an obscure Japanese actor? Especially in this particular war climate."

"I don't know, but you're right. It's a lead, and we've got to follow every one we can."

At the late hour, with the roads mostly empty, they arrived in the defunct Little Tokyo in less than a half an hour. Elton pulled up in front of the tiny Japanese restaurant but it was dark inside. "Damn!" he declared.

"We'll come back tomorrow," Cassandra suggested.

"Wait a minute." There was a sign on the door. Elton went to examine it. Upon it was scrawled Japanese lettering, and below it, the words, in English, "Closed Indefinitely."

As he walked back to the car, a grizzled white woman leaned out of a window above the shop next door. "What do you want?" she cried suspiciously.

"I'm looking for the Wakais."

"They're gone," she yelled.

"Where did they go?" he returned, a cold chill

creeping up his spine.

The woman eyed him for a moment before replying. "Why should I tell you?"

"I'm a friend of their son, Hiro. I'm looking for him."

"Well, you won't find him here. They all been shipped off. The whole family. I say, good riddance. You can't be too careful of them yellow bastards."

Elton swallowed his disgust. "Do you know where they were sent?"

"Most of the japs around here sent to one place. Manzanar."

Chapter Nineteen

Hiro Wakai - June 22nd, 1942

The class I'm teaching is actually not a bad way to spend my time. We meet Monday through Friday from five to six. While I'm waiting for the camp director to come up with some books of plays, I've been doing acting exercises with my students and they seem to be having fun with them. Most of them are so reserved it's hard to get them to come out of their shells, but the exercises and games help. Once I get them laughing, they're able to relax and not be so self-conscious. I'm also using the classes as an opportunity to help some of the Issei with their pronunciation—kind of a losing battle with those old folks, but they seem to appreciate it.

There's a really pretty girl in the class too. Her name is Kanako. She always smiles shyly at me, but she's quite game when it comes to participating. I can't wait to get a hold of some materials so I can place her in a scene. In the meantime, I asked if anyone might be interested in writing one themselves and Kanako showed up today with something she'd written in hand. It was about a girl and her grandfather so I paired her with an older guy named Mr. Matsuda. He was pretty bad, but she's a natural.

During the day, the hours are long and boring though I spend part of it doing the translations of Pop's diary, which keeps me out of the heat. Everyone has their own way of keeping busy. Some of the older gentlemen have begun carving out small gardens here and there. Most of them are vegetable gardens, and there's a large communal garden too. Some of gardens are purely ornamental —the kind of simple, elegant spaces I've seen in the back yards of our friends in Little Tokyo. Mr. Matsuda has started working on one himself so I asked if I could help him, and he seemed glad for the offer. So now, in the cool of the evenings in between supper and lights out, I work with Mr. Matsuda in his garden. It's very therapeutic. God knows, we need all the peace of mind we can get and, here, getting it isn't easy. We don't know how long we will be at Manzanar or if something worse is on the horizon. The uncertainly of it all, besides the humiliation, is one of the worst things.

It was a long and boring five-hour drive from Los Angeles to Manzanar, most of it desert and farmland. The highways were barely that, and some of them were nothing but dirt roads. At one point, Nick grew nervous about a grey sedan that seemed to have been behind him since he left the L.A., but it drove past without slowing down when he turned off to the camp, so he figured he was probably just being paranoid. He drove slowly on the street that ran alongside the facility and gawked at the buildings and the people inside the tall, barbed-wire-topped fence. The structures were basically army-type barracks, made of wood and tin. Japanese men, women, and children shuffled along inside with haunted looks in their eyes. Some trudged along in lines, probably going to eat, shower, or use the bathrooms. Others worked in a big garden, hoeing and shoveling in the setting, but still very hot, sun. Nick knew exactly what Wakai looked like from the old, print-style actor's headshot he'd seen when researching him online but it was impossible to make out any one face from the distance.

He pulled up at the guard station and presented his counterfeit ID badge to the man stationed there.

The guard looked it over carefully. "A government inspector?"

"Yes," Nick replied impatiently.

"Well, I'm gonna have to call your name in. I know all the inspectors already."

"I'm new."

"Sorry, it's protocol."

"How long is that going to take?"

"Well," the man glanced at his watch. "Oh yeah, it's Sunday. They'll be closed. It'll have to wait until tomorrow."

Nick knew that would be the case and had waited to come out until Sunday on purpose. "Look, I've got a job to do. If your superior officer gets wind that you didn't let me in, it'll be your head on the block, not mine."

The man appeared to ponder this. Then his eyes roved to the X sticker on Nick's windshield. Soon after Nick had arrived in 1942, knowing he was going to need to get around without worrying about rationing, he'd sniffed someone out and paid them to bribe someone else to get one for him. With enough money, you could do anything.

"Yeah, okay," the guy said, "you can go on in." He unlatched the big metal fence and opened it up.

Nick drove through and parked in a line with some government vehicles. He grabbed a clipboard and pen out of the car and walked purposefully toward the barracks, his ID badge now pinned to his jacket. He knew that families were housed together, but single men were in their own quarters. Would he find Hiro with his parents, or in with the single men? The only way to find out would be to look everywhere.

It being dinner time, the first place he looked was the mess halls, walking up and down the rows of people quietly eating rice and vegetables in scant portions at long tables and benches. Suddenly, he froze. What if Akito Wakai was here too? Nick hadn't thought of that. If he was, would he recognize him? It had, after all, been twenty years, and the man couldn't have gotten more than a glimpse of him at the time, but what about his wife? He looked all around the room. Everyone ignored him. He didn't see anyone that resembled Akito so he began to question people with just the name: Hiro Wakai? From a worker, he learned that the people ate in shifts, which meant he could conceivably just wait in the mess hall for all the shifts to come and go but, if he did, Akito or his wife would be more likely to spot him—if, indeed, the parents were even here. Finally, after a discussion among some prisoners who knew Hiro about who had last seen him and where he was at the moment, one of them pointed Nick toward a building on the outskirts of the camp. He marched across the dusty compound to the building with as much purpose as he could muster. Once there, he eased the door open and stepped inside. Only one dim bulb hung from the ceiling. It took him a minute to orient himself. He was in a sort of classroom. Two people were standing at the front of the room, a young woman and an older man, papers in hand, reading a scene of some sort together. A man was seated in the front row of a group of chairs, his back to Nick, watching eagerly. No one else was in the room.

Nick cleared his throat and the readers turned to look at him.

The man rose from his chair and turned to look as well. It was Hiro Wakai.

"Can I help you?" he asked with annoyance.

"I'm so sorry," he said, "I'm an inspector. May I interrupt you for just one minute?"

"Certainly," Hiro said coldly.

"Just one moment of your time."

Hiro walked to the back of the classroom and stood there, arms folded, while the two readers waited.

"Forgive me, this will just take a moment," said Nick. "We're trying to get a sense of the activities provided for the..."

"The prisoners?"

"Um, well, we don't like to call them that. Anyway, can you just tell me how often you teach this class?"

"Every night from five to six, Monday through Friday."

"But it's Sunday."

Hiro sighed. "We're having a special rehearsal if you must know."

"Oh, I see. Thank you."

Hiro sighed again and walked back up the aisle. The young woman who had been reading the scene smiled at Hiro and he smiled back as their eyes met. That could be his future wife, Nick thought, the one who died giving birth to their child. Hiro died two years later from polio, contracted in the camp—that much information he had. But the child—it was the child who he had to assure would never be born. In reality, it wouldn't matter which one of them he killed, Hiro or the child's mother, as long as one of them died before the baby was conceived. Nick wasn't a monster though. He wouldn't kill a woman if he could avoid it. Anyway, he had the information he needed. He glanced at his watch. He turned and left.

He would go check into one of the seedy motels in nearby Independence, and then he'd come back tomorrow. His plan was simple and clear, and when it was done, he'd head back to his portal exit without delay. He nearly laughed out loud with the anticipation of carrying out the deed.

Chapter Twenty

Hiro Wakai – June 24th, 1942

Kanako stayed after class today to help me rearrange the benches and clean up the classroom. It has to be ready for the high school students in the morning, so it's my job to clean it when I'm done in the evening. If I'm not mistaken, I think she purposefully wants to spend extra time with me. We chatted as we cleaned and, though I had to keep up most of the conversation myself, I was able to get a glimpse into her character. She was sent here with her family, and she, like the other young women, is housed with them. I asked about them. They are five altogether, her parents, a sister, and a little brother. It must be terribly cramped in the space allotted them. She says her sister goes to school with the other children during the day but that her brother is still too little, so she helps her mother care for him. She described him to me with such joy in her voice. I can see that he and her younger sister, who is eight, are the apples of her eye. Interestingly, their mother is not hers, though she calls her "Mama." Her real mother died when she was young and her father raised her himself until he met another woman and they married. That's why her brother and sister are so much younger than Kanako. She loves her stepmother with all her heart, I can see that. I think, in some ways, they are more like sisters than mother and daughter. She says, at home, they made clothes together, and still do each other's hair. They cooked the family meals together, and went to the movies sometimes in the evenings after the kids would go to bed since Kanako's father doesn't speak English well and didn't like to go. I didn't ask her age, of course, but I think she must be around twenty. I imagine her stepmother isn't much more than thirty so that does make them close in age. I didn't ask about her actual mother and she didn't talk about her. Maybe she doesn't remember her well.

When we were done cleaning, I walked Kanako back to her quarters, not far from mine. I have to admit that I like her. Rather a lot.

As Cassandra and Elton drove home after Betty Grable's party and their failed attempt to find Hiro Wakai in little Tokyo, streetlights throughout Los Angeles and Hollywood began to blink out one by one.

"What's happening?" Cassandra wondered out loud.

"I don't know." Elton answered. "Rolling blackout to save electricity?"

"In the middle of the night?"

They drove up their street, the half-headlights on the Hudson barely penetrating the complete darkness. They said good night and went into their respective houses. Cassandra began getting ready for bed, brushing her teeth and going through her skin routine. She stripped off her clothes and was about to get into bed naked when she remembered her pajamas, sighed, and went to put them on. She only slept clothed when time traveling, though, she thought with a warming of her skin, never had with Lauro. Usually, when visiting other eras, she was obliged to wear long, frilly nightgowns of silk or linen—the only choice for a woman of the wealth and stature she always pretended to have. Though the night dresses changed in style from one century to the next they were always bulky and uncomfortable to sleep in. The comfy PJs were definitely an improvement. She was just pulling the covers down to get in when a siren pierced the air.

What the hell?

A moment later, Elton was pounding on the front door. She ran to answer it. "What's going on?" she shouted to him.

"Air raid drill!" he said, running around the bungalow closing curtains and turning off the few lights she still had on. Through the open door she saw his cottage was dark. He came back and closed the door as the siren continued to whine.

"What do we do now?" she cried.

"Hunker down, I guess, until it stops."

They both flopped onto the sofa.

"What time is it?" he asked.

"Midnight, I think."

"Oh! That's what she meant!"

"Who? What?"

"Betty Grable. As we were leaving the party I heard her say, 'Don't forget about midnight.' She must have known about the drill."

"How did she know?"

"I guess they must advertise it. Maybe on the radio. Maybe with flyers or in the paper. We haven't been paying attention. That must be why the streetlights went dark."

"Oh! Wow. I don't feel as prepared for this trip as I should be," she said.

"I keep having that feeling too," he said.

It was hard to talk with the siren blaring in intermittent bursts from somewhere nearby. Cassandra drew her legs up under her and curled into a ball. With the drapes closed, it was very dark. She could barely make out Elton sitting next to her but was aware of the heat of his body.

"Are you cold?" he asked.

"No. I'm okay." There was no source of light in the room at all, which felt strange. In the future, there was always light in a dark room whether you particularly wanted it or not: digital clocks on appliances, the tiny green or red lights on just about every piece of electronic equipment that filled everyone's home, and light filtering in from the outside either by streetlamp or the general illumination of light pollution. Environmental pollution had finally been gotten under control after the World Wide Crisis of 2080, but light and noise pollution were still problems the modern world had to contend with.

Finally, the blare of the sirens ceased.

"Now what?" she whispered to him, keeping her

voice low though she wasn't sure why.

"I don't know. I don't know how long we're supposed to keep the lights off."

"I guess we'll know when the street lamps start to come on."

"Yeah. Well," he paused. "We might as well go to bed. I mean, I might as well go back to the cottage."

"Yes. We should get some sleep," she replied, "though it will be hard now. My heart is still beating fast." His presence next to her was comforting. Something made her want to snuggle into his arms, but she wouldn't. She could hear him lightly breathing. Then his hand touched hers where it rested on the sofa.

"Okay," he said. "I'm going.

"Okay."

He didn't move. His hand remained over hers. She imagined him kissing her.

He stood up. "Good night. Sleep well."

"You too." She stood and took a step toward him. He took her in his arms. It was only a brief hug, but it felt wonderful. "Good night," she whispered, and he went out the door.

In the morning, the world had completely returned to normal. Cassandra was dressed, making breakfast, looking out the kitchen window, wondering when Elton would be over. A warm breeze blew in. The sky was blue without a cloud. Birds sang and the smell of freshly cut grass wafted in from somewhere. It was a perfect California day. Then she saw him, walking across the lawn, and smiled, thinking about the night before.

As he came through the door, he said, "I've been thinking about what Nick's interest could be in Hiro Wakai and I can't find the connection."

"No, it doesn't make sense. Is it a coincidence that the Wakais were sent away, and that Nick was asking about him, then has suddenly taken a mysterious trip to the desert? It might mean he went to Manzanar after him, but why?"

"That's what I was asking myself. Anyway, we have two choices here as I see it," said Elton. "We either go back through the portal and research Hiro Wakai—see if we can find a connection there, or we drive out to Manzanar and see if we find anything out that way. I think it's about four or five hours from L.A."

"Going back through the portal will probably take longer," Cassandra remarked. "And it's riskier in a sense—making sure we get in and out of the warehouse undetected. But we could get the information we need and end up being more prepared."

"Yeah, but we're wasting time debating it. I say we go to Manzanar."

"How will we get in?"

"I have no idea. Say we have a reason we need to see the Wakais?"

"Do they let visitors in?"

"I don't know. Who would know? Someone must know."

Cassandra paused, spatula in hand. "I feel like we're at a dead end. Going to Manzanar is a shot in the dark."

"I think we should at least give it a try. We'll bring something...food, or toilet paper or something. We'll say we're donating supplies for the prisoners."

"No, it's a waste of time if we don't even know whether we can get in."

"Hey, what about Bogart?" Elton said.

"What about him?"

"The Wakais told me he had helped them. Because his son was friends with Bogart, they were spared being sent away—at least at first."

"Do you think Bogart would know something about the internment camps?"

"He might. Do we know how to get in touch with him?"

Cassandra felt a flush creep over her cheeks. She went to her purse on the kitchen sink and extracted a match box. On the back was scribbled a phone number. She showed it to Elton. "He gave me his number."

"Oh, I see," said Elton with a tease in his voice.

"So, I guess I'll give him a call." Cassandra went into the living room, picked up the receiver of the phone, and began to dial.

Elton hovered in the doorway.

Bogart's unmistakable voice drawled, "It's your

dime."

"Mr. Bogart, hello, it's Cassandra Reilly."

"Red! To what do I owe the pleasure?"

Cassandra paused over his use of the nickname, then went on. "I have something I'd like to talk to you about."

"How about you have dinner with me tonight?"

She hesitated. "It's rather urgent."

"Lunch then. Give me your address and I'll send a car."

"We could just speak about it now, if you don't mind."

"Nah, I hate these contraptions. I like to do my talking in person. It's nine-thirty now. I'll send the car. It'll be there in a half hour. We'll have Sunday brunch. Brunch—god, I hate that word. Anyway, how's that sound, Red?"

"Sounds great, Mr. Bogart."

"Call me Bogie, everyone does."

"Ok...Bogie." She gave him the address. "I'll see you soon." She hung up the receiver, appreciating the satisfying clunk it produced when being set back on its cradle.

"So?" Elton queried.

"I'm meeting him for brunch. He's sending a car."

"I could drive you!"

"Elton, let me do this on his terms."

"Well, I don't trust him," her boss grumbled.

"What do you mean?"

"He obviously has designs on you, Cassie."

"So what? It's not like he's going to get anywhere."

"You sure about that?"

"Elton!" Indignation rose like bile in her throat. "What are you saying?"

"Nothing, it's just…you know, when we time travel, we often…I'm the same, it happened to me too."

Her ire calmed a bit. "No. I feel no temptation when it comes to Bogart if that's what you're saying. He's charming, but I'm not attracted to him. And even if I were, I wouldn't…I mean…I'm here with you."

His face brightened. They stared at each other for a moment from across the room.

"Ok then," he finally said with a shrug. "I guess I'm eating breakfast alone." He wandered off toward the kitchen.

"I'm going to change."

"Wait," he said. He returned from the kitchen with a piece of buttered toast in his hand. "So you don't get hungry on the way."

She took it and smiled. She nibbled it in her bedroom as she looked through her clothes, suddenly distracted. That feeling she'd experienced last night had been creeping into her heart, she realized, since this journey had begun. No, since they had started planning it. It was a feeling that she'd pushed away because, after all, her love for Lauro was still burning bright. Yet that love brought with it a bitter-sweetness she'd rather not have to carry around. It was becoming easier, in Elton's presence, to just let it go.

She chastised herself as she decided on what to wear. She had no time for confusing feelings at the moment, and yet there was no denying how attractive Elton was—was becoming to her—the more time she spent with him here in 1942.

A black Bentley pulled into the driveway right on time. Elton watched her go from the doorway of the guest house where he had retreated to. She was not mistaken that he was irked by her meeting Bogart alone, and now it was growing clear to her why. She wasn't the only one, it seemed, who was struggling with feelings of attraction. As the car sped onto the Pasadena Freeway, she had some time to reflect on what she'd tried to discount just a few moments earlier. The hours they had spent preparing for this trip had thrown them together more than any other one period of time in their fifteen-year acquaintance and she was enjoying it—so much it surprised her. He, however, seemed to be more than just enjoying being with her as a friend or close colleague might. He seemed genuinely drawn to her, and really, there was no point in denying it: every time she looked at him, she felt a surge of...attraction at least. Maybe more. As much as she felt guilty at the thought of someone else replacing Lauro in her heart so soon after leaving him, her heart was tugging her in the direction of Elton Carver, a man who was strong, kind, brilliant, good to his soul, and let's face it, she thought, gorgeous.

As the scenery rolled by out the window of the luxurious car, Cassandra realized they were heading toward the beach. "Excuse me," she said to the driver, a distinguished white man of middle age, "where are we going?"

"San Pedro Marina, Ma'am," was the reply.

"Oh." She sat back in her seat. Why a marina? It seemed far to go for a brunch and she didn't have time to spare. At least it gave her an opportunity to think up a story to tell Bogie.

The drive had taken about thirty minutes when the car finally pulled up to a series of docks where large elegant yachts were moored in rows. There, leaning on a low wall, was Bogart, dressed in white slacks, a black and white striped boating shirt, a navy-blue blazer, and a matching captain's hat upon his head, smoking, as he nearly always was.

The driver came around to open her door and Bogart came to the car to meet her.

He kissed her hand in his inimitable way and winked. "Welcome to the California Yacht Club. You are radiant as always, Red," he said to her.

She was glad she hadn't overdressed. She was wearing the simple green frock she'd worn when she'd come through the portal. She didn't want to give Bogart the idea she was interested by dressing provocatively. "You didn't tell me we were having brunch on a boat."

"It's a surprise." He tucked her arm through his

and led her along one of the docks. He pointed to a large streamlined yacht. "It belongs to a friend of mine who lets me use it. Maybe you've heard of Cary Grant?"

She laughed. "Um, yes. I believe I have."

"Well, baby, this is his. Complete with chef and waiters at our beck and call. You can't take these boats out anymore though. Not enough fuel. Also, security, you know?"

She nodded.

A steward met them at the gangplank and gestured for them to come aboard, holding his hand out to assist Cassandra. The vessel was beautiful, the deck and railings of shining teak, every detail classic and elegant—but not ostentatious, just like Cary Grant himself. They were led to the fore deck, which was overhung with a canvas awning, and were seated at a roomy table set with fine silverware, china, and crystal.

"Listen, Bogie, this is lovely, but I have something pressing to talk to you about."

The waiter poured chilled champagne into their glasses and she paused until he had moved off.

"Shoot," Bogie replied when the man was gone.

"I was told you were friendly with Hiro Wakai. I need some information about him."

"Hiro? Yeah, he's a swell guy. But what do you want with him?"

"Well, it's a little too complicated to explain, but, remember that Elton and I told you we were looking for Nick Stockard? We think there may be a connection between him and Mr. Wakai."

Bogart frowned. "I don't get it."

"Veronica Lake told me that Nick had been asking about Mr. Wakai on the set; that Nick was upset he wasn't there. Recently, she learned Hiro was sent away. I'm not supposed to tell anyone, as it's a secret, she said, but—"

"What do you mean, sent away," Bogart interrupted, trepidation creeping over his face.

"We went by the Wakais' restaurant last night and the neighbor said the whole family was sent to Manzanar. We suppose that means Hiro too."

"Damn it!" Bogart slammed a fist down on the white linen tablecloth and the dishes jumped. He leapt to his feet and paced around the deck. "I tried so hard to keep that from happening. I pulled all the strings I knew how to pull."

"I'm sure the family appreciates that very much," Cassandra said, repositioning the tableware. "Here's the thing. We're really worried about Nick." She was improvising now. "He's kind of the jealous type if you know what I mean. Maybe he thought Hiro was having some kind of affair with Veronica, and has gone out to Manzanar to rough him up. I don't know. I can't think of any reason for his going off to the desert in coincidence with Hiro and his family being sent away."

Bogart placed one hand on the back of his chair and gestured with the other. "Ronnie wasn't having no affair with Hiro. I'm pretty sure about that. Hiro was very respectful of women. He worked around a lot of beautiful actresses but he knew the studios wouldn't look kindly on him messin' around with any of 'em. He valued his job."

"Okay, so, here's my question. If Nick did go to Manzanar to find Hiro, would they let him in? Do you know?"

He slumped into his chair. "No, no way. Not a civilian. I've heard they don't let anyone in—or out."

The waiter reappeared with a tray, on top of which were two plates covered with silver, domed lids. He set the tray down and uncovered the lids to expose entrees of chilled, poached salmon with dill sauce, whipped mashed potatoes, and asparagus spears. He set them in front of the guests. It looked great and Cassandra couldn't resist.

"Well, if they don't let us in," she said after having a bite, "I'm sure they wouldn't let Nick in, so maybe we're worrying for nothing." This was not true, of course. Nick would find a way to get into the camp if that were his aim. She just didn't know what it would be, and why he might have any interest in Hiro.

Bogie was now tucking into his food too. "Yeah, maybe."

"This is delicious." She applied herself to the meal too, suddenly very hungry.

"Only the best for you, Red." He clinked his

champagne glass with hers.

They ate silently for a few minutes.

"I just don't get it," Bogart finally said. "What do you care if Nick roughs up Wakai—not that I think he'd be able to get near him anyway."

She thought for a moment, and then said, "Look, I didn't want to say this before, but, Nick is unstable. We only have his best interests at heart. I promised his family we would find him and bring him home."

He regarded her with a sidelong glance. "I see. Well, I hope you find him before he does anything crazy."

"Me too."

He paused before saying, "But, you know, I'd rather talk about you. Better for the digestion," he smirked. "Tell me about yourself, Red. Word has it you're an heiress, huh? Of a textiles company? I don't get that. You're way too glamorous to be runnin' some factory."

"Well, thank you. I don't exactly run it though. I hire people to do that. I oversee the finances. I have a head for business." That wasn't at all true, but she may as well develop her character.

"A head for business and a bod' for pleasure. My favorite type of dame."

His directness took her aback, but then, as a time traveler, she was used to men of previous eras thinking of women as objects. It was one of the most difficult things about time traveling for her. She smiled with some effort. "I'm much more than a pretty face and body, Mr. Bogart."

"Ooh, we're back to Mr. Bogart, huh? I'm sorry, Red, most gals like my compliments."

"I'm sure they do. Here's the thing though, if I want respect as a business owner, I've got to get men me to see me as their equal. Otherwise, no one will ever listen to me."

He nodded as he looked her over. "Yeah, I get it. Makes you all the sexier."

But he didn't get it. He didn't get it at all and probably never would. Anyway, it was time to get out of there. She hadn't gotten much information from the actor about Manzanar, but it was probably as much as anyone knew who wasn't a military official. She and Elton would just have to go and take their chances they'd find Nick there. It was their only lead. Now, she needed an excuse to make her escape. "Can you tell me where the powder room is? I'd like to freshen up."

He snapped his fingers and asked the waiter to escort her. They went up a flight of steps to the master suite. In the beautifully appointed room there was a door to a bathroom. She went in, made use of it, re-applied some lipstick, and came out. When she did, Bogart was there, leaning against the doorjamb of the entrance to the bedroom.

"Oh!" she cried.

He slowly walked toward her. "And now, Red, why don't you tell me what this really is all about?" He stood close to her. In her heels, they were about the same height.

"What do you mean?" she challenged.

"I don't think you're a friend of Nick's. And I don't think you're a 'textiles heiress'. I can read people, and I don't think you're shootin' straight with me. I think there's something else going on here. What are you, a spy for the government? Maybe for the japs? Somethin' about your story doesn't sit right with me."

"No! I'm telling you the truth!"

"Really. I can tell an actor when I see one, and you're a good one. Still, this is an act. Now give me the skinny."

"Fine. You guessed it." She took a deep breath to buy a few seconds of time, then went on. "I am working with the government. It's Nick who's the spy." She suddenly found herself channeling Bette Davis. "We think he's a double agent and we're here to roust him out."

"We? Your boyfriend too?" He asked doubtfully.

"Elton is along to keep me safe, and to drive, of course."

"You must be a pretty tough broad if they sent you out here to nab a spy."

"My job is to seduce him. To get him under my spell, and then turn him in to the authorities. I'm the bait. Elton is the muscle."

"Now that makes sense. Ain't many red-blooded males could resist you." He pulled her into his arms and laid an open-mouthed, and very tongue-y, kiss on her.

She pulled back and slapped him across the face. "How dare you!"

He rubbed his face, but smiled. "Oh, so that's how you like it. Rough, huh?"

"No, Mr. Bogart. I do not. And now, I'm leaving." She stalked past him, but he grabbed her arm.

"Come on, Red," he said pulling her towards him again. "Don't tell me you really are soft for your bodyguard."

"Yes," she said, it ringing true in her heart. "I am. You can imagine what a difficult situation that puts us in, but such is the case. Nevertheless, we are professionals and we're here to do a job. And that job, Mr. Bogart, is to keep the American people safe from ne'er-do-wells like Nick Stockard."

This obviously appealed to his sense of patriotism. He let go her arm, and nodded appreciatively. "Okay, Red. You go do your job. But if you ever change your mind about your boyfriend, I'll be here."

She raised one brow like she'd seen Davis do. "You are a married man, Mr. Bogart."

"I told you, it's an open relationship." He grinned.

"And what about Miss Bacall?"

"Lauren? She's just a kid. Maybe in a couple a' years," he said with a suggestive smile.

And that, thought Cassandra, is exactly when they will get together, ending his current marriage. She was glad she and Elton hadn't done anything to alter that particular time line.

She walked back toward him and kissed his cheek where it glowed red. "I'm going, Bogie. Thank you so much for your help. I'll never forget you."

"I ain't goin' nowhere," he said, still smiling that wry smile.

"Glad to hear it. Can I ask your driver to take me back?"

"Yeah. I got my own car. I like to be the one in the driver's seat."

"I bet you do," she countered seductively. Though Casablanca hadn't yet been released in the U.S., she couldn't resist. "Here's lookin' at you, kid," she uttered. She winked at him, then turned and sauntered away in her best movie star style.

She was at the stairs when she heard him say out loud to himself, "Wait a minute, how in the hell...?"

Chapter Twenty-one

Hiro Wakai - June 25th, 1942

I've spent most of today trying to comfort my mother. Pop has barely said a word since we got here. He sits on the front step of their barrack in the bit of shade that the overhang provides, just staring. When I got to their room this morning, Mom was shaking out their blankets and using a piece of cloth to try to dust the meager belongings on the few shelves that have been tacked up. She didn't look at me when I came in, but just kept dusting. Then she grabbed the broom and started sweeping.

"No, Mom, let me do it," I said. I practically had to pry it from her hands. She looked completely exhausted. I sat her down on her cot. "Are you sleeping?" I asked her in Japanese.

"No, no sleep," she replied. "Too much noise. I can hear everything. People coughing, snoring, crying...babies, old people."

I sighed. "Mom, I'm so sorry."

"When can we go home?" she pleaded, looking into my eyes. "What is happening to the restaurant, and all our things? Are they safe? Will our home still be there when we go back?"

"I don't know, Mom, I don't know," I said. "But I don't

want you to worry. I will take care of you and Pop no matter what."

"How will you take care of us? You cannot work! They will not let you work!"

"I'm sure that's not true," I said, though I wasn't sure at all. "We will all go back to work. You'll see. After the war, they will see we are not the enemy. You will go back to the restaurant, and I will go back to Hollywood. It will be the same as before."

"No, not the same. Never the same. Nothing will ever be the same." She went limp and her head dropped into her hands. She started sobbing. I'd never seen her cry like that before. She'd shed tears, yes, especially in the recent weeks, but never this display of emotion. The Issei, the first-generation Japanese, have a stoicism about them that we, the Nisei, the second generation, didn't inherit. Well, at least I didn't, which is why I'm a good actor. I'm able to show emotion. But my parents and their generation consider it shameful to be open with their feelings, which is why I didn't know what to do for a moment. Finally, I went and put my arms around her. I stayed there holding her for a long time. She didn't return the caress, but it seemed to comfort her because eventually her tears dried. Finally, I persuaded her to leave her quarters and go to the mess hall for lunch. As we passed Pop, sitting on the front step of the barracks, I said, "Pop! Come and eat!"

He just shook his head.

"He won't eat," said Mom. "He will die."

"No he won't," I replied, and tried to think of how I could get him to come and have a meal, horrible as I knew it was going to be.

I sat down next to him. "Pop, we have to be brave." His eyes showed some sign that he'd registered what I'd said.

"I know you know what it's like to experience hardship. You must show these people that you are above their treatment of you. You served in the Imperial Navy. You are a noble Nipponese man. You must not give in. You must not let them think they are winning."

He looked me directly in the eyes for the first time in days. He didn't know how I knew about what he'd experienced in his life because I hadn't yet told him that I was translating his diary, but what I said got through to him. I stood up and held my hand out to him. He took it and I helped him to his feet. Mom smiled, also for the first time since we'd come to Manzanar. She put her arm through his and they walked toward the mess hall. I followed, glad I could be of some help to them.

Elton hopped into the Hudson soon after Bogart's car had picked Cassandra up, and headed toward Compton. She probably wouldn't be thrilled if she knew what he was up to.

He parked outside of Joe McGee's soda fountain, and walked in. Joe was there, just as he had been a few weeks before, serving his customers in his spit-and-polish establishment. A flicker of recognition passed over his face as Elton sat down and ordered a cup of coffee and a slice of pie. Once Joe was done with his other customers, Elton called him over again.

"Don't know if you remember me, but I was here a couple of weeks ago. I was looking for a car, and you steered me in the right direction."

"Oh yeah! Sorry, I don't remember your name."

"Elton," he said with a smile.

"Yeah, that's a funny one."

"So I've been told. So, listen," he lowered his voice and leaned toward Joe. "There's something else I need and I was wondering if you knew where I might find it."

"Lay it on me."

Elton whispered, "I need a gun. There ain't no trouble," he hastened to add. "Just for protection. My boss is a very important lady and worth a lot of dough. I just want to make sure I'm ready for anything that might come up. It's my job to keep her safe."

Joe nodded. "I know what you mean." He grabbed a paper napkin and jotted an address on it. "Just down the avenue here. It's a junk shop in the front…"

"Open on a Sunday?"

"He lives there. Just knock. Tell him I sent you.'

"Gotcha." Elton drained his cup of coffee and wolfed down the rest of his pie. "That is good," he said truthfully.

"I make all the pies myself," Joe said proudly.

"You're a regular artist," Elton replied. "Thanks again for your help."

"Don't mention it."

Elton drove down the avenue, found another parking place, and knocked on the junk shop door. After a few minutes, an old man, grizzled and scruffy, came and peered through the barred, glass door.

"Joe McGee sent me," Elton said loudly.

The man frowned, but slowly unlocked the door and let him in. Fifteen minutes later, Elton exited with a 1937 Beretta pistol, stolen off an Italian soldier, the shop owner had said, that had made its way to the States. It came with sixteen rounds. It was tucked discreetly into Elton's left inner jacket pocket. When he got into the Hudson, he put it and the box of bullets into the glove compartment.

Soon after he returned to the bungalow, Bogart's car pulled into the driveway, and Cassandra stepped out. Elton went outside to meet her.

She walked swiftly to him and said, "He wasn't much help, but I think we'd better head out there and see what we can find."

"Great." He paused and stared at her for a moment.

"Nothing happened, if that's what you think," she said huffily, and walked past him into the house.

"I don't think anything," he replied, following her.

"Good, because it didn't. Let's throw some food in a basket and bring it along. Who knows if we'll find anything to eat along the way."

"I'm ahead of you." He'd bought some chicken and mac & cheese from Ivie's Chicken Shack, plus had picked up some fruit from a farm stand because he knew Cassandra would appreciate it. They put it all in a picnic basket they found in the kitchen, plus a half a loaf of bread and a jar of peanut butter from the fridge, and filled a couple of thermoses with water.

They both went to pack up a few changes of clothes and other necessities, not knowing how long they'd be gone. When Cassandra emerged from the bungalow with an oversized purse on her arm, she had changed into a pair of lightweight trousers and a white blouse, the same thing she'd been wearing the day they'd had their impromptu picnic on the beach. She had a bandana tied around her head and looked jaunty. He smiled approvingly to show her he wanted to be on friendly terms and held the rear door of the car open for her.

"Wait!" Cassandra cried, and ran back into the house, emerging a few minutes later with a newspaper in her hand. She hopped into the back seat, flopping the newspaper in the front.

It was the paper with the picture of Nick at the Brown Derby.

"You never know," she said. "Might come in handy."

He started the car and she leaned forward as she was prone to do now, with her chin resting on her arms on the back of the front seat. Elton could smell her particular fragrance: lavender and lemongrass.

They meandered north through the San Fernando Valley, which was nothing but farms, fields, and arid land, until they connected with

Highway 6. They drove over the San Gabriel Mountains and came down the other side into desert. There were no other cars on the two lane expanse of asphalt that seemed to stretch straight ahead into infinity. He kept glancing at Cassandra in the rear view mirror. She looked hot and uncomfortable, the air blowing in from the open windows like a hair dryer. It was impossible to talk.

After a while, he felt a tap on his shoulder. "Can you pull over?" she yelled over the roar of the wind. He did, and she got out and jumped into the front seat.

"No, no, no," he said. "You can't do that."

She slammed the door with finality. "I can and I will. There's no one out here. If we see a cop, I'll dive into the back seat."

He laughed, imagining her doing such a thing. "It's not just cops you know; some redneck could give us trouble."

"Elton," she said, laying her hand lightly on his. "I would never put you in a compromising position, but I can't stand to ride the whole way out there in the back. I can't talk to you and I'm bored. I tell you what, if we pass any car at all, I'll duck down."

"Okay," he relented, and drove on. After a moment, he spoke. "You mind if I ask you something?"

"No, of course not."

Should he really start this conversation? Finally,

he said, "What was it like—falling in love over and over again each time you traveled to the past?"

She paused before responding. "I think you're exaggerating a bit. Yes, the first time I traveled, I fell in love with Ben. With Thaddeus, it was a little different. More lust than love, if you want to know the truth."

He chuckled. He knew what that was like.

"And with Lauro," she sighed. "Yes, that was true love. Still is. But that's over." Her voice cracked.

His heart tore in two a little. Could he be the one to help her get over Lauro? "And Nick?"

She paused before continuing. "I was never in love with Nick. I thought maybe he and I could have had something real, but...no. Thank god I realized it when I did, though it was too late to avoid his wrath. Thaddeus paid the price for Nick's jealousy, as well as those who died in Italy..."

"Nick is going to get his this time if it's the last thing I do," Elton said under his breath. More loudly, he continued, "I don't want to talk about him though. I want to know more about the others. I've read your publications on your travels; I certainly have a sense, but I want you to tell me things you wouldn't tell the public."

He didn't know why he wanted to torture himself, but, if he was going to be with her someday, if he dreamed of being with her one day, he had to know everything.

"Wow, well, I don't know where to start."

"Start with Ben."

"Ben..." was all she said for a moment. She took a deep breath. "Well, he was beautiful for one thing. I don't generally go for fair complexions, but he was special. He had this sandy, blond hair peppered with gray. His eyes were sea green, but they changed with his mood or the weather—sometimes bright blue, sometimes gray..."

"Like yours." He glanced at her and she smiled.

"Yeah, I guess. He had a compact body, fit and muscular, but he wasn't a big man, or bulky."

"Was he tall?"

"No. Just a little taller than me. Not tall like you."

Somehow this gratified him.

"He was so sweet, too. A real gentleman, like only gentlemen could be in Regency England. He was proper, but not too proper..."

Her voice trailed off, and he hoped she wouldn't go into detail.

"...and such a brilliant musician," she went on. "When he played his violin, my knees went weak."

Elton smiled to himself. He hoped someday she would hear him play the trumpet. She was an accomplished pianist in her own right and he knew how important music was to her. "Do you miss him?"

"No. I'm over him. I realized I was when I went with Evie to 1853 and met his family—Evie's ancestors—after he had died. Meeting the woman that had ultimately become his wife, and their grown children made me able to put his life into context. Obviously, I had a huge impact on him; he named his daughter after me, and his son after my son."

"And then you met Thaddeus Evans."

"Yes. Oh my goodness, he was so charismatic. Not traditionally handsome, really, but had a lot of character in his face. He had such nice, thick brown hair and lovely hazel eyes. And boy, he was tall. He always reminded me a little of pictures I've seen of Ralph Waldo Emerson. He certainly had similar values. What really attracted me to him, though, was his passion and his strong sense of right and wrong. He put his life on the line to help escaped slaves over and over. Yes, he spoke passionately about abolition to many audiences around the country at that time, but it was the action he took that really made the difference."

"I remember you writing that he wanted you to stay with him and help him carry on his work."

"Yes," she laughed. "I was tempted for about half a second if you want to know the truth, Elton, but I never would have. He was so compelling... and sexy...but that life wasn't for me—not to mention the fact that I would never have stayed in the past and left my future life behind. Not for anything. Not even for Lauro."

"Lauro was really the one, wasn't he?"

"Yeah."

Out of the corner of his eye, he saw her turn to look out the window. She wiped a tear from her cheek. He let her have her moment.

Finally, she spoke again. "After Franklin died, I never thought I would love anyone like that again."

"Franklin was an amazing man and a wonderful husband to you."

"And a great father to James. Lauro, I have to say, was an equally amazing man in his own way, though honestly," she laughed now, "he was better looking than Franklin ever was."

Elton swallowed and forced himself to laugh. He was beginning to wish he hadn't started this conversation after all.

She continued, "But I don't really need to tell you about Lauro. You met him; you know."

"Yes, that's true. I'm glad I had the privilege."

They were quiet for a few minutes.

"I wonder how things ultimately went for Evie, living out the rest of her life in the 1800s," Cassandra mused.

"We know she was happy with Caleb because of that painting of hers that surfaced. We know she didn't have any children because she took permanent precautions against that. You can't have a time traveler creating people that never should have existed."

"Or that might end up being their own ancestors."

They both laughed at the thought for a moment though it was rather disturbing.

"Wait a minute," Cassandra said, leaning forward and grabbing the dashboard.

"What!" He looked around to see if there was something on the road he should be aware of.

"I just thought of something. Oh my god!"

"What, what is it?"

"Evie had Japanese ancestors...Japanese American."

"Yeah.... Oh, shit."

"Elton! What if that is Nick's motive? What if Hiro Wakai is Evie's ancestor? Do you think it's possible that Nick found out and that's why he came here? That Hiro, trapped in an internment camp, is a sitting duck?"

He caught on to her train of thought. "Nick started to flip out when you decided to travel back in time with Evie, without him to 'protect you' as he put it. He started becoming irrational at about that point."

"What if," she said, her voice trembling, "he wants to erase Evie from history. If she never existed, I would never have left him to travel to 1853. I would never have met Thaddeus and realized I wasn't happy with Nick—or, at least, his sick mind would tell him that. I would have left him eventually whether I'd made that trip or not, but he must think that he and I started to fall apart because of that trip."

"And if he's successful," said Elton, "not only

would many other people not exist, but we would never have Evie Johnston, one of the greatest artists of her generation. Could he really be that diabolical?"

"You know he can be. He's already proven it. He doesn't care who lives or who dies in the course of history. For god's sake, he was willing to kill William Shakespeare!"

"Goddamn it," Elton growled as he stomped on the accelerator, "what if we're too late?"

"I could be wrong, you know," Cassandra uttered.

"Yeah. But what if you're not?"

The road turned to dirt and the clatter of driving on it made it impossible to talk further. Suddenly, there was a pop, and the car swerved.

"Damn it!" Elton yelled. "We have a flat."

"Oh, crap," Cassandra said as he pulled over to right. "Do you know how to change it? I hate to say it but I haven't got a clue."

"Actually, I do. I'm old enough to have once had a car with rubber tires. Now, let's see if the tools are the same."

"I'm actually old enough too, but I never had one. I'll help if I can though."

"No, that won't do. You'll get dirty. Just stay put. According to the guy I bought the car from though, this will probably be the last tire we can get, due to rationing, so I hope it's the last flat we get too." He jumped out, walked around the car, opened the trunk and peered in. He took out the spare and examined the tools. They looked familiar enough.

He set about changing the tire, finding it more or less intuitive. The only real problem was the heat beating down from the relentless sun. He'd just finished when he saw a car approaching from the way they'd come. "Cassandra," he warned, "get in the back."

She hurried to obey. As the car got closer, Elton spied a light on top. A cop. Great. The car pulled up behind them—highway patrol. An officer got out and approached Elton.

"Can I help you, son?" The officer said in a decidedly unfriendly tone. He was definitely not old enough for Elton to be his "son." He was white, with closely-cropped light blond hair under his hat; red-faced, strong looking.

"Just fixing a flat, officer. I've got it under control."

The officer looked over the Hudson. "This your car?"

"No, sir," Elton replied, hating the tone of subservience that had crept into his voice. "It belongs to my boss." He gestured to Cassandra in the back seat.

She nodded to him. He went around to her window and leaned in. "Really. This is your car and you're that boy's boss."

Elton could see Cassandra's body stiffen. "That's right," she said defensively. "He's my driver."

"What are you two doing out here in the middle

of nowhere?" The officer demanded.

Cassandra paused.

What would she tell him?

"We're going to Manzanar," she replied. "Official business."

Elton flinched. How would she explain that?

The officer laughed, his mouth stretched into a sneer. "Now, what official business could a white lady and a colored boy have at Manzanar?"

Cassandra went to open the door and the officer stepped back. She got out and faced him. Elton wasn't sure that was a good idea.

"I don't believe you have the clearance for that information," she said.

"Listen, little lady," he said, grabbing her arm, "I'm the law out here, and you answer to me."

"Let go of her!" Elton shouted, instinctively moving toward Cassandra.

The cop took a gun from his belt and pointed it at Elton. "Don't take another step!"

Elton halted, seething with frustration.

"Officer," Cassandra said, her voice softening. "There's no need for a ruckus. Let me show you my I.D. Do you mind if I get my purse?"

"I guess not," the officer said, letting go of her.

Elton's heart pounded.

Cassandra reached into the car and pulled out her purse. She extracted her wallet, and took put a blue card, showing it to the officer.

"Strategic Scientific Reserve? What the hell is that?"

"A secret branch of the military, that's what," Cassandra said mysteriously. "See that sticker on the windshield?"

The officer looked. He obviously hadn't noticed it yet.

"Oh," he said.

"That's right. I know you must think it's strange, a woman in such a high government position, but we all have our roles to play in this war, don't we?" She threw him a sexy glance which irked Elton to his soul.

"I...don't know," responded the officer, his brow creased in confusion.

"I suggest you let me and my driver be on our way," she said. "There's a lot at stake here; however, I'm not at liberty to go into detail."

"Uh." The officer thought about it for a moment. "Okay," he said. And then added, puffing up his chest like the hero he thought he was, "Do you want me to escort you?"

"No! I mean, that won't be necessary," she told him.

"Alright then, you have a good day ma'am. But be careful out here. If you didn't have this boy to help you with your tire, you mighta been in a lot of trouble; that is if I hadn't come along." He laid a hand on her shoulder.

"I appreciate it," she said, smiling at him sweetly.

The officer walked back to his car, throwing Elton a dirty look. Elton and Cassandra both got back in the car. Without meaning to, Elton stomped on the gas and the car fish-tailed for a moment before straightening out.

"I'm sorry," Cassandra said from the back seat.

"What are you sorry about?" Elton said more angrily than he meant to. The fact was, he was furious.

"That you had to go through that."

"Well, thank god I had you to rescue me," he spat.

"What's that supposed to mean?" She sat forward and leaned on the back of the front seat.

"That whole femme fatale thing you used on him? Was that really necessary?"

"Look," she said, her voice angry now too. "I did what I had to do. I'm not proud of using feminine wiles but I've done it before to save my ass and I'd do it again. By the way, I saved your ass, too."

"I didn't need saving. I could handle the situation just fine."

"Really? Is that why he pulled a gun on you?"

"You can't know what it's like to be in my shoes," Elton shot.

"No, you're right. I can't. Which is why I apologized. I apologize for the entire white race. But you have to admit, humankind will finally get it right in about a hundred and fifty years. We don't deal with this in our day and age."

"It's just...humiliating," he finally admitted.

"I can well imagine."

"Can you?" His anger flared again, irrational as he knew it might be.

"Well, let me put it this way. You were annoyed at me for using my sexuality with that cop. How humiliating do you think that is for me? How do you think it felt being a second class citizen, meaning, a woman, in every time period I've travelled to? My being strong-willed and independent made me a freak more than once. But it was dangerous for me to behave that way so I learned to curtail it, to be deferential to men. Do you think I liked that? Do you think I like Bogart treating me like an object? Or those boys at the Hollywood Canteen? I've had to get used to it and basically just go along with it. We're not in a very different boat, you and I. Yes, black people may have been on the bottom rung throughout U.S. history, but women were a pretty close second, black women lower than anyone."

He was silent, mulling her words. "I know. You're right," he relented.

"Elton, please," she said quietly. "We're on the same team. We shouldn't be fighting."

"I know," he said again.

She placed a hand on his shoulder, and he took one off the wheel to squeeze it back.

"By the way, what was that card you showed him?" Elton asked.

Laughing, she replied, "During those two weeks while I was waiting for you to come back through the portal and get me, Shannon and I were mulling over what kinds of things a lady would have in her wallet in 1942. She made up a few different things—a driver's license, like you have, a library card...and, just for laughs, she made me an ID card for the Strategic Scientific Reserve—you know like Agent Peggy Carter would have."

"Who?"

"You never watched that old television series? It's from the early twenty-first century. Came from the Marvel comics."

"Um, no. I knew you were a nerd, but..."

She smacked his arm and he laughed.

"Well, good," he said. "It will probably come in handy again."

They sped on toward Manzanar, arriving at the dismal camp around seven PM. Cassandra got out of the car. Newspaper in hand, she walked purposefully past the wooden sign that read "Manzanar War Relocation Center," to the guard gate. Elton could hear the conversation.

"Hello," she said in a friendly voice.

"You lost?" the guard asked gruffly.

"No, actually, I'm looking for someone who might have come by here."

The guard looked her over doubtfully. She flipped the paper open to the picture of Nick and showed it to him. Though he was partially hidden in the photo, one could still make out his face. "This fellow," she said, pointing to Nick.

The guard peered at it carefully by the light of the glaring electric bulb that hung from the ceiling of his station and the waning light of the sun.

"Oh yeah, he did come by. Just left as a matter of fact, about ten minutes ago."

"Damn it!" Cassandra hissed through her teeth. "Do you have any idea where he might have gone?"

"No clue, sorry. He was a government inspector. Had an ID badge, but I couldn't call his name in to headquarters 'cause they're closed today. I let him through—hey, am I in trouble?"

"Oh, no," said Cassandra. "It's just that...I'm afraid he was not with the government. He's an imposter."

"For real? I knew I shouldn't have let him in," the guard grumbled.

"I won't tell anyone," Cassandra said to him. "It's just that...well, if he comes back, do not let him in under any circumstances. As a matter of fact, you should detain him if at all possible."

"Who are you?" The guard wanted to know, glancing over at Elton suspiciously.

"I'm surveilling him for the U.S. Government. He might be a spy." Cassandra said dramatically. Elton saw her take the blue card out of her purse again and flash it at the guard, who peered at it for a moment, brow furrowed.

"They sent you?" he asked doubtfully.

"We all have to do our part during war time, sir," she said with indignation.

The guard glanced over at the car. Elton could see him taking in the X sticker.

"Oh. I see."

"He's unstable," Cassandra continued. "I don't know what he's intending to do here, but he might want to cause one of the...detainees... harm."

"Oh, boy," the guard said, obviously annoyed at himself.

"Well, no harm's been done...yet," she said. "Thank you for your help. Say, what's the nearest town near here where we might be able to find a motel."

He again glanced doubtfully at Elton. "Well, you would have passed Lone Pine on your way here."

"Yes, my driver and I didn't see much there," she indicated Elton.

"You might have more luck in Independence, about another ten miles up the road."

"Thank you."

He nodded to her and she returned to the car, getting into the back seat.

"So, what do we do now?" she asked Elton.

"Let's drive the road alongside the camp. We have to make sure he's not anywhere in the area."

They did, and saw no signs of Nick or his Daimler. Elton had left the binoculars in the glove box of the Hudson so he got them out and scanned the area all around the camp. There were no cars, no people, nothing in the vast desert but the camp itself, the high mountains of the Sierra Nevada looming in the distance, some trees, and a few outcroppings of rock. "I say we come back tomorrow and stake the place out," he said. "He may not be here now, but he might very well come back tomorrow, or even tonight."

"Yeah, he may figure if the guy let him in once, he'll let him in again. Seems he didn't cause any disturbance here though, or the place would be up in arms."

"Do you think he might have gone to one of the nearby towns to get a room for the night?"

"Maybe. But which one? If we knew, we could show the innkeeper the picture. Say he's dangerous. If he's there, maybe they'll lead us to him, then we go back to the plan with the sleep elixir, which I brought, by the way."

"Good thinking. You said you didn't see a motel in Lone Pine?"

"There was only one main street and we drove down it. I didn't see any place to stay there," Cassandra said.

"Then let's go to Independence. Your plan is good. How many motels could there be? We'll go into all of them and show them his picture."

"I think I'll have to do it Elton, if that cop's attitude reflects that of the people around here."

"Oh. Yeah."

"I'm worried about covering all our bases though. If we look for him in Independence, we might miss him coming back here tonight. But if we stay here, we might miss him there."

"I have an idea," Elton said. "Let's, I mean, you, go and ask around about him at the motels there. Also bars, restaurants, wherever. If we don't find him, maybe we should come back here and park on the road next to the camp for the night. Stake the place out."

"Okay. If that's the case, we're gonna need some coffee."

Chapter Twenty-two

Hiro Wakai – June 26th, 1942

Today after our acting class, Kanako walked with me to the mess hall. We chatted about little things: movies we'd seen and liked, books we'd read. We didn't talk about the war or the camp. We didn't complain about the food or the lodgings. Something about Kanako seems to rise above this place. Her dresses are simple and light, but she wears them with grace. While everyone else is sweating, she looks cool. She wears her hair in a long braid down her back. Of course, the women here don't have much to style their hair with, but I notice that most still attempt to wear it in the fashion of the day. Kanako does not, and she's all the more beautiful for it. She doesn't laugh easily, but she smiles a lot.

She asked me what it's like being an actor in Hollywood, something I hadn't wanted to talk about before because the loss of my career is devastating to me, but I told her a little bit about it. She had just finished her first two years of college when they sent her and her family here, and she hopes to return when this is all over. She said she was studying marine biology and wants to be a scientist, studying ocean creatures. This fascinates me. I don't think I've ever known anyone as smart as she is. I know it's ridiculous to say I'm falling in love with her, but I can't deny it's happening. She is loveliness itself. She is beauty in the very essence of the word.

Cassandra and Elton had no luck finding Nick in Independence. There were only two small motels, and the person on duty in each said no one had checked in all day. There was only one restaurant, and one bar, which was closed. Cassandra asked in the restaurant, but no one had seen him. She had one of the thermoses filled with coffee and then they drove back to the camp. She told the guard they would park on the side road in case Nick showed up.

"I'm gonna have to call Mr. Merritt, the camp director. He's not here now, but I can't okay this on my own."

They waited while he phoned his boss. It seemed like a long time before the phone picked up on the other end. The guard explained the situation but the conversation was brief and hurried. Elton thought that maybe they hadn't made clear the gravity of the situation. They probably just seemed like a couple of nut cases to these people.

"Alright," the guard said after he'd hung up. "I'll alert the next guy on duty, who works the graveyard shift. I'll let the tower guards know too, and give him that fellow's description. I'll also tell 'em that you two will be staked out over there on the road in a Hudson."

They thanked him, and made their way to the road that ran along the south side of the camp, stationing themselves just off the shoulder where they could take in the full sweep of the area.

Cassandra prepared for a sleepless night. They ate some of the chicken Elton had brought and the cold macaroni and cheese. She ate an apple for dessert, and sipped the hot, bitter coffee. The desert had started cooling off by the time they'd first arrived at the camp that evening, and now it was growing cold. They sat in the front seat together, covered by the couple of blankets Elton had stowed in the trunk.

As darkness crept in, floodlights illuminated the camp. Cassandra wondered how the prisoners could sleep with all that light. Her heart went out to these people, held against their will for no reason whatsoever. Though the American government didn't purposefully harm or kill the Japanese who were detained there, were they really that much better than the Germans who were imprisoning the Jews? She had read enough about the Japanese internment camps to know that these people suffered many humiliations: waiting in long lines to bathe and eat, living in cramped and dirty quarters with hordes of other people and virtually no privacy, toiling long hours in the heat at various kinds of manual labor—most of their belongings left behind and then lost or confiscated. Though the prisoners ultimately managed to create some modicum of civilization at Manzanar, growing vegetables and orchards; learning skills such as carpentry, sewing, and English (though many already spoke fluently, being American citizens to begin with); families and individuals were released from the camps at the end of the war with no more than twenty-five dollars and nothing to return to. So many left behind homes they owned, businesses...entire lives and livelihoods, never to recoup those losses again. It was such a blow that many, especially the older people, would never recover from the trauma of those camps and the loss of so much.

Cassandra and Elton spoke of it for a while until they grew sad, then they fell quiet. Sleep began to overtake her in spite of the coffee. Against her will, her eyes closed.

"Cassandra," Elton said.

She opened her eyes.

"I need to tell you something."

She was awake now. "What is it?"

"I don't know how to say it."

"You can tell me anything, Elton."

"It's just that...I've been feeling so close to you since we've been here together, you know, here, in 1942."

"I feel closer to you too," she said softly. Was he going to say what she hoped he was?

He leaned in closer to her. "What I mean is that, oh god, I don't know how to say this. I mean that, I have feelings for you, and I have for quite a long time."

She didn't know how to reply.

He went on. "Jeannine may have picked up on it while we were still together. I'm not saying it's why she left me, but it may be why a distance began to grow between us, I mean, besides the physical distance my work required."

"Elton..."

"You don't have to say anything. I'm sorry. I shouldn't have spoken. I know you're still in love with Lauro. We can just forget I said anything. I don't want things to be awkward between us, and I never want to lose you as a friend."

She reached down and took his hand. "I wish you would have said something before. How long have you been feeling like this?"

"I think...I think since before you went on your first time journey."

"That long? Five years ago?" *How can this be? He's hidden it so well!*

"Yes. I'm an idiot. I'm sorry."

"You don't have to be sorry. Of course you couldn't have told me. You were still married. But, I suppose if I had known, I might have done things differently."

"What do you mean?"

"Elton, I've had a crush since the moment I met you." She was able to express now what she realized she'd always felt. "I just passed it off as a student crush for a professor and ignored it as much as I could. These things happen you know; you can't always control who you're attracted to..."

"You're attracted to me?"

She laughed lightly. "Well, of course! Who wouldn't be?"

"I—I don't know what to say."

"But you were married; I married Franklin...I just pushed it aside. There was no other choice. And yet, after Franklin died, maybe I wouldn't have been so, you know, ready to fall for the men that I became involved with on those journeys if I had known how you felt—"

"No. I wouldn't have wanted you to do things differently. Those experiences were important to your journeys. I wouldn't have wanted you not to."

"But that must have been hard on you, seeing me fall in love with other men, and then writing about it, telling you about it! Oh my gosh, how I've been going on about Lauro!"

"It's okay, Cassie," he said, squeezing her hand. "I wanted to be there for you."

"Let me tell you this," she said returning the squeeze, "though I will always love Lauro, I can't be in love with him anymore. I'm letting those feelings go."

"Is it that easy?"

"No, of course not, but now I can see that the reality of being with you far outweighs carrying around memories of a man who is forever gone to me."

"Don't rush it, Cassie. I can be patient."

"Elton, you are amazing."

"No, I'm not. I'm just a boy, standing in front of a girl…"

She giggled. It was a line from an old movie they both liked. "Oh, Elton." She put her hand on his face. He looked at her softly with his dark brown eyes. He was one of the most handsome, brilliant men she had ever known. She was flattered and happy.

He moved closer still. She closed her eyes and his lips met hers. She opened her mouth slightly and the kiss intensified. She moved into his arms as he drew them around her. Passion flared within her breast. He pressed his mouth to hers with more urgency. The kiss took over her whole being. She was on fire for him.

He was the one to finally pull away. "We better not," he said gently.

"You're right," she said, though she didn't want him to stop. She moved a few inches away. "We better stay focused."

He chuckled. "Yeah."

They both turned to look toward the camp. There was no movement there. The guards on top of their towers seemed motionless. As night turned into early morning, sleep overcame them.

Chapter Twenty-three

Hiro Wakai – June 27th, 1942

I tell you, it feels like these people are watching everything we do. Guards watch us from towers, inspectors come through our barracks, and through the mess hall. We have no privacy. If, for a moment, like when I'm with Kanako, I forget that I'm in a concentration camp, I'm reminded every time some jerk barges into the barracks at three in the morning, shining a flashlight in our eyes, or whenever I walk across the compound with a rifle pointed in my direction.

There's been one good development though—Pop decided he was fed up with the food and went to volunteer as a cook. I went with him, since his English isn't great. I told them he ran one of the most popular restaurants in Little Tokyo, and has experience cooking for a lot of people. I just came back from dinner now, his first time cooking, and what a difference! Though he doesn't have all the ingredients he would normally use, and so can't really cook food in the way we're used to, the rice was steamed to perfection, the vegetables were crisp and flavorful, and he managed to tenderize the meat and disguise it so that it was at least palatable. One of my mother's friends asked her to bring him out of the kitchen, and when she did, everyone stood and bowed reverently to him. He bowed in return, and tears came to his eyes. Mom cried. I think this is a turning point for him. Maybe now, he will not feel so hopeless. To have purpose is all he really needs.

The sun was high in the sky when Cassandra jolted awake. "Elton!" she exclaimed. He woke with a start. "We were asleep!"
He looked at his watch. "It's just after ten. Damn it!"
"I don't think Nick has shown up. The guards are on the alert. We would know."
"Good point."
"Want some gum?" She reached into her purse and pulled out two minty sticks.
"Thanks," he said, taking it from her with a chuckle. He unwrapped it and popped it into his mouth.
"Now for a bathroom of some kind," she said. She looked around and spotted a clump of small trees not far off that might shield her.
"Here, take a blanket," he said, "you could sort of hide under it."
"Good idea." She went, and then he did.
After that, they stood outside the car for a few minutes, stretching their legs.
"It's hot already," she observed, wondering how they were going to broach the topic of what had happened between them the night before.
"And it's going to get hotter as the day goes on. We're going to need more water. I'll walk to the guard station and ask to fill our thermoses up.

They must have a spigot there somewhere." He poured the last of the coffee from the one thermos, grabbed the other, and headed off down the road.

She got back in the car, rolling all the windows down. There was very little breeze. She picked up the binoculars and scanned the length of the camp, seeing nothing but prisoners going about their dismal routine. Then she scanned the desert in every direction. There was nothing there but sand, rocks, and a few shrubs. Far beyond the other side of the camp was a large rock outcropping, big enough, it occurred to her, for a car to hide behind. She observed it with the binoculars for a while, but nothing stirred. Only the occasional bird flitted by, and one tumbleweed rolled along by the fence of the camp.

She was hungry. She ate another piece of chicken, saving two for Elton, another apple, and made herself a half of a peanut butter sandwich, regretting she hadn't waited for Elton to come back with the water.

Soon, he returned and let her know there was another guard on duty who had been filled in on their presence by the one from the night before. No one had shown up at the camp at all that day so far, the guard had said, but he had given Elton a walkie-talkie so they could communicate if necessary. He opened the door and laid it on the seat, and then said, "Here, give me your bandana."

She suddenly realized her hair must be a mess. She checked the mirror on the visor, and gave her hair a shake, revitalizing her curls. Her wavy, Veronica Lake hairstyle had long since disappeared due to the wind and having been slept on, and was now reverting to its usual, shoulder length crop of spirally tresses. She touched up her sparse makeup from what she carried in her purse and popped another piece of gum in her mouth.

Elton was pouring water onto her bandana. He then squeezed it out and handed it back to her. "Tie it back on your head," he said. "It will keep you cool."

Using the mirror, she repositioned the wet bandana on her head so that it at least still looked halfway decent. Elton moistened his handkerchief and laid it on the back of his neck. He got in the car with her and she made him eat.

"What if he doesn't show up?" she wondered out loud. "I mean; how long can we hold out here?"

"That's a good question," Elton replied. "At least we can feel fairly certain he doesn't know we're here. If he was snooping around yesterday without success, I think he'll probably try it again today. This time though, the guard is on the alert. Hopefully, he'll be able to hold him, and turn him over to us."

"I think I'll be able to persuade the guy that Nick is supposed to be in my care."

Elton turned to her. "I think it's safe to assume

Nick won't be detained easily. He likely has a weapon, and we know he won't hesitate to use it."

Cassandra's stomach knotted up. Does this plan make any sense? "I wish we had something more powerful than sleep elixir."

"We do." Elton opened the glove compartment and showed her the pistol.

Cassandra gasped. "Where did you get that?'

"Compton. When you were off with Bogart. You're not mad?"

She hesitated before replying. "No. Maybe under other circumstances I would be, but we need to make sure we get Nick this time, no matter what. I don't want to kill him but—"

"We may have no choice," Elton agreed.

The yoga class Suhan took every day was drawing to a close, and she and the others were lying in Savasana, or corpse pose. She tried to let her busy thoughts evaporate and her body completely relax as was the point of the asana. She had always found this aspect of yoga the most difficult. She liked the exercise part of it—liked that it made her body stronger and more flexible, but mastering the meditation was a challenge for someone like her, whose mind was always racing at a million miles an hour.

In the next room, music was playing. There was a ballroom dance class that happened in the room next door to yoga. Suhan had tried it, but didn't like dancing exclusively with women. The song that was playing was familiar. She focused on it and, as recognition sparked, her mind flooded with memories. It was "Sweet Georgia Brown," and they were probably using it to learn the Charleston, as the rhythmic stomping of feet indicated. She had done that dance too, with Nick. He had taught her in their Parisian pied-a-terre, the both of them laughing as she fumbled her way through the steps at first, the Victrola playing that very same song. And they had danced to it at the Bricktop Club, with Louis Armstrong himself on trumpet. On one of those nights they had met Josephine Baker, and Nick, in his sneaky way, had asked her if she'd met Elton Carver in New York. She had, of course, and Nick knew it because Suhan had told him. It wasn't supposed to be general knowledge that Carver had come close to having an affair with the young dancer, but there was nothing Suhan wouldn't tell Nick. Baker was clearly heartbroken that Mr. Carver, as she called him, had left town, never to return after his month of hobnobbing at the Cotton Club, where she often performed, as well as at other clubs in Harlem. The poor thing had fallen hard. Nick drew out her tears as she spoke of him. He was like a cat toying with a wounded bird. Why hadn't Suhan seen how despicable he was?

She hadn't seen it because Nick kept her high on passion, excitement and "love." The man became like a drug to her. They roamed Paris together like royalty. He bought her the most expensive clothes during the two months they were there, designed just for her by the likes of Coco Chanel and Jean Patou. He bought her jewels, all of which she still had, squirreled away in a safe deposit box, worth a fortune by today's standards though she hadn't been able to get to them since she'd stored them there. He held court in their beautiful apartment in Montparnasse, entertaining Django Reinhardt, Gertrude Stein, Ezra Pound, F. Scott and Zelda Fitzgerald, Isadora Duncan, Hemingway, and more with champagne and caviar and the wittiest of conversation. Nick was smart; he was educated; he could keep up with the greatest intellectuals on the topics of art, music, literature, philosophy, and world affairs. Suhan was always checking herself on these occasions, worried she would make some reference that was anachronistic for 1925. So she mostly kept quiet, smiling and serving drinks. She was beautiful—she knew that—and her Turkish heritage exotic to those people. With her black hair cut short in a bob, smoky eyeliner, raspberry-colored lipstick, and the elegant flapper-style clothes which suited her slim body as if she were made to exist in that era, she was a sensation in her own right.

And when those parties would end, at four or five in the morning, he'd take her to bed and make love to her with the ultimate expertise. Her body tingled through and through as she lay there on her mat thinking about it. Her counselor was right. She wasn't completely free of his spell, but she was hoping Mark Stein would help with that in more than one way: both by eliminating Nick from existence, and by fulfilling her physical needs. He wasn't the lover Nick was, but he could be trained.

She joined the other students in a seated pose, did three last, deep-cleansing breaths, and uttered Namaste to the instructor. She stood and rolled up her mat, placing it in the bin with the others. She went to the yard to clear her head. This was not some dismal, concrete enclosure surrounded with a chain-link fence, topped by barbed-wire, like you saw in old-time movies and shows. It was more of a garden, with a vast green lawn for exercising, a stream, a pond, flowers, and low trees. It was surrounded by a tall cedar fence, slatted so one could see through but not get out. The security was there, it just wasn't obvious, which gave the inmates a sense of freedom. She looked up at the clear, blue June sky. Where was Nick right now, a hundred and eighty or so years in the past, and what was he doing? Equally important, where was Mark, and was he having success? She wouldn't know until he came back—if he came back. If he didn't, she would have to assume that Nick had turned the tables on him somehow, adding him to the list of his victims. Suhan said a silent prayer to Allah for Mark. He had to succeed. He just had to.

Chapter Twenty-four

Hiro Wakai – June 28th, 1942

Just a short entry because I'm feeling annoyed. I was spending some extra time working with Kanako on the scene she was doing with Mr. Matsuda so they could be ready to do it in class tomorrow. Some guy barged in asking me questions like he owned the place. It really riled me too because Mr. Matsuda was finally starting to get it, but the interruption threw him off and then we had to start all over, and the second time he fumbled and stammered and the whole scene was ruined. But then really, why should I be surprised that these people feel they can disrupt anything we're doing anytime they feel like it? They've already upended our lives through no fault of our own. The acting class, or any of the activities they have us doing are nothing but ways to distract us from the reality of our situation. We are animals, no better. We are kept in a large cage, fed, and our basic needs tended to, but we are just like creatures in a zoo—maybe not even as well off because at least people like the animals in a zoo. We are reviled and mistrusted. It's everything I can do to not fall into complete despair but I have to stay strong for my parents. And then, of course, there's the other thing that keeps me going in spite of everything, and that is Kanako.

One other thing, I finished translating Pop's memoir.

Now, it's a matter of telling him, and praying he won't be angry with me. Reading about his early life with my mother has made me feel closer to both of them— like I know them in a way I never could before. I hope he'll understand.

After Nick's encounter with Wakai in the classroom, he drove to Lone Pine, since it was the closer of the two small towns nearby, had a meal, got some extra food packed up to go, and then, once it was dark, drove back to Manzanar, cutting his lights before he was in sight of the camp. He wanted to be in position well ahead of time—to keep an eye on the camp in case anything changed. He could not miss the opportunity to do what he'd come here to do.

He slowly drove past the fenced-in area, into the desert. By moonlight, he found his way to the large stand of rocks he had observed earlier in the day. It was like a small hill, really— wide enough to park his car behind and have it completely hidden from the guards at the camp. He slept comfortably on the wide back seat of the Daimler, awakening in the morning as the interior of the car began to heat. He opened the windows, took a piss against the rocks, and ate some food. Then, he found a position within the mound of rocks from where he could observe the camp and all its surroundings, using the powerful scope on his rifle. Ideally, he would have brought a far superior instrument from the future, but he hadn't known he was going to have to shoot his target from so far away. As it was, it had taken several days and a lot of bribery to find this black market, military grade sniper rifle, an M1 Garand, scope attached. He wished he hadn't had to waste those days but it would have taken more time and would have been riskier to go back through his portal again to get the rifle he really wanted, the kind he had given the shooter he'd employed in Siena, Italy, when he'd had the winner of the Palio horse race killed. That had been a beautiful plan to start with, he mused, his mind wandering. Too bad it had been foiled by that idiot candidate for mayor, Franco Marino who'd ratted Nick out. All Nick had wanted to do was to screw things up for Cassandra and her lover, Lauro, that Italian prick, and yet, his plan had failed. He'd found everything out from Suhan...the beautiful Suhan who had been under his spell for years. She would have done...did do...anything for him. Well, she'd ended up in jail, and he'd gotten away scot-free. He'd get away this time too.

He snapped back to the present moment. When all this was said and done, and when Hiro Wakai was dead, the past would be neatly rearranged just the way he wanted it. He laughed softly to himself at the thought. He was just a day or two away from a whole new life in which not even he would be aware of what he had done to make it that way. He went back to the car and dozed for a while—there was no need to remain alert for the moment. He had plenty of time before he needed to be in position—until almost five o'clock before he would need to take action. He sat back and did what he always did when he had some time to kill—watched the video of Cassandra on his wristwatch, a special instrument he'd had made to look like those they wore in the forties, but with modern-day technology inside. He had taken the video a few years ago, during the glorious time when they were together and she had loved him. It served as an entertainment device when he got bored with the limited media available to him in this era. Did these people know how uncivilized they were, even with all their glamour and finery?

He switched it on. It was the only footage he had of her. He'd shot it during the summer they'd taken a vacation to Maine for a week. They had been hiking along the shores of the Bay of Fundy and she decided to go swimming. It was growing dark and there was no one around so she stripped down to nothing and dove in. He stayed on the shore. He didn't like to swim. Without her knowing, he filmed her with his palm-link as it automatically enhanced the light. She was an excellent swimmer—did several rigorous laps back and forth, all of which he caught in close up. Then she began to frolic. As the sun set, she dove in and out of the gentle undulations of the waves like a mermaid. Her hair fell across her shoulders like strands of golden sea plants. Her breasts, wet with the salt water, glimmered in the rose color of the setting sun. The shape of her hips and derriere shone like a luminous white lily. This went on for at least a half an hour and he had caught it all, surreptitiously closing the palm link as she emerged, like a goddess, from the bay. Then, they made love on the shore. Now, in the back seat of the car, he gave in to the usual urge he experienced when watching the video and remembering their exquisite coupling.

After another brief nap, he went back to the rocks and scanned the camp. The rifle's scope was so powerful he could easily make out the faces of each prisoner. They were boring to look at though, and there was no point trying to find Wakai now in that mass of people. Nick raised his scope to take in the desert beyond the camp. He noticed there was a vehicle parked along the road on the opposite side of the fenced enclosure. It was a nice car; a Hudson maybe? There appeared to be two people inside, but not even his powerful scope could make them out clearly. It was possibly a man and a woman, but they were in shadow and he couldn't tell anything more about them. What were they doing there? It was odd that a car would be parked there in the heat of the day. He glanced at his watch. It was two o'clock. Less than three hours to go.

He watched the car for a while, but nothing changed. The people did not emerge. It was becoming too hot to stay poised within the rocks much longer. He went back to his own car and settled down into its hot, but at least shady, interior. He had brought plenty of water, and kept himself relatively cool by pouring it on his handkerchief and laying it on his head. He let himself doze again. He had set the alarm on his watch for four-thirty. He'd need to be sure he was alert and in place well before Wakai would be heading to his classroom.

Around two-thirty, Cassandra scanned the camp and the surrounding desert with the binoculars for what seemed like the hundredth time that day. Both she and Elton had been taking turns looking, but nothing had changed. Suddenly, she saw a glint from the rock formation far on the other side of the camp. She took the binoculars from her eyes and looked again. "Elton, take a look at that hill of rocks over there. I thought I saw something." She pointed toward it.

He took the binoculars and looked. "I don't see anything."

He handed them back and she looked again. She scanned the rocks over and over, from top to bottom, side to side, for about fifteen minutes, but whatever she'd seen was gone. She sighed, and stepped out of the car to stretch her legs, then made another visit to her make-shift latrine. How long could they keep this vigil up? The sun was beating down and, though she was always covered with a layer of sunscreen she'd brought from the future in a carefully disguised bottle, it was way too much for her red-headed complexion. She got back in the car.

"I'm so hot," she complained.

"Yeah. It's getting bad." He took the gum he'd been chewing out of his mouth, put the tiny ball back into its wrapper, and set it in the car ashtray. "I think we should wait at least until the end of the day. If he doesn't go back by the guard station in the front, and if we don't see any sign of him out here, I think we'll have to give up and assume he's changed his plan, whatever it was."

"Hmph, it's not like Nick to give up so easily."

"I agree. For all we know, he's gone back through his portal, wherever it might be, to regroup. Maybe he's decided to kill off another of Evie's ancestors. It would only take one."

"Oh, this is so frustrating!" Cassandra cried. "If he's successful in obliterating Evie and changing the past, he changes so many things. You and I will suddenly not even be here, in this moment. We'll just suddenly be back in the future, living some alternate life, without even knowing what happened. I might even be with him, if that's what he wants to happen." She shuddered just thinking about it.

Elton put his hand on her leg. "I don't think, even if that were to happen, that I would give up the idea of being with you. Jeannine and I would still have broken up for the same reasons and, if I saw that Nick was not right for you—and nothing would ever change his basic personality—I would try to do something about it."

She looked into his eyes. "Are you serious about wanting to be with me, Elton?"

"I am. Would you want that? Could you want that?"

She nodded. "Since last night, I've been wondering if we've been meant to be together all along, despite Lauro, despite Ben, despite any of it."

He leaned in and kissed her. His lips were cool. His breath tasted of the minty gum.

Suddenly, Lauro seemed like a beautiful dream, a dream that was over, and that she could put away in a small place in her heart, like a picture in a locket. She could treasure it now as the memory it was. He'd lived five hundred years in the past, and she was never going to go back there again. Finally, that felt just fine to her. She wrapped her hand around the back of Elton's neck and kissed him again.

Chapter Twenty-five

Hiro Wakai – June 28th, 1942

It's late…nearly midnight, but I had to make one more journal entry today because the day has been salvaged, and so much more. Kanako and I met after supper tonight and took a walk together around the compound. It's hardly the most romantic place to be together when you feel like you have eyes on you all the time, but what choice do we have? The thing is, our surroundings didn't matter. All I saw was Kanako and I know all she saw was me. We talked and talked. She told me about her studies and how fascinating life under the sea is to her. I can understand that. The ocean is still such a mystery to we humans, and yet a place of such overwhelming beauty.

One thing I really like about her is that she's not at all star-struck when I talk about my work even though she likes movies. She sees the people like Humphrey Bogart, Veronica Lake, Bette Davis and some of the other stars I've worked with just as people doing their job to entertain the public—which is exactly the right way to think of them because that's all they really are.

We talked about what we would do when we finally are released from this nightmare. If I'm not mistaken, the conversation seemed to veer towards ways in which we might find ourselves in proximity to each other in the future. She goes to UCLA and, hopefully, if I return to acting, I'll be in Hollywood most of the time. I think there's definitely a way to make our lives interconnect.

I finally walked her back to her barracks. The camp was mostly deserted. And even though bright lights shine down on the buildings all night long, I spotted a shadow and pulled her in. Then I kissed her. She melted into me. We didn't stay there long—if her father got wind of her fraternizing with a man, I'm sure there would be hell to pay. We said goodnight, as our hands lingered in each other's. It's official: I'm in love.

This time, it was Elton who caught a glint of something out of the corner of his eye. It was now four-thirty. He and Cassandra had fallen asleep in each other's arms, but had woken a few minutes before. He grabbed the binoculars and looked toward where it had come from: that large stand of rocks in the distance.

"What is it?" she wanted to know. "Do you see something?"

"You were right. Something is glinting over there. It can't be water. There isn't a drop around here anywhere."

Sure enough, the faint flash of light came again and Elton fastened the sights of the binoculars on it. It was round, like a lens. "Cassie. There's something there."

"What should we do?"

"If that's Nick; we don't want to arouse suspicion. We don't want to scare him off; we want to trap him." He picked up the walkie-talkie and pushed a button, causing it to crackle to life.

"Elton Carver, here, the driver for Mrs. Reilly. We think we've spotted something—over."

"I'm not hearing anything from my guards—over," the static-y voice returned.

Elton said to Cassandra, "Those guard stations are only two stories high and that hill of rocks is too high and too far away for them to see over." He pushed the button and spoke again. "We think it's worth investigating. What we're seeing is light bouncing off something that could be a lens. Could be a camera, could be a telescope, could be the scope of a rifle, behind the hill of rocks north of the camp—over."

"We'll send someone to investigate—over."

"If that's Nick, and he sees someone coming," Cassandra began, "he'll bolt. We've got to get over there so that if he does take off, we'll be able to close in on him. We've got to make sure he ends up in our custody."

Elton engaged the walkie-talkie again. "The man is under Mrs. Reilly's jurisdiction. Let us investigate first. We'll call for back up if we need it—over."

"Roger—over and out," was the reply.

"This could get dangerous."

"I'm ready," she said, looking him in the eye.

He started the engine and eased onto the road, driving slowly back toward the main highway. Once at the intersection, he turned right, so that now they were driving past the turn-off that led to the guard station and the front gates of Manzanar. He continued to drive at a moderate pace, but not too slowly, so as to not to appear like anything was out of the ordinary. Cassandra continued to scan the hill of rocks with the binoculars. The road veered away from the outcropping, but she kept her eyes trained on it.

As they passed it, though it was farther off now than before, she shouted, "There's a car parked out there, Elton! It's behind the rocks. I can just see it now! That's the car Nick was driving before —that Bonnie and Clyde car!"

"Hang on!" he cried, wishing for the life of him that there were seatbelts in the vehicle. He peeled off into the desert, leaving the road, and headed full speed toward the car that was now visible to him too. The Hudson bounced and jolted over rocks and ruts but the thing was as sturdy as a tank. He hoped to god the tires would hold out.

There was a flash from the out-cropping and the sound of a gun-shot. Cassandra shrieked.

"Son of a bitch!" Elton yelled.

"We're still here, Elton, we're still here!" Cassandra screamed over the noise of the car. "He must have missed Hiro!"

"Or we're wrong about his motives..." He held onto the steering wheel with all his might, punching the clutch with his left foot as he shifted, pushing the huge car as fast as it would go while watching out for rocks, shrubs, and dips in the terrain.

Cassandra was managing to hold the binoculars up to her eyes. "I see him! I see him!" she cried. "He sees us. He's climbing down the rocks."

Was the Hudson fast enough to catch him?

"He's getting in the car!"

"Call for back-up," he said. "We've got to head him off."

She grabbed the walkie-talkie. "We need help!" she yelled into it. "He's getting away! Over!"

"Roger that. Sending reinforcements—over and out," the voice squawked on the other end of the phone.

She scrambled for the binoculars again as the car bounced and jolted her around on the front seat. Nick's car peeled across the desert in a cloud of dust. Elton pushed the Hudson as fast as it could go on the uncertain terrain. They were gaining on Nick but were still too far to shoot out one of his tires. One of their own hit a rut and sent them both bouncing. Cassandra nearly hit the roof. She shrieked.

"Hold onto the armrest," he yelled. "Forget the binoculars. We don't need them now." She grabbed onto whatever she could to keep from flying around the car. The windows were open and dust was filling the interior.

Nick headed around the east side of the camp, the one farthest from the guard station, toward the road where they had been staked out earlier. Elton followed, gaining every minute, thanking

God for the powerful engine on the car.

As Nick's Daimler approached the road, a military jeep sped toward him from the other direction.

"Here they come!" Cassandra cried. She grabbed the walkie-talkie and yelled into it. "Tell them not to shoot to kill! Over!"

"They'll do what they have to do. Over—" the voice on the other end acknowledged.

"Crap!" she exclaimed. "I don't want him dead!" she said to Elton. "I want him to face justice for his crimes!"

Elton said nothing. They'd thought Nick was dead once; what difference would it make if he died for real this time? The world would be better off without him. They were closing in now.

"I'm going to try for a tire!" he yelled to Cassandra.

"Let me do it," she returned. She grabbed the gun and aimed it out the window.

There was a bang, and a cloud of dust erupted from just behind the Daimler.

"Damn it!" she said.

"Try again," he urged.

She fired again, and this time the bullet pinged off the right rear fender.

The rear window of Nick's car suddenly blew out and a small explosion blasted the dirt just in front of the Hudson. Cassandra screamed.

"Get down!" Elton yelled.

She ducked onto the floor.

"He's got a handgun," Elton cried. "He shot out his own window!"

Cassandra was gasping for breath. At least she was safer on the floor.

The army jeep sped toward Nick. They would head him off. He'd have no choice but to surrender now. "They've got him, Cassie!" he said to her. "I think they've got him. Stay down!"

A shot was fired from the jeep, and returned by Nick.

"Shit!"

The Daimler now veered off the road and into the desert, heading away from the camp. The jeep followed, as did Elton. Cassandra clutched at the seat, still crouched on the floor.

Another shot came from the jeep. The windshield of the Daimler shattered. It spun around, out of control, then hit something, a large rock perhaps, and flipped into the air and onto its side.

"What happened?" Cassandra shouted, crawling back up onto the seat.

"They hit him."

"Oh my god." She was on the seat now, looking at the wreck.

The soldiers closed in from one side and Elton's vehicle approached from the other, skidding to a stop near the upside-down car. Nick was trying to scramble out of the passenger side-window.

"Stop right there," a soldier yelled, leaping from the jeep and taking aim.

Nick fired and he went down.

"Stay here!" Elton called to Cassandra as he jumped out of the car, pistol aimed at Nick.

Nick turned at the sound of Elton's voice and pointed his gun at him. Elton hesitated, but a ready soldier did not. There was a gunshot and Nick clutched at his chest, slumping back into the car.

Elton, the soldier who had fired, and his comrade cautiously crept up on the Daimler, guns drawn. Another attended to the fallen soldier who appeared to be hit in the arm. More military vehicles sped toward them.

"Be careful!" Cassandra called to Elton.

He nodded, gun at the ready. He was taking no chances. Nick was nothing if not wily.

The soldiers got to the car first and began examining the situation. "We need a medic, over—" one of them said into his walkie-talkie.

Elton decided to let them handle the situation for the moment, but stood close by, ready to do whatever was necessary to make sure Nick couldn't escape now. It didn't look like that was going to happen. Two soldiers gingerly lifted the limp man up and out of the passenger side window. Blood had soaked through his shirt. The soldiers laid him carefully on the ground as Elton approached. Nick had no gun now; it must have fallen from his grasp. His eyes were closed. He looked pale and small. But was he still alive? Elton bent down and felt for a pulse. It was there, but just barely. Before he knew it, Cassandra was beside him.

"Is he dead?" she asked softly.

"Not yet," Elton replied, not sure what else to say.

Cassandra bent down in the dust next to Nick. As if sensing her presence, his eyes fluttered open.

"Cassandra," he croaked. He reached out a hand for her but she pulled away. "Cassandra," he repeated. "You came to me."

"I came to find out what you were up to. And to stop you. I guess we did if we're still here. Was it Hiro Wakai you were after?" Her voice was shaking.

"I did it for you." His voice was barely audible. "It was only for you."

"That's what you always say," she replied. "But it's not for me. It's for you. You don't care about me. You just want to possess me."

"I love you."

"No, you don't."

He looked into her eyes. Elton shivered with disgust. But then a darkness settled behind Nick's pupils and he stared straight ahead, lifeless. Elton took his pulse again. "He's gone."

"Are you sure?" Cassandra asked. She was trembling.

"Yes." He closed the dead man's eyes.

"What if he's taken nano-healers?'

"He probably has. But that can't fix a hole in his heart. He's gone, Cassandra. He's gone for sure this time."

"I wish we could have brought him back with us."

"I know. But that would have been hard to do and he might have gotten away again. Or worse, hurt one of us. It's better this way, Cassie, I hate to say it, but it is."

"I guess you're right," she said softly.

The soldier who'd killed Nick came close. "I know you said not to shoot to kill, but we didn't have a choice."

Elton stood and looked him in the eye. Cassandra rose too and was staring at him.

"You saved my life," Elton said to him. "Thank you." He put his hand out to shake and the soldier took it. Then Elton had a thought. "We need to confiscate his weapons," he said. Without waiting for a reply, he stalked over to the Daimler. As tall as he was, he could open the door on the side that was facing up. The rifle and the pistol were on the floor of the front seat. He grabbed them. One was authentic to the day, the other was not, and would raise questions among anyone who examined it. He quickly looked around and didn't see any other weapons. There was a thermos, some clothes and some trash, but that was all. He grabbed a shirt and wrapped the rifle in it; the pistol he stuck in his pocket. The trunk had flown open upon impact so Elton took a quick look there. It was empty save for a spare tire.

"Sir," the other soldier called to him. "I'm not sure we should disturb the scene any further..." Just then, the walkie-talkie on his belt cracked to life.

"We have two casualties among the evacuees," the voice on the other end said. "Repeat. Two casualties. Over—"

Cassandra gasped, but didn't take her eyes off the soldier who had killed Nick.

He seemed disconcerted by her gaze. "I think we need a superior officer here," he said. "I'll go get him."

The other soldier was still on his walkie-talkie. "We have a man down too, but he'll make it. We'll need another medic truck. Over—"

"Do they have the names of the...evacuees...that were hurt?" she anxiously asked him as Elton walked back toward them.

"I'm not sure they'll release that information to you, ma'am," he said. "You'll need to go see Mr. Merritt. He's the man in charge. He's going to want to talk to you."

"Yes, of course," said Cassandra, wiping her face with the back of her hand.

"I'll turn these over to your superior, soldier," Elton said, indicating the weapons.

The young man nodded.

"Let's go," Elton said to Cassandra.

As they walked toward the Hudson, Elton saw a large crowd of prisoners staring at the scene of the accident through the chain link fence. More people were running around in the background, medical vehicles making their way through the throng. He looked at Cassandra. Her cheeks were wet.

"Elton," she whispered, "what if he got Hiro?"

"Like you said, we're still here."

"But someone was hurt…or killed." She was crying.

He wished he could take her in his arms.

"I feel sick," she continued.

"I do too. I have to admit; I wanted Nick to die. I've never felt that way about anybody in my life and I'm not proud of it. I don't like feeling vengeful. I wish we could have brought him back alive and made him face his crimes in a civilized society. But the fact is—he gave up any right to be considered civilized a long time ago. He was a monster. A sociopath. I guess this was his choice, in a way."

"Yes," she replied, tears still streaming down her cheeks.

"And you're traumatized," he said. "You shouldn't have had to see that."

"I've seen people die before, Elton."

"I know," he said quietly. "You've been through a lot these last few years."

A small sobbed escaped her lips. "It's really over now though. And I'm done traveling. Done for good."

"Me too."

Elton put the weapons in the trunk. He had no

intention of giving them to anyone. They drove to the station, where the guard pointed them in the direction of the director's office. Just then Elton noticed a car pulling out onto the main highway leaving the camp road. He squinted. It looked like the old grey sedan that had been behind them the night they'd left the gala and followed Nick into the Hollywood Hills, but he couldn't be certain. He didn't have a chance to point it out to Cassandra though, because she was already walking ahead toward the director's office. He hurried to join her and they soon found themselves knocking on the door of one of the barrack-like buildings. A young soldier answered and directed them to his boss's desk. The name plate on it read Ralph Merritt. He rose to greet them and shook Elton's hand. He seemed like a decent fellow and Elton wondered how he had gotten assigned the job.

"I'm sorry things ended badly for your suspect, Mrs. Reilly," Merritt said to her. "But WRA Headquarters will want to talk to you."

Cassandra had dried her face and taken on a professional demeanor. "WRA?"

"War Relocation Authority," he said with a tone that indicated she should know. "Can you get back to L.A. by tomorrow afternoon, three o'clock?"

"Yes. We'll drive tonight. It won't be a problem."

The man was scribbling something. He handed her a paper. "Here's the address."

"I'm sorry, we want to know about the casualties here at the camp." she said.

"Yes, there were two: a Hiro Wakai..."

She inhaled sharply.

"Do you know him?"

"No. Was he killed?"

"No, as a matter of fact, he was barely wounded. He came to the aid of an elderly gentleman that was hurt quite badly though, a Mr. Koichi Matsuda. They've been taken to a medical facility."

"Here? At the camp?"

"Mr. Wakai is being treated here. Mr. Matsuda is being taken to a hospital in Sacramento."

Elton could see she was trying to stay calm.

"May we see Mr. Wakai?" she asked.

"You want to see him?" Merritt seemed confused.

"Yes. If he's up to it, I'd like to ask him a few questions. We're trying to figure out what motivated the shooter, Nick Stockard. Whether it was Wakai he was after, Mr. Matsuda, or someone else. And if so, why?"

"Certainly. Let me call over there and I'll ask."

"Also," Cassandra blurted, "what arrangements will be made for Stockard's body?"

"Well, um," Merritt said, "do you know if he has any next of kin?"

"No, he does not," Elton interjected.

"I think it's best if he's cremated," Cassandra said. "My agency will cover the cost." Anticipating any objections, she took several twenty dollar bills from her wallet and handed them to him. "This should be enough."

He looked at the money, wide-eyed. "Yes, yes it will. There's a funeral home in Independence that'll take care of it. I'll have to clear it with the WRA though."

"Very well," Cassandra said.

"Do you want any of the deceased's personal effects? Though we'll have to confiscate the weapons, of course."

Cassandra looked at Elton who subtly shook his head. She took the hint and whipped out her Strategic Scientific Reserve card. "Mr. Merritt, we are an extremely secret branch of the government, concerned with uncovering espionage here on American soil. The weapons must come with us. We cannot take the risk of them falling into the wrong hands. I'm sure you understand."

Merritt frowned, examining the card.

"Let me use your phone," she went on. "We can call headquarters and you can speak to my commanding officer. Oh, wait. It's twenty-thirty hours in Washington D.C. They aren't there. We cannot wait until the morning, Mr. Merritt. As you say, the WRA wants to see us tomorrow. We'll discuss the matter further there. We would like the rest of Mr. Stockard's effects though."

She was authoritative and he was a man who had been taught to respect authority.

"Okay, I guess that arrangement will be acceptable. We can collect Stockard's other items while you're visiting the evacuee," Merritt offered.

"That would be fine," she said. "Thank you."

A few minutes later they were being escorted to the medical facility at the camp. It was strange and sad to be walking among all those Japanese faces—people who by all rights should be out in society, dealing with the war like everyone else instead of sequestered like criminals. This episode in American history had always disgusted Elton, but now he felt enraged.

Inside the building, they were led to the bed of a handsome young man whose wounded shoulder had already been bandaged up. Elton recognized him from the picture on the wall of his parents' restaurant. He was sitting in the bed, a beautiful woman next to him on a chair, holding his hand.

"Mr. Wakai?" Cassandra said.

"Yes," Hiro asked, looking at the mixed-race pair wonderingly.

"I'm Mrs. Cassandra Reilly. I'm with the government. This is Mr. Elton Carver, my…assistant. We're here to question you about the incident if you're up to it."

"Yeah, sure, I guess," said Hiro with some trepidation. "Shoulder hurts, but I'm okay. Bullet just grazed me. What about Mr. Matsuda? Do you know anything about his condition?"

"Just that they took him to a hospital in Sacramento."

"Oh gosh, I hope he'll be okay."

"We're very sorry for what you went through. Could you describe the attack for us?"

"Um, well, Kanako and I…this is Kanako Takahashi…"

The young woman nodded.

"Nice to meet you," said Cassandra.

"Anyway we were walking together, heading toward the building where I hold my acting class —I teach an acting class here. We were almost to the door when it opened, and Matsuda-san, Mr. Matsuda, came rushing out, excited, saying he'd learned his lines for his scene. He almost knocked me down. Then, all of a sudden, we heard a bang, and he fell. At the same time, I felt a sharp pain on my shoulder that knocked me to the ground too. I saw that Mr. Matsuda was bleeding from his chest. Without thinking, I pressed my hand over the wound, something I'd seen in a movie I was in once. Anyway, then people came running over to help me. Someone handed me a bandana and I used that to staunch the wound as best I could. Then there were sounds of other gun shots and everyone hit the ground all around me. I pulled Kanako down. We thought the guards were firing at us. Everyone was screaming and yelling, and then people were running to the fence. Someone yelled something about a car accident, and there was more shooting. That's all I know. Then the medic trucks came and one brought me here. The other took

Mr. Matsuda."

"Do you have any idea why someone would want to harm you?" Cassandra asked, and then added quickly, "or Mr. Matsuda?

"No. Not at all. I'm not even sure they were after either of us. Maybe it was some crazy person who just wanted to kill Japanese."

Kanako lowered her head and a tear rolled down her cheek. Hiro squeezed her hand.

"I'm very sorry you had to go through that," Cassandra said. "We do know who the shooter was, but we don't know why he attacked you or Mr. Matsuda, or, as you said, if it was either of you, specifically, that he was after. We don't know of any reason why he would have had you in mind."

"I guess I could have been killed," Hiro said somberly. "I just hope Mr. Matsuda will pull through. He's a tough old guy."

"We're very glad you weren't hurt any worse," Cassandra replied. "We'll find out which hospital he was taken to and make sure you get updated about his condition."

"Thank you. I'm sorry I can't be of more help," said Hiro.

"That's okay. We appreciate your time. We'll let you get some rest now. If there's anything we can do for you..."

Elton cleared his throat. There was no point making promises they couldn't keep.

"Anyway," Cassandra went on, taking the hint, "we wish you a speedy recovery."

"Thank you Mrs. Reilly, Mr. Carver," I appreciate it.

"Very nice to meet you both."

"Nice to meet you," Kanako said, her gaze still lowered.

Cassandra offered Hiro her hand and he took it with his uninjured arm and shook it.

The same soldier who'd escorted Elton and Cassandra to the medical building took them back to the guard's gate, where they were given a box of Nick's effects.

Elton opened the door of the car and put it in the back with Cassandra as she got in. "Shall we pick up something to eat in Lone Pine? I'm not hungry now but I'm sure I will be."

"Same here," she said, "that's a good idea."

He started the Hudson and they pulled out from the camp road.

"Elton," Cassandra suddenly said from behind him. "I have to tell you something. The soldier that killed Nick? He's the one I saw in the crowd outside the gala. The one who was following us afterwards in the grey car. I'm sure it was him."

"I thought I saw that same car leaving the camp when we were at the guard station! I wasn't sure so I decided it couldn't have been."

"Elton, there was something different about him. Different from the other soldiers. His hair cut wasn't like what other soldiers are wearing in this time period. Also, the color of his uniform was just slightly different. You could almost write it off to having been washed too many times but, usually, soldiers' uniforms are identical. I just felt like there was something odd about him. Also, what was he doing at that gala? I didn't mention it at the time, but I almost thought he was about to pull a gun on Nick there."

"What?"

"Yeah. And then he was following us, and parked outside of Veronica Lake's house like he was waiting for Nick too."

"Right. We thought maybe he was a jealous boyfriend."

"Could be. But then, could he have followed Nick out here and posed as one of the camp soldiers so he could get a shot at him?"

"It doesn't make sense," said Elton. "And then he took off like that. A soldier can't just leave their post."

"I don't think he was really a soldier." Cassandra remarked.

They were both silent for a minute, then Elton heard Cassandra rifling around in the box that contained Nick's things. "What's in there?"

"A thermos, a bandana, some binoculars, a ring..." Cassandra replied. "I remember him wearing this. I think it's a school ring. I know he went to Princeton. A comb, sunglasses, his wallet.... It's got some money in it, a driver's license, replicated, I'm sure, like ours. A government ID. Wow, it really looks official. A condom package.

Ew."

Elton chuckled.

"And a picture of me."

The back of Elton's neck prickled.

She was quiet for a moment. "He must have had this made into a print. It's from about four years ago, in Boston. I don't remember him taking it." Another pause. "And there's a watch. Oh boy."

"What?"

"Yeah, it's a replica of a 1940s watch but it's got all kinds of gadgets inside. A camera, a video recorder..." She was silent for a few moments. "I don't want to look at this stuff anymore." He heard her throw the watch into the box with a loud thump.

Elton wondered what she'd seen on the watch but didn't ask. They were silent for a long time as they drove south along the highway, into the evening, toward L.A.

Chapter Twenty-six

Hiro Wakai – July 1st, 1942

I write this, grateful to be alive. Though the government fed us the line that we'd be safer under confinement than among an American public who might want to harm us, as it turns out, that is as much a lie as we always suspected it was. Mr. Matsuda was shot in the chest by some crazy person and I was grazed on the shoulder. They say the bullet missed Mr. Matsuda's heart, that he's come out of surgery, and is recovering now. The people who came to ask me questions about it seemed to imply there might have been a vendetta against me or him. Could it have been someone who saw one of the movies I've made who thought I was a spy or something? And either Mr. Matsuda just got in the way, or it was he they were after, though why anyone would want to kill a seventy-year-old fisherman, I can't imagine. It all seemed so absurd I couldn't make any sense of it.

Then, when Mom and Pop came to visit me here in the hospital, something else occurred to all of us. They were, of course, very shaken by all of this, but were calmer once they saw that I was fine. We couldn't talk about it in front of Kanako, but she stepped outside the door so we could be alone, and then, my eyes met Pop's.

"Did you know," Pop began, speaking Japanese, "that

someone tried to kill me once? At home, in Los Angeles, before you were born?"

I then told Pop about reading and translating his memoir. He was speechless at first, and I thought he was going to be angry, but then he said. "So you know."

I nodded.

"Did you see the man who shot you?" He asked. "Do you know what he looks like?"

"No," I said. "It was from very far away.

"I saw him," Pop said. "I was in the kitchen, but when we heard the gunshots and an explosion I went running to see what was happening. I saw them carry the man away. It was far away, but, I swear, it was that same man."

I shook my head. "It's crazy to think it could be the same person. First of all, that was twenty years ago, and he'd be much older. Second, from your memoir it sounds like you barely caught a glimpse of him so you probably wouldn't recognize him. And, anyway, if he still wanted to kill you, Pop, and took the trouble to come all the way out here, why not just try for you? There's no way it was him, Pop." I said to him, taking his hand. "Anyway, they don't know what the guy's motive was, and there's no reason to think he was after me."

Pop nodded slowly.

"You're right," said Mom. "It just scared me so much. I suddenly remembered that day as if it were yesterday."

"Listen, I have something to tell you both," I said, and suddenly felt timid. "It will help you forget about that." I called out to Kanako and she came back into the room.

She was shy—barely spoke a word—just as they would expect, and I could tell they were very pleased with her demeanor. I think they ended up being happier about

Kanako than worried about my wound and the shooter. They, especially Mom, have been pushing me to find a nice girl to settle down with. I think Mom was worried that, being an actor, I'd end up with some Hollywood floozy who wasn't Japanese, so she seemed very relieved. After Kanako left, Pop gave his blessing on our relationship which leaves me open to go to Kanako's father and ask his permission to marry her. I realize we met less than a month ago but, why should we wait? If I know anything now, I know that life is short, and we must seize the moment.

"About your writing, Pop," I said before he and Mom left. "You're not angry? I'll show you the translation when I get out of here."

He told me he was happy I had read it, and happier still I had preserved it when we were sent away, and translated it. He said he would read it again, that he wanted to relive both the terrible and beautiful times from his past.

"Will life ever be the same again?" he wanted to know.

The War Relocation Authority wasn't exactly the military, even though military troops manned the camps. Upon meeting the man in charge, a Colonel Myers, at his office, Cassandra showed her S.S.R. card yet again.

"We're a branch of the F.B.I.," Cassandra told him. Elton had not come in with her, but remained outside in the car. After all, she was the supposed person in charge of Nick's "case." "It's a highly secret organization," she continued, having had time to perfect her act since dealing with Mr. Merritt at Manzanar the day before. "We deal with rousting out spies on American soil, and that's exactly what the deceased, Nick Stockard, was." Never had she been more grateful that computers did not yet exist, nor electronic databases with records of citizens' information. They had no way to trace her or Nick.

Colonel Myers kept squinting at her as if he couldn't believe a 'dame' would have such a high level of responsibility. Well, he'll just have to get over it.

"We did not want him to die," she continued. "We needed him alive for questioning. I told your people that at the camp, but they did not exercise caution. My organization is most displeased. We could have gotten a lot of information out of Mr. Stockard but, now, that opportunity is lost. We don't know what he was doing at Manzanar—never will. That's on you, now, Colonel Myers. However, I will make sure you and the soldier who fired the deadly shot do not receive a censure, since, in the end, it saved my driver's life." *And, since we have no idea who the soldier is.*

"Thank you, Mrs. Reilly, thank you," he stammered.

He must have been hoping to find some reason to censure her, but she had turned the tables on him. "I'll tell my people the casualty couldn't be helped. We'll end the case there. Can you tell me the condition of the man who was badly injured, a Mr. Matsuda?"

"Yes," he said, "they said he'll pull through."

"Does he have family at Manzanar?" She was curious.

He rifled through some papers. "No, he was a widower. No kids I guess."

"I see, well, I'm glad to hear he'll be okay. I'd also like to talk to you about the other prisoner who was hit, Hiro Wakai."

"We refer to them as evacuees."

She sighed. "Fine."

"Go on," he said.

"It seems to me it's the job of your agency to keep the people in these camps safe. You failed in that respect."

"Mrs. Reilly, there was nothing we could do."

"Well, if you'd had people patrolling the perimeter of the camp on a regular basis, Nick Stockard would never have had the chance to hide out there in the desert and stake out his prey."

Myers' face began to turn red. "We simply don't have the manpower. The government doesn't give us those kinds of funds. It would be impossible to have all that area around the camp patrolled day and night. That's what the guards on the towers are for. It's a big camp; you saw it. What does any of that have to do with Wakai?"

"Well, it all sounds like excuses to me," Cassandra rejoined. "And it sounds like Mr. Wakai saved Mr. Matsuda's life. Surely he deserves to be rewarded for that. He acted quickly, and with valor."

"What would you have me do?"

"Release him and his family."

"No. There's no possibility of that."

"Well, I could bring my team of attorneys to look into the situation. I could also let the New York Times know about the incident. Even though the American people couldn't care less about the Japanese who are being held against their will all over the country," she paused, trying to control her temper, "it would certainly make it look like you're running a shoddy operation out there at Manzanar. You've left the 'evacuees' not only vulnerable to outside forces, but to perform emergency aid for each other because you don't have anyone on the ground to do so."

They stared at each other. Cassandra didn't blink. "Oh, and one other thing. Hiro Wakai is a personal friend of Mr. Humphrey Bogart's as am I. You know who Humphrey Bogart is, don't you?"

Myers' face brightened. "Of course, he's a swell actor. A war hero too."

"Yes, well, I think he would also be very disappointed to hear about what happened to his friend, and the friend of his friend."

He stared at her a moment longer. "I'll see what can be done."

"Thank you." She wasn't about to give him the opportunity to ask about the weapons. "And now," she said, rising from her seat in front of his army-green metal desk, "I must be going. I must file my own report about the shooting. My agency will be waiting."

He stood too. "Of course."

She held out her hand to him and he took it gingerly. She gave his a nice, firm shake. "Good day."

She strode from his office, exhaling deeply once she was outside. She got in the car with Elton, debating whether she should tell him everything she said to Mr. Myers. She decided to wait until later. Instead, she said to him, "I want to go out tonight. Is it possible?"

"Maybe…" Elton replied with a grin, and headed toward their Hollywood Hills home.

When Cassandra walked into the house, she saw the matchbook with Bogart's number on it lying by the phone.

"I should call Bogie," she said, "and tell him something about Nick. We can't just disappear and leave that loose end. Everyone will wonder what happened to us. And to him.

"What will you tell him?"

"I have an idea." She picked up the phone and dialed.

"Red!" Bogart cried, upon hearing Cassandra's voice. "I knew you'd come back to me!"

She laughed lightly. "No, Bogie, not exactly. Listen, I have some really sad news to share with you."

"What's up?" he replied gently.

"Nick Stockard has died," she began. "He was in a

car accident."

"Oh boy," he said on a long exhale.

"Yes. It's terrible. Worse, in some ways though, is that I wasn't able to determine what he was up to, and if he was, indeed, a spy."

"So, you'll never know, huh?"

"Not unless we're able to apprehend someone else with information on him. That's always possible." She was making it up as she went along. "Anyway, we were working with the police, and it was they who informed us of his accident. Apparently, he never even made it to Manzanar, if that's even where he was going."

"Gotcha. Whew."

"So, I'm letting you know, partly because I thought you'd want to, and also because I'm wondering if you can be in touch with Bette Davis, or Lena Horne, or Betty Grable, one of those who knew him and liked him, and fill them in. They'll pass the word around. And of course, we'll want Veronica Lake to know."

"For sure. Is there going to be a service?"

"A service?" she looked at Elton.

He shook his head.

"I mean; I hadn't planned to..." Cassandra said into the phone

"Seems like the right thing to do," Bogie urged. "He was a popular guy. And generous. The others don't know he was a spy, if he was, and you don't want 'em to, right? So it seems to me you oughta treat his life like it mattered to you."

"It's not that it didn't matter," Cassandra said, looking at Elton who frowned. "He was a friend…until he turned—"

"But you see what I mean. No one knows that but us."

"I do see what you mean, Bogie, but, I don't know how I'd begin to organize it."

"Lemme handle it, Red." he replied. "I'll call Davis. She'll put the word out and get it done."

"Thank you so much. And let her know, the sooner the better. It would have to take place in the next couple of days, if possible. I have to get back east with Elton."

"I'll be sorry to see you go."

"Likewise. But I'll see you at the service. Just let me know when and where."

She set the phone back on the cradle.

Elton was still frowning at her. "A memorial service? Really?"

"Listen," Cassandra said gently, going to him. "I don't feel any need to honor him, that's for sure…"

"On the contrary," Elton agreed.

"But I need closure too. I thought he was dead once, and now I know he really is. This will be a way to say good-bye to his influence over my life once and for all. Let others eulogize him if they want. You and I will know the truth." She took his hand and squeezed it.

He brought her hand to his mouth and kissed it. "So you want to go out, huh?"

"Is there somewhere we can be together?"

"I think I might just be able to arrange that." He picked the phone up and dialed a number. "Calling to see who's playing tonight," he said into the receiver. "Mm-hmm, great. Thank you. Can I get a reservation for two under Elton Carver for the ten o'clock show? Excellent. Thanks." He hung up and winked at her mysteriously.

They made dinner and lingered over it, talking over all that had happened. Afterward, they went their separate ways to dress. Elton told Cassandra to put on her finest so she donned the black evening gown, complete with gloves and diamonds, and arranged her hair in her best Veronica Lake style. She took extra care with her makeup, applying burgundy-red lipstick, smoky eyeshadow, lots of mascara, and subtly penciling in her arched brows. She took a look in the mirror, finished it off with pale powder, and was pleased with the effect.

When she entered the living room, she found Elton waiting for her in a black zootsuit, black fedora on his head. "Wow," they both said simultaneously.

"You are stunning," Elton, breathed.

"Thank you," she said, looking down, suddenly feeling shy. "So are you."

They both laughed.

She took her requisite seat in the back of the car, glad they wouldn't have to repeat that scenario too many more times, and watched out the window with curiosity as they drove. Elton wouldn't tell her where they were going—it was to be a surprise, he'd said. Soon, she realized they were heading toward Compton. He turned the car onto S. Central Avenue and finally pulled up in front of Club Alabam. She'd seen it once before as they driven past on their first foray to the neighborhood, but now, all lit up, elegant people streaming in, it was like something right out of movie. Elton motioned to a valet who came running over to park the car. She saw him stop the young man and talk to him for a moment, gesturing toward the trunk. He then handed him a bill, and came around to hand Cassandra out. Everyone within sight, save herself, was black.

"Are you sure this will be all right?" she whispered to him.

"I've got it covered," he replied, smiling.

At the door, the Maître d' said to him, "Glad to see you again, Mr. Carver."

Elton slipped him a bill, though Cassandra couldn't see how much, and he said to the man, "This is my lady friend, Mrs. Reilly. I'm sure there won't be any trouble about it?"

"No, sir," the Maître d' replied practically clicking his heels. "Of course not."

"Oh, and could you deliver this for me?" Elton surreptitiously handed him a folded piece of paper.

The man glanced at what was written on the front and said, "Immediately, Mr. Carver. Follow me, please."

He led them to a table right next to the dance floor with the best possible view of the band, which was beginning to take their place on the stage. It was just before ten o'clock.

Cassandra noted the signature lettered on the front of the blocky white music stands in front of each musician's chair. "Duke Ellington?" she marveled.

"Nothing but the best," Elton replied, grinning. He ordered a bottle of Moet et Chandon from the Maître d', who then scurried away.

The famous band leader took the stage, and the musicians arranged themselves in their seats. They struck up the first song, one she recognized, though she didn't know the name. It immediately had her tapping her feet. She smiled at Elton. She so wanted to dance, but didn't know if doing so would be correct. She enviously watched other couples take the floor. He just smiled back at her. The champagne came and was poured. She sipped at the light, frothy bubbles, perfectly dry and delicious.

The band launched into another, faster number, and Cassandra watched in awe as the couples on the floor not only kept up with it, but danced with such flair and grace it took her breath away. During the song, Elton excused himself. By the time it had finished, he still hadn't returned. She noticed that people were staring at her. She was the only white face in the club. She now understood how Elton must have felt, existing in a white-only world since she'd arrived.

Ellington came to the mic, breaking her train of thought. "Ladies and gentlemen," he announced, "I like to introduce a special guest artist joining us tonight. Please welcome, Mr. Elton Carver!"

Elton walked onto the stage to enthusiastic applause. He had a gleaming trumpet in his hand.

"What the...?" Cassandra whispered to herself.

He went to stand with the trumpet section and the band launched into a piece Cassandra loved, "Take the A Train." Her mouth fell open. About half-way through the song, Elton stepped around to the front of the band and took the improvised solo, playing with style and flair, wowing the crowd. How had she not known he was a first-rate musician? There was something so... sexy...watching and hearing him play. The solo lasted about thirty seconds, then he took his place with the rest of the horn players. The song wound up to even greater applause, Cassandra clapping harder than anyone.

Elton looked at her from the stage and grinned. Then, a beautiful young woman took the stage; Elton crossed to her, took her hand, kissed it, and went to make his exit.

"Mr. Elton Carver!" Ellington said again, gesturing to Elton as he left the stage. Elton waved at the crowd. "And may I introduce," Ellington continued, "Miss Sarah Vaughn!"

Cassandra gasped. Ellington's smooth piano was

the intro to a slow, romantic number. Once Vaughn started singing, Cassandra recognized the song. It was "Prelude to a Kiss."

Elton was suddenly at her side, trumpet case in his hand. He placed it under the table and offered her his hand. "Do you care to dance?"

She looked around nervously. "Is it okay?"

"It's okay," he said with a smile.

She stood and he led her onto the floor. He took her in his arms with authority. One hand rested on the small of her back, the other held her right hand in his as he guided her to the music. She already knew he was an excellent dancer, but they had not danced this closely before. She gazed into his eyes. He was amazing in every way though there was one more thing about him she was dying to find out.

As they danced, she could feel the warmth radiating off his body. She glanced at the other dancers on the floor. Some of them, the women in particular, sent angry glances her way. Though she loved being in his arms, she was glad when the song ended and the band launched into the classic, "It Don't Mean a Thing If It Ain't Got That Swing." Elton swung her out, twirled her around, and they fell right into the steps of the Lindy Hop, though it was a fairly contained version of the dance. No one on the floor was dressed for the acrobatics sometimes associated with it, nor was there room. Just as they'd done at the bungalow, Cassandra and Elton partnered together smoothly, without a missed step. He was a confident lead, and she'd been well taught how to follow. Of all the dances she'd ever learned, this was her favorite and the one she'd studied the most. She never thought she'd have a chance to dance alongside people of the actual era in which it became popular, but now, here she was, experiencing a dream come true. They danced to one song after another until the band finally took a break.

"You wanna get outta here?" Elton whispered in her ear.

She nodded enthusiastically. They stopped at the table to get her purse and his trumpet, swigged down one final glass of champagne each, and headed for the door. On the way, a lady bumped into her, shooting her a resentful sneer. Cassandra tried an apologetic smile in return.

The valet fetched the car, and soon they were on their way back to the Hollywood Hills.

Once inside the bungalow, there was a moment of awkwardness as they stood in the entryway and stared at each other.

"How about a swim?" Elton finally suggested with a mischievous grin.

"Last one in is a rotten egg," she cried, and ran from the room, Elton close behind.

Outside in the back yard, the air was warm, the breeze light. She turned her back to him, indicating the zipper of her dress. He drew it down and she shrugged it off her shoulders, then shimmied it to the ground. She pulled off one glove, and then the other, as he watched. She took her jewelry off, then, one by one, her foot resting on a chaise lounge, unfastened her garter and slipped her stockings off. Her underwear was fairly complicated, as it included a strapless bra/girdle in a sexy, bustier style, the garter belt itself, and underpants. Before removing the final layer, she grew shy. "What are you waiting for?" she challenged.

He began to undress while she removed the last of her undergarments. While he was still fumbling with his suspenders, she dove into the pool, naked. The water was cool but she warmed up with a quick, underwater lap. She came up to the edge to see him slipping his boxer shorts down.

She looked away before she could catch more than a glimpse, smiling. He dove in next to her.

"Agh!" he cried, coming up for air. "It's cold!"

"You'll get used to it," she said, backstroking away.

He swam to the far end of the pool, then glided across the water to meet her. He pulled her close with one arm, treading water with the other, and kissed her. She felt him harden against her thigh. "Mmm," she murmured.

He slid his hands over her slick body, gently cupping her rear. He pressed her hips against his. "Elton," she whispered.

"Come on," he replied. He swam to the steps and

she followed. Holding her hand, he led her into the bedroom. He grabbed a towel from the bathroom, and, as she stood dripping, he dried her off from head to toe. Draping the towel around his shoulders, he paused at the triangle of soft hair at the meeting of her legs. He knelt and kissed her there. She gasped.

He stood and dried himself quickly, then threw the towel aside and backed her toward the bed. She sat abruptly and then slid along the bedspread toward the headboard. He leaned over her, pressing her onto her back. She sighed as his body lengthened against hers. He kissed her, slowly and deeply, then his kisses traveled down her neck to her shoulders, and to her breasts. He took each nipple in his mouth in turn, taking his time, teasing and nibbling.

"Oh!" she uttered, intense pleasure overtaking her.

He lingered on her breasts, then kissed her belly, her hips, and again, that triangle. She let her legs open, enjoying every sensation of his tongue and lips. He was expert—knew every way of bringing a woman pleasure. Unable to contain her desire, she grasped his broad shoulders and drew his face back up to hers. His hips now lay between her open legs. Before she knew it, he had slid himself inside her, filling her completely. Slowly, and sensually, he began to rock his hips back and forth, all the while kissing her mouth and her neck. She gave into him utterly, running her hands over his muscular arms and back. It wasn't long before her release came. She arced in ecstasy as he increased the speed of his rhythm. With every pulse she experienced another wave of sheer bliss that washed over her, making her tingle through every pore. Finally, he reached his own climax, his body arcing as hers had. She ran her hands over his beautiful, strong chest until he collapsed on top of her, spent. She grasped his head with its closely shorn hair and kissed him over and over. He rolled to the side and they continued to kiss.

Finally, they lay still, gazing at one another. "I never imagined this would happen," she said quietly.

"I did," he said with a soft laugh.

She smiled. "Well, I can't say I haven't fantasized about it," she coyly admitted. "I just didn't think it would ever become a reality."

"I'm so glad it has," he said.

"Me too."

She closed her eyes, breathing in his presence. She felt herself slipping into sleep. She opened them again to see his were closed now too. She let herself relax, happier than she'd been since returning from Italy.

Chapter Twenty-seven

Hiro Wakai – July 5, 1942

I'm happy to say we've heard Mr. Matsuda should make a full recovery. I was only in the hospital a few days. Yesterday, as soon as they released me, I went to Kanako's father and asked his permission to marry her. He said yes without hesitation (I suspect there was some influence from her step-mother because she stood in the background during the interview, smiling slyly). Anyway, after that, I planned my proposal though she must have known I had gotten permission from her father. I found a spot behind the building where I teach my class, an out of the way nook where no one ever goes that's shielded from the guards by the angle of the building. We brought a blanket, some food, and a small bottle of rice cooking-wine, all of which

Pop put aside for me. It was he who suggested the picnic. I don't think I ever realized how much he loves me, but being at this camp has brought us closer and I'm grateful to know that he wants this for me almost as much as I do.

Kanako and I sat on the blanket, the sun setting over the Sierra Nevadas, and ate for a while, both of us feeling timid. Then, I took her hand and asked if she'd marry me. She shyly said yes, and we kissed. We then talked about whether we should wait to get married until we get out of

Manzanar or not. But, since we don't know how long that will be, we decided to do it here. The traditional Shinto ceremony is a small one, just family present, and there is more than one Shinto priest here who can perform it. I believe that father is already brewing the sake! Then, when we finally get out of here, we will make a home and have children together. I now have hope for the future that I didn't have before.

Bogart called the next morning to tell Cassandra the memorial for Nick had been arranged for that evening at the Hollywood Canteen. Bette Davis had the authority to close it to the public when necessary and so she'd secured it for their event. She'd arranged for food, drinks...the works, Bogart said, and had sent the word out through the grapevine to all the people who had known Nick in the few weeks he'd been in Hollywood. Bogart had said Davis was devastated, which made Elton cringe. He wasn't sure how he and Cassandra would play the parts of bereaved friends, but they'd have to give it a go.

They'd woken that morning in each other's arms and made love again. Their bodies fit together like pure magic. Hers was so beautiful, like marble, a Grecian statue. Her auburn hair fell across the pillow like a Renaissance painting as they made love. She responded to him with the slightest touch or kiss. After all the years of knowing her, he finally knew what it was like to taste her, drink her, caress her, be inside her, and it was more wonderful than he'd ever imagined. After they'd dressed and breakfasted, they drove to the realtor's office to tell Betsy they would be giving up the house the next day. They told her that, of course, the owner could keep the full six months' rent, and they'd leave the key under the mat. Betsy couldn't have been more gleeful, knowing she'd get another commission on the place if she could rent it again soon.

Next, they drove to a car wash and had the Hudson cleaned to shining, and then to Sam Jones's car lot in Whittier to let him know they wanted to sell the car back to him, but that they'd need it for one more day. Elton told Sam he'd meet him at Joe's soda fountain the next day when Sam got off of work, and they'd exchange the car and money then. Elton actually had a reason for doing the transaction at Joe's, but didn't tell Sam why. Sam agreed on a fair price for the vehicle —certainly not what Elton had paid for it, but not a paltry sum, given that he'd only driven it a few weeks. The whole time the deal was being made, Cassandra stood outside the office in the lot, leaning against the Hudson. When the men finally emerged, Sam regarded her with deference, lowering his gaze in her presence. In his mind, she was Elton's rich boss.

Cassandra immediately went and took his hand, shaking it and smiling at him warmly. "Thank you, Mr. Jones," she said to him, "for taking care of Mr. Carver, and providing him with just the right car. We've loved driving around in the Hudson. I'm sorry to let it go."

"It's my pleasure doing business with y'all," Sam replied, now looking her in the eye.

Elton and Cassandra then went back to the bungalow and began to pack up their things. When Elton had finished up in the guest house, he walked through the main house, into Cassandra's bedroom, to find her gazing at the beautiful gowns she'd bought, as well as some of the other clothes she'd needed to purchase during their time there.

"This isn't all going to fit in my suitcase, Elton, and, besides, there's no point taking it back with me."

He picked up the black gown. "Bring this one," he said. "I hope to see you wear it again," he added with a wicked grin.

She smirked at him. "Alright. I'll wear this one tonight," she said, indicating the beige formal with the gauzy skirt. "I haven't worn it yet. Is it too light colored for a memorial?"

"No," he replied, "not for this kind of memorial. I'll wear my grey suit."

She nodded. "And all these diamonds and things? What am I going to do with them?"

He thought about it for a moment. "Why not bring them tonight and tell Miss Davis you'd like to donate them to the cause? The clothes too. They can sell them or whatever. I'm sure they'll find a use for all of it."

"Good idea," she nodded, and began to fold the things up, placing them with the jewels in one of the Bullock's shopping bags she'd kept.

"I'll do the same with mine," he said, turning to go gather the extra clothes up, "but I'm keeping the blue zootsuit," he added over his shoulder.

At seven o'clock they got in the car and made their way to the canteen. It was clear this was to be a quiet affair; there were no photographers, no limousines dispensing stars at the curb. People were walking in without fanfare, but they were all there: Grable, Davis, Horne, Tierney, Cassini, Gable, Bogart, and even Cary Grant; as well as Katherine Hepburn, holding court at a table in the corner. Elton glanced at Cassandra who grinned like a schoolgirl upon seeing her idol. Poor Veronica Lake sat at the bar, dabbing at her eyes, surrounded by a phalanx of lesser known male actors who'd nabbed an invitation to the event.

Bogart spotted Elton and Cassandra right away and made a beeline for them. "Red!" he cried, taking her hand and kissing it. And then, "Mr. Carver..."

"Nice to see you again, Mr. Bogart," Elton said, shaking his hand.

"Really sorry about your 'friend,'" the star replied.

Cassandra smiled at him with feigned sadness though only he and Elton knew it wasn't genuine. "Thank you," she replied.

The other celebrities they'd met came to say hello and offer their sympathies, all singing

Nick's praises for the charming and generous person they'd thought him to be. Elton and Cassandra received them all with due grace. Cassandra took Bette Davis aside and whispered to her about the donation of clothing and jewelry she wished to make and Elton saw the star clap her hands with subdued delight. Davis sent her date, a man considerably younger and prettier than she was, out to fetch the bags.

Finally, Hepburn approached and uttered her condolences in her clipped, New England accent. "I'm so very sorry about Mr. Stockard," she said more to Cassandra than Elton. "I only met him once, but he seemed like a fine sport."

"Thank you Miss Hepburn," Cassandra said, her eyes wide.

"If there's anything I can do, please let me know," the movie star replied.

"I think there is, but I'm sure Mrs. Reilly is too shy to ask," said Bogart, who was still hovering around Cassandra like a dragonfly.

Cassandra glanced at him, brows raised.

"I mean, it ain't related to Nick," he continued, "but I bet she'd give anything for an autograph."

"Oh no," Cassandra cried, "I would never assume —"

"Nonsense," Hepburn said. "I would be delighted."

Cassandra fished the small notebook out of her purse, along with a pen, and handed it to the auburn-haired legend. In Elton's mind, Hepburn wasn't what he considered beautiful, but she shimmered with stardom, and that, in itself, made her handsome. Hepburn signed her name with a flourish.

"My turn," said Bogart, and took the notebook and pen. "Something to remember me by, Red," he said with a wink.

Before Cassandra could take it back, he'd begun to pass it around the room and all the celebrities added their autographs, one by one. Then, once plenty of food and alcohol had been consumed, those who'd known Nick the best, in particular Grable, Tierney, and Horne, got up to deliver short speeches in Nick's praise.

Veronica Lake was the last to speak: "I loved Nick," she said tearfully, "though I didn't know him long. He was so kind and...sweet."

Elton marveled at the man's capacity for dissemblance.

"I will remember him the rest of my life," Lake continued. "Whenever I look at the stars, I'll see his eyes shining back at me; whenever I see the ocean..." and on and on she went, obviously quite tipsy. Finally, Cary Grant went up to her, thanked her for her words, and led her to a seat. Elton didn't know what Grant's marital status was, or lack thereof, but he was sure that if anyone could make her forget Nick, it was that charismatic actor. As a matter of fact, he looked like he already was. Lake gazed into his eyes with puppy dog gratefulness and Grant seemed to be eating it up.

Elton whispered to Cassandra. "I want to go."

She nodded, then stood as the room grew quiet. "I just want to thank you—that is, Mr. Carver and I want to thank you, for showing Nick what a real Hollywood welcome is like. You brought him into your fold, and made him one of you, and I'm sure he was grateful for it." She at least wasn't saying anything that wasn't true. "Mr. Carver and I are headed back east tomorrow," She continued, "but we will always remember this wonderful community of artists, and how you embraced Mr. Stockard. Thank you so much, for your kindness to us and our…friend."

Her speech was met with applause as she and Elton made their way, smiling, to the door. On their way out, she took Veronica Lake's hand and slipped Nick's ring into it. "I think he'd want you to have it," she whispered to her.

"Oh!" Lake cried, and burst into tears while Cary Grant comforted her.

Bogart met them at the door. "And I want to thank you," he said to Elton, "for taking such good care of this gal." He wrapped an arm around Cassandra's shoulder and handed her the notebook full of autographs.

Elton knew it would be a prize she would treasure always.

"You are one lucky man," Bogart said to him, shaking Elton's hand with his free one.

"I know," said Elton sincerely.

"I'll miss ya, Red," he said to Cassandra, finally letting her out of his embrace.

"I'll miss you too, Bogie," she said, and kissed his cheek.

He grinned like a little boy. "Hey, I meant to ask you, how did you know about that line from Casablanca? Nobody's seen it yet in the states."

"That's my secret," she whispered to him.

She then took Elton's arm, blew Bogie a kiss, and, waving to the crowd, they made their exit.

"What was he talking about?" Elton asked as he helped her into the car.

"I'll tell you later," she replied with an enigmatic smile.

On their final day in 1942, Elton and Cassandra said good-bye to the cozy bungalow. With just Cassandra's suitcase, Elton's satchel, and his trumpet, they prepared to leave forever the place that Elton now considered their own little love nest.

They were bringing Nick's watch and wallet back with them, and the guns were stored in Cassandra's suitcase, but the other things Elton left in the box and put on top of the trash can, Then, as he was loading their luggage in the trunk, the neighbor lady, Mrs. Watson, who had stopped them the first morning of their stay, came along, walking her dog.

"Going on a trip?" she said to Cassandra while eyeing Elton suspiciously.

"I'm afraid I'm leaving for good," Cassandra said. "Obligations back east."

"Oh, how too bad," the woman said with a sniff. She cast a superior glance at Elton, and walked on without another word.

Cassandra gave her the finger behind her back.

"Mrs. Reilly!" Elton whispered to her, amused.

"I won't miss that kind of attitude, that's for sure," said Cassandra as she got in the back seat. "And I won't miss having to pretend you're my servant."

Elton settled himself in the driver's seat. "I'll always be at your command," he said, winking at her in the rear view mirror.

She leaned forward and kissed him on the cheek, not caring who might catch a glimpse. "And I yours," she whispered.

A thrill ran through Elton's body. Was she really his? Would this go on after they returned to the future? He worried for a moment. The spell of the past was powerful, and sometimes made you feel and do things you wouldn't do in your real life. He could only trust that the feelings she'd said she had him for would remain as true then as now.

They drove off toward Compton, the windows open, the warm summer air blowing over his skin. He would miss it. Of course, they could come back and visit L.A. whenever they wanted, but they'd never see it like this again. He took in the sights, memorizing them as best he could.

Finally, they arrived in front of Joe McGee's soda fountain, Elton unloaded the trunk, moving the luggage close up against the big windows of the restaurant. Cassandra stayed with it while he went in and handed Joe the keys. "When Sam gets here, he'll take the keys and give you the money. He thought I'd be meeting him here, but my boss doesn't need the money. She wants you to have it."

"What? I couldn't!"

"Sure you could. Maybe use it for a down payment on another restaurant. Or a house."

"Boy!" Sam exclaimed. "Please thank her for me!"

"I will."

At that moment Cassandra turned and waved to Sam, who waved back. "She sure is a swell dame," Sam declared.

"She sure is," said Elton.

He and Cassandra walked to the trolley stop, luggage in hand, then hopped on the Red Line over to Alameda, the driver and passengers all staring at the white woman. Then they got on the Alameda line with the same result. Finally, they arrived at the warehouse. They had discussed their plan of action.

They knocked on the front door, and it was opened by a worker with a surprised look on his face.

"Is your supervisor here?" Cassandra asked with authority.

"Um, yeah, hang on."

"No, that's all right, you can bring me to him."

The befuddled employee nodded and led them to a small office that was situated toward the front, inside the huge building.

"Hello, I'm Mrs. Cassandra Reilly, government inspector." She flashed her S.S.R. card at him. "This is my assistant, Mr. Carver. We are here to do a surprise assessment of your work."

"What? You?" the man queried.

"Yes. Me. We have all our equipment here." She indicated their luggage. "Don't mind us; you may all go about your jobs. We won't disturb anyone, and we'll let ourselves out when we leave."

"I think I'd better call my boss," he said picking up the phone.

"I thought you were the supervisor," she said, annoyance lacing her voice.

"Well, I am, but…"

"Then you are the authority here. You're welcome to call my headquarters and check my credentials if you like. It's a long distance call to New York, but I'm sure your boss won't mind the expense."

Elton held his breath.

"Oh, no, no. That's ok," the man said. "How long will you be?"

"Not long. Maybe a half an hour. You won't even know we're here."

"Alright then. Do you need someone to show you around?"

"That won't be necessary. Thank you."

As they left the office, Elton saw the supervisor looking at his trumpet case inquisitively. Oh, well. Just have to let him wonder.

He and Cassandra marched straight back to the hidden corner where the portal exit awaited them. There would be someone on duty at the portal lab who would operate the transfer, and bring them back as soon as they saw the outlines of their bodies appear on the infrared sensor.

The time travelers ignored the stares of the workmen and walked briskly through the warehouse as though they belonged there. Once near the portal exit, they stopped and spoke quietly as if they were conferring about the job. There was only one person operating a forklift nearby. He stared at them for a moment, and then returned to his work. As soon as the man's back was turned to them, they hurried into place, standing close together. Elton felt the dizzying sense of the transfer beginning, and then the warehouse disappeared from sight.

Chapter Twenty-eight

Suhan watched from the window as Mark Stein marched across the grounds to the main building. She appreciated his strong frame even more now, now that she had held him, naked, in her arms and made love to him. But those thoughts were secondary to what was making her heart pound. Had he done it? Had he been successful? In the days since June 23rd, she had searched and searched the historical archives but had found that the photo of Nick at the gala was still intact (if it hadn't been, she wouldn't have ever known it existed in the first place, and she wouldn't be standing there waiting for Mark—she knew that, but she had gone through the motions anyway). Neither was there any mention of Nick Stockard being shot, or killed, or his name on record in any way during the war era. That didn't mean anything though. If he was staying undercover, no one would know about him.

She knew Mark had done it the moment she locked eyes with him. He was smiling ever so slightly—she might even say it was a triumphant smile in its understated way. He took her in his arms briefly. They weren't allowed long embraces in the recreation room. He whispered in her ear. "It's done."

She kissed his cheek, then took a step back. "Have you checked your bank account?"

"Haven't had a chance," he said, still smiling.

"You'll be pleasantly surprised. And you're set. Set for life."

"Will you be in my life after you get out of here?"

"If you want me to be. I don't know if you'll want to wait. It will be another year at least."

"I can wait."

She wondered if that were true. It didn't matter that much though. She'd enjoy him for now. "Why don't I go sign you in for a private visit, and you can tell me all about it in my room."

"There's a lot to tell. I had to track him for several days, but, in the end.... Anyway, I think you'll appreciate hearing about it."

"That, and more," she said smiling.

Alex, Yoshi, and Sara were on hand to welcome Elton and Cassandra back. The first thing Cassandra did was to assure them the mission had been accomplished, that Nick was dead, and that they were certain he had gone to 1942 to eliminate a man named Hiro Wakai from history. The fact that nothing had changed in their own timeline indicated that such was surely the case.

"There is something you should know," Sara said to them. "There was, actually, a slight shift in the historical timeline while you were gone. We didn't know who Hiro and Kanako Wakai were, or what part they played in all this until just now, but suddenly a bunch of information popped up on them. We were wondering what it meant."

Cassandra activated her computer, and spoke the name Hiro Wakai. Sara was right. There was a huge amount of information about Hiro and Kanako's family that appeared as a hologram in the air before them. All five scientists looked it over. The first thing Cassandra noticed was a record of the Takahashi family's release from Manzanar on July 25th, 1942. "But not the Wakai's?" She said out loud, her heart sinking.

"This is odd," said Elton, reading. "It's indicating there is no record of the Wakais ever being at Manzanar."

They tried entering several different spellings in the WRA database, and finally came up with information about the Akai family—Akito, Mai, and Hiro, released from Manzanar on July 25th.

"That's it," said Cassandra. "It must have gotten messed up when a database of the list of evacuees was created several decades after the war.

I guess that can happen easily when transposing from a manual list to computerized one. Amazing how a simple misspelling can practically erase someone from history.

"But why would they release them?" Elton queried. "That's bizarre."

Cassandra could feel heat rise to her cheeks.

Elton looked at her. "Cassie, what did you do?"

"Well, I might have threatened the Colonel from the WRA with legal repercussions for not keeping his prisoners properly protected."

Elton laughed. "And how were we going to follow through with that?"

"I also might have told him I'd give the story to the New York Times...and that Hiro and I were friends of Humphrey Bogart's and that he'd be very upset to hear about what happened."

"You met Humphrey Bogart?" Sara squealed.

"Yes," Cassandra said, "and so many more stars. I have their autographs!"

Sara made another squeaking noise.

"Anyway," Elton cut in with a serious tone, "it looks like you put the fear of God into the guy." He crossed his arms and looked at Cassandra under his brow.

"I really didn't think he'd do it," she said. "I mean, I hoped he would, but..."

Elton looked back at the holographic images. "So it looks like Hiro and Kanako got married on September 3rd, 1942. They had a son on July 4th, 1943. Huh," he grunted. "Ironic."

Sara cut in. "Though their son would have been born anyway if they had remained in the camp," she said, reading from the information in the original timeline, "Kanako would have died in childbirth and Hiro would have died of polio a couple of years later."

Cassandra glanced over the documents. "Look at this!" she cried, "there's a diary here." She told the computer to show her the pages and it did. "Hiro wrote this!" she exclaimed. "He kept a journal!" They skimmed through it quickly. "They went back to Los Angeles after they were released from Manzanar, but Hiro couldn't get work in Hollywood, he says. Not great, but better than dying of polio." She read forward a bit. "They reopened the restaurant, and he helped his parents run it. He says it didn't do very well during those war years but they managed to keep it going."

"It was probably the black folks in Compton who ate there," Elton said. "I'm sure the white people wouldn't go."

"Here's something else!" Sara said, pointing to the hologram. "Another journal, written in Japanese, and...it looks like it was translated into English. It's Akito Wakai's."

Cassandra, skimmed it. "Wow, what an intense beginning. An earthquake, escaping Japan by boat...and he met his wife saving her life."

They all read quietly for a few minutes.

"What's this?" Elton said. "Someone tried to kill

Akito Wakai in 1920. The killer just came out of nowhere."

They all looked at each other and a chill ran down Cassandra's spine. "You don't think..." she said to Elton.

"That Nick first went to 1920 to kill the father, and failing that, came back in 1942 to kill the son?"

"If so, he was busier than we thought," Yoshi commented.

The room went silent. Nick's determination to eliminate Evie Johnston's existence, just so he could be with Cassandra, made her feel ill. It was incredible the lengths he'd been willing to go to. She read on and saw that Akito and Mai recovered from the shock and went on to have their baby and live their lives, as Hiro's existence proved. She switched back to Hiro's journal.

"Kanako went back to school after the war ended," Cassandra said out loud, reading, trying to shake off her feeling of disgust toward Nick, "and got her degree in Marine Biology. This says she got a job at UCLA after that. I wonder what happened to Mr. Matsuda."

They entered his name but there was no information about him, other than that he was sent to Manzanar in 1942.

"He might have opted to go back to the camp once he recovered," said Elton. "An old guy like that might not have had anywhere else to go."

Cassandra sighed.

Yoshi was still skimming the documents. "Looks like Hiro and Kanako only had the one son," Yoshi commented, "Naoki. It was a difficult birth according to doctor's notes in the medical records. Kanako did almost die."

"He stops writing after about 1950," Cassandra said. Then she ordered the computer to research the Wakai family tree and found that, indeed, Naoki Wakai married, he and his wife had a daughter, who had a son, and on and on with information about the descendants of Hiro and Kanako, until the line reached Evie.

"If Nick had killed either Akito or Hiro," Elton mused, "Evie would never have been born." Elton took Cassandra's hand. She squeezed it, looking into his eyes.

"What's this about?" Yoshi asked, glancing at their clasped hands and smiling.

Cassandra didn't know what to say, so she just smiled back.

"Well, your rooms are ready for you," Sara said, taking Yoshi's hand.

"We've had a little development of our own here," said Yoshi, his handsome face turning pink.

"I hope it's not catching," Alex said with a laugh, and went to prepare them all a meal. Then, Elton and Cassandra retired to her room in the big house that was both portal lab and L.A. headquarters, a place which stood on the same spot as the war machinery warehouse had, almost two hundred years before.

Though Cassandra didn't quite feel ready to step out into Los Angeles of 2126 after having just left the same city in its simpler time, she and Elton agreed there was no reason to delay. The shock was great, but she adjusted quickly, partly because that area of Long Beach had become a quaint neighborhood of what might be considered middle-class homes, if there were really such a thing as class differences anymore, pleasantly cooled by the ocean breeze. Elton and Cassandra had decided that, as long as they were in L.A., they might as well revisit some of the sights they'd just left behind to see if anything of the past was left. They knew that Grauman's Chinese theater was still there, though it had undergone many different names, as well as the iconic Hollywood sign, though it had said Hollywoodland back in the forties. More than anything, Elton wanted to drive through Compton. He told her that one hundred years earlier, neither one of them would have wanted to venture there. It had been a hot bed of crime and gang activity, but Sara had assured them it was an entirely different place now.

He and Cassandra took a driverless car to S. Central Avenue and 42nd Street and hopped out at the corner. Though it was still a largely African-American community, there seemed to be people of every race co-existing there peacefully. Cassandra and Elton strolled north. None of the buildings of the past were there, but there were vegetable markets, clothing stores, movie theaters, restaurants, and all kinds of various specialty stores run by people of every possible background. Sara had told them that Little Tokyo still existed in a sense, though it was more just a smattering of Japanese restaurants now, mixed in with many other kinds.

Cassandra enjoyed the walk, taking in the sights and basking in the beautiful weather. As they entered the environs of what was once Little Tokyo, Elton began carefully observing the street names. Finally, he led her down Second Street, and then came to an abrupt halt in front of an elegant-looking establishment, called simply, "Wakai's." They looked at each other in astonishment. "It's still here!"

They went in and asked for a table. Elton described to her the restaurant as it had been when run by Hiro's parents under the name Rakuzen. As they ordered a sushi meal, they gazed around at photos that were of people who must have had significance to the restaurant and its history from long, long ago to present day.

"Look!" Cassandra cried. "There's Evie!" The artist's photo hung in a place of prominence.

"And there's Hiro!" Elton pointed to the actor's headshot, a photograph that was yellow and faded with the nearly two centuries that had passed since it was taken. It hung next to a photo of a middle-aged Japanese couple, and a placard underneath that said, "Akito and Mai Wakai."

The waiter came by and they struck up a conversation with him. He told them the restaurant had been passed down generation after generation, and was still owned by descendants of the original Wakai family.

After dinner, Cassandra and Elton took a car to Venice Beach, where they got out and walked along the sand. The waves crashed on the shore under the bit of twilight left in the sky. Some people had lit a bonfire that burned not far off. It was chilly so Elton took off his jacket and put it around Cassandra's shoulders. They stood and gazed at the horizon.

"Some things never change, do they?" observed Cassandra.

"Thank goodness for that," said Elton. He turned to her, took her in his arms, and kissed her. "Is it too soon to say I love you?" he asked.

"No," she replied. "We've loved each other as friends, and then some, for nearly two decades. I'd say it's rather more late than anything."

He laughed his big, contagious laugh.

"And I love you too," she said. Their lips met again and they drank each other in.

Life had come full circle. All Cassandra had been through in the previous five years quickly passed before her closed eyes. She was the mistress of her own fate now, and would no longer give herself up to the uncertainties and dangers of traveling to past eras. A wonderful future stretched before her, and it was all she needed.

Books In This Series

The Time Mistress Series

Dr. Casssandra Reilly travels to different eras in the past, finding unexpected romance, danger, and adventure.

Book One – The Time Baroness

A romantic, time-travel adventure set in Jane Austen's England, The Time Baroness is the story of Dr. Cassandra Reilly, a scientist from the year 2120 who embarks upon a journey to England of 1820. Her purpose is to conduct an experiment: living for a year in the guise of a wealthy widow and interacting within the Regency world. Though she has painstakingly prepared for the experience, her unusual ways arouse both ire and interest from her neighbors…and attract an unexpected admirer. Ultimately, circumstances beyond Cassandra's control plunge her into a dangerous situation, and she learns that people, and love, aren't always what they seem to be.

Book Two – The Time Heiress

Dr. Cassandra Reilly is surprised to find herself time-traveling again, this time to New York of 1853, accompanying the internationally acclaimed artist, Evie Johnston. Evie has funded the trip, explaining that she wishes to meet her ancestors, activists in the Underground Railroad. However, the beautiful painter has another agenda altogether.

Book Three – The Time Contessa

The Time Contessa is an adventure to Siena, Italy, 500 years into the past and 100 years into the future. Something has gone wrong with an historical timeline, causing a famous painting to disappear from the world's conscious memory, surfacing only in people's dreams. Two members of MIT's Chronology team, Dr. Cassandra Reilly and her colleague Jake, must go to Renaissance Siena to repair the timeline so the artist who painted the portrait of a beautiful woman known as Giuliana will ultimately live to complete it. However, the past holds many pitfalls, both dangerous and romantic, that Cassandra must stay clear of, while trying to prevent Jake falling prey to them as well. The time-travelers' problems follow them to the future, where love takes such a strong hold it becomes impossible to resist, and past adversaries resurface to create new threats.

Book Four – The Time Duchess

"Did I just kill William Shakespeare?" The question hammered through James's mind as he fled the arena, gasping for fresh air, of which there was none in that hell-hole of a city... Sometimes, time travel isn't all it's cracked up to be as James Reilly discovers when he journeys to Elizabethan England to solve a long debated question: Did Shakespeare really write the plays attributed to him? When his investigation leads to nothing but a violent confrontation between him and the Bard, he returns to the future to ask the most renowned time-traveler of the day, who also happens to be his mother, Dr. Cassandra Reilly, to go with him to London of 1598 and use her charms to make inroads where he has failed. Once immersed in the era, Cassandra finds herself becoming intimate with the key players of the time: Shakespeare and his troupe, Queen Elizabeth, Ben Jonson, Robert Cecil, and Edward De Vere - the Earl of Oxford. However, navigating the perils that lie around every corner of London of that day, as well as the whims of the unpredictable queen, makes it a hazardous undertaking, especially when three men are vying to win Cassandra's heart, and a mysterious presence seems to be stalking her.

Book Five - The Time Mistress

In this fifth and final book in The Time Mistress Series, Cassandra must travel to Hollywood, circa 1942, to investigate why criminal and fugitive Nick Stockard mysteriously showed up in a newspaper photo of the era, when she'd thought he'd already died. The only explanation is that he cheated death and time-traveled there, but how and why? Dr. Elton Carver, inventor of the time machine, goes with Cassandra to help her in her hunt for Nick. While in 1942, Cassandra and Elton rub elbows with stars like Humphrey Bogart, Bette Davis, and Lena Horne, but they also have to deal with the complications of Elton being African American in a segregated and racist Los Angeles—and with the feelings they begin to have for one another.

This final novel in Georgina Young-Ellis's fascinating time travel series satisfies in every way with romance, danger, excitement...even celebrities from Hollywood's golden age! It's an entertaining yet poignant look at the World War II era, with all its glitz and glamour, as well as it's harsh realities. It's a page turner to the end! - Barbara Silkstone, author of the Cold Cream Murders series.

Time traveling to the past can be so romantic...

except when there's a murderer on the loose

Made in the USA
Columbia, SC
07 September 2021